The Resurrectionist

THE RESURRECTIONIST

James Bradley

ff

faber and faber

First published in Australia in 2006
by Picador, Pan Macmillan
First published in Great Britain in 2007
by Faber and Faber Limited
3 Queen Square London WCIN 3AU

Printed in England by Mackays of Chatham

'Four Quartets' from *Collected Poems 1909 –1962*
by T. S. Eliot, Faber and Faber Limited, 1963 Edition.

A CIP record for this book
is available from the British Library

ISBN 978-0-57123275-8
ISBN 0-571-23275-2

2 4 6 8 10 9 7 5 3 1

'We are born with the dead:
See, they return, and bring us with them.'
T. S. Eliot, *Four Quartets*

A Thing Lighter Than Air

London, 1826–7

IN THEIR SACKS they ride as in their mother's womb: knee to chest, head pressed down, as if to die is merely to return to the flesh from which we were born, and this a second conception. A rope behind the knees to hold them thus, another to bind their arms, then the mouth of the sack closed about them and bound again, the whole presenting a compact bundle, easily disguised, for to be seen abroad with such a cargo is to tempt the mob.

A knife then, to cut the rope which binds the sack, and, one lifting, the other pulling, we deliver it of its contents, slipping them forth onto the table's surface, naked and cold, as a calf or child stillborn slides from its mother. The knife again, to cut the rope which binds the body to itself, the sack and rope retained, for we shall use them again, much later, to dispose of the scraps and shreds.

Together then we take hold of them, forcing their bodies straight once more. Although their limbs do not loll, neither are they stiff, despite the chill that lingers in them, their rigor already broken by the graveside as they were bent and bound for sacking. Instead they shift beneath our grasp, moving with the peculiar malleability of a corpse caught midway between death and putrefaction. It is an ugly task, yet what ugliness it has lies not in the proximity of the dead but in the intimacy it demands of us, this closeness with the flesh and substance of their bodies.

When they are done, laid pale and naked on the table, we begin. First we turn them on their faces, exposing the flesh of the back and buttocks, mottled purple and green as if with bruises where the blood has pooled in the hours after death. If the flesh has begun to spoil there will be blisters forming soft, pale pouches of fluid which break when they are disturbed, but even if their flesh is sweet the skin will be moist with the liquid that seeps from them like sweat. Sometimes those who dressed them for the grave will have plugged their anuses, and if they have the obstruction must be removed and disposed of. Then, taking rags, and water, and vinegar, we begin the work of cleaning them, our hands moving carefully across their skin, the smell of the vinegar mingling with the darker scents that cling to them, the movements of our hands economical yet not without tenderness as we wipe and wring.

Once the back and legs are done we turn them over again, working from feet to groin, groin to chest, arms and hands, coming at last to the face. Here our work is most careful, cleaning around the bones and ridges with our folded rags, wiping the cheeks, the sunken pits of the eyes. Sometimes the lids will be open, caught in the stillness of death, the eyes beneath cloudy and colourless like the eyes of the very old, pale with cataracts.

The washing done we draw fresh water in the yard, fetch soap and razor. Cold water still, cold for the cold. Then, pulling the loose skin taut, we begin to shave; first the scalp and face, the hair coming away in wet clumps to expose the knobbled dome of the skull; then the chest and armpits; then finally the cold instruments of their sex, the blade of the razor rasping across their skin. Sometimes we will nick them as we work, but no blood comes, the wound pale and empty.

How we know this is work to be done in silence I cannot say. Only that this is how it is, how it must always be. At other times we move amongst them as if they were not there, talking and laughing as we lug and cut and tidy the pieces, pushing them aside as casually as we might a book or a jacket which lies where one means to sit. But here we work quietly, speaking no more than we must. It is as if this is a ritual, this washing of the dead: as one washes a baby clean of its mother's flesh, so we wipe the grave from these stolen dead, bring them new into the world.

When our work is finished the sacks are tidied away, the buckets emptied, the rags rinsed and left to dry, the books begun. Our master is most particular about the keeping of accounts, and the money paid to Caley and Walker must be noted: eight guineas for a man or woman fully grown, or what we call a *large*; four guineas for a child, or a *small*; a shilling by the inch for what we call a *foetus*, or a baby less than a foot in length. And so, while I mop the cellar floor Robert works quietly on the ledger, making notes of payments made, checking the balances against the contents of the cashbox, his face masked behind the look of quiet sadness he wears when he thinks he is unobserved.

Tonight there were three, two larges and a small, and by the time we are done, and we climb the stairs to the yard to wash our pails and hands at the butt, the sky has begun to lighten the high roofs which surround us. From far off there can be heard the ringing step of a horse upon the cobbles, but otherwise it is still, the air cold, the water from the pipe colder as we scrub our arms, over and over.

———

5

Mr Poll slips two fingers into the dead man's mouth, pulling the jaw open once more. Glancing up he surveys the watching students.

'Death is a mirror,' he says, 'in which life is reflected for our edification.'

Beneath his fingers the dead man's tongue can be seen, purplish-grey like an oxen's on a butcher's slab, the darker mass of the tumour swollen beneath. Pressing down on it he tilts the head, staring in as if he has seen something that interests him. Then, his curiosity seemingly satisfied, he withdraws his fingers and pulls the lips back to expose the teeth, yellow and brown, higgledy-piggledy in the ulcerated flesh of the gums.

If death is a mirror, I find myself wondering, what lies behind it?

Finished with the mouth, he turns to Robert.

'We will begin with the chest. The state of the vital organs must be ascertained.'

A tremor runs through the body as the scalpel pierces the skin. Almost like a sigh, the gas that has swollen in the cavity is released, escaping in a soft breath. The smell is not quite foul, more the clinging scent of the butcher's yard, that peculiarly clammy scent of cut meat intermingling with the first sweetness of putrefaction. I no longer choke on the smell, indeed there is scarcely a smell a body can produce which still turns my stomach, but although I do not gag I am aware of it, even after all these months.

The skin divides in a wake behind Mr Poll's scalpel as he slices in one smooth motion from neck to groin. Carefully he makes more cuts at the top of the incision and at the bottom, then, with a practised motion, he pushes his fingers into the incision and peels back the skin, revealing the red flesh beneath, the white ribs and yellow fat.

Laying the two flaps of skin over the arms, he takes the

saw Robert holds ready. Steadying himself with a hand upon the shoulder, he places the saw against the ribs and begins to cut. The teeth bite into the bone with a wet, splintering rasp, small flecks of meat and bone scattering before it, spattering the aprons we each of us wear. When he is done he lifts the sternum and ribs away, exposing the organs nestled in their broken cage of bone; grey, blue, black. Extending a hand he touches the heart, his thin fingers lingering upon the bluish muscle.

'It does not beat,' he says. The statement seems incontrovertible. But after a moment Mr Poll looks up, his watery blue eyes fixing me with their cold stare.

'Why not?'

I do not answer.

'Do you think it a foolish question, Mr Swift?'

I shake my head. 'No, sir,' I say.

'Perhaps you think its author a fool instead?'

'No,' I say again.

'Then why does it not beat?' he asks once more, and as so often, I feel there is some simple thing expected, something which eluded me. Across the table I see Robert watching, his eyes steady.

'Because he is dead,' I say abruptly, knowing this sounds half-witted. Mr Poll regards me disappointedly, then returns his attention to the corpse.

'And I suppose when once it beat, it beat because he lived.'

———

When our work with them is done, we sack their remains, pile them in the cellar until we may be rid of them. Even now, in November, they grow rotten as they wait, the limbs and torsos swelling and turning foul, though Robert tells me this is the best of it; in the summer the sacks may lie until they are almost liquid. And so each Thursday before dawn we wake and load the sacks into the cart in the half light. The houses opposite standing silent as we work, still sleeping, for though our neighbours know our business it is wisest not to remind them of it more than we must.

The man who brings the cart is a former soldier called Miller. He does not speak as we load the sacks, just grunts when we are done and thrusts out a hand for his fee. Robert has told me that once, two years ago, it was Mr Poll's wish that he travel with Miller to see that the remains were disposed of discreetly and completely. The day chosen was in late spring, a fine, summery day. Robert rode beside Miller, his companion barely speaking, so they travelled in silence, the cart jolting beneath them. All through the long morning and into the afternoon they travelled east along the river, until they came to a low field, bordered by trees on one side and on the other by the river flats. The place was silent, no birds singing, save for a flock of geese, who rose as one, honking and shrieking as the cart approached. In the centre of the field the grass was burnt away, the barren earth scorched and filthy. Robert helped Miller unload the wood he had heaped upon the sacks to disguise them for their passage through the streets, and together they built a pyre. Then, one by one, they shook out the sacks, spreading their contents thinly across the piled wood. Finally he set it burning, stoking and tend- ing the flames. The fire spat and crackled where it took the fat, the flesh bubbling and blackening where it lay. Robert said hell might look like this, legs and arms and heads, jumbled and broken and burning. The smoke that rose from the pyre was oily black, and evil, and Robert said it clung to his clothes like a stain.

It was dusk before the fire was done, the embers glowing in the fading light. And in the gathering darkness Miller took up a post from the cart, and, stepping out across the remnants of the pyre, brought it down again and again upon anything that remained, sparks rising in clouds around him, like fireflies or shooting stars against the great space of the night.

WE WAKE EARLY with the maids and the market boys. Downstairs Mrs Gunn will have risen half an hour since to stoke the fire in the kitchen; sometimes she can be heard, clattering at the door to the yard or conversing with the milk-carrier, but otherwise, high in the eaves the house might yet be asleep. From the streets come the cries of the last revellers of the night before, or the sounds of the first barrows and carriages making their way past the silent windows, but these sounds echo through a world that is, for this brief moment at least, both quiet and still.

Shivering with the cold I hurry from my narrow bed, pulling on my boots and trousers. Gathering the rest of my clothes I make my way downstairs, careful lest I wake Mr Tyne in his room beside the stairs. By the fire Mrs Gunn stirs her pot or converses with Robert as he dresses. Sometimes I will steal a slice of bread or compliment Mrs Gunn upon her hair to watch her blush; if I do Robert will tease her too until she slaps the two of us aside and spoons the porridge out into our bowls.

We have an hour, seldom more. An hour before Mr Poll arrives, and the business of the day begins. But I have come to love this brief time, poised between the dawn and the day's beginning. There is only porridge, and tea, or sometimes bread and milk, but it is enough, for in it we have conversation, and laughter, both coming freely and easily. Of what we speak it would be hard to say – little of any consequence, I am sure – the business of the house and our neighbours, the gossip of the marketplace. Sometimes Mrs Gunn, who has a habit of forming attachments to patients she has glimpsed or whose names she has heard out of all proportion to her contact with them, converses of these poor souls as if they were close acquaintances of all present, offering homilies and advice directed to their happiness, a habit which will often bring Robert and me to tears of hilarity. But of that business which occupies our days and nights, the cutting and the probing of the dead, we do not speak, not here, not now, for in this time we are but men again, as any others, and for that we are content.

———

It is three months since I came here, apprenticed to my master's side so I might learn his trade. That first night the sky overhead as red as fire. Or blood. Robert met me in the yard at the Bell, where the coaches disgorge their cargo of bodies into the city's roil. I knew him by his suit; black like the one I wore myself, new-cut for the life that lay before me.

'You are the partner of my master, Mr Poll?' I asked, and he laughed and shook his head.

'No, that is Charles,' he said, 'I am but a prentice, the same as you.'

Shouldering my bag he led me out into the city streets. Since then I have come to know its avenues and alleyways, but that evening it seemed to me a maelstrom, a tangled maze of yards and passages, of windows heaped with meat and bread and millinery, of gaslight hissing high above the moving crowds. Never had I seen such a place, so many faces, so many bodies pressing by, and though as we went we spoke, I do not recall what words they were that passed between us, only the way the noise of it thrilled inside of me.

It was dark before we reached the house, closed tight against the night. Opening the door he led me up into the room that was to be my own. Placing my bag upon the floor he watched as I crossed to the window, looking out upon the roofs outside. And when I was done he smiled again.

'Come now,' he said, 'we will see if Mrs Gunn is still awake. You have travelled far and will be hungry.'

'BUT WHAT OF the soul?' Marshall demands, his voice breaking across Mr Poll's.

Looking up from the corpse Mr Poll pauses.

'My apologies,' he says, 'you have a question?'

'I asked what of the soul?' Marshall replies, less certainly this time.

Mr Poll stares at him, letting the moment play out at his expense. Charles has set down his scalpel.

'Ah yes,' says Mr Poll, 'the soul.' With a sideways look he surveys his audience. 'And where do you think this soul might have its seat? Here?' he asks, tapping the bisected heart with one finger. Lifting his pale eyes he gazes at Marshall.

'No? Then perhaps it is here?' he suggests, scooping up the brain from the dish in which it lies. From behind Marshall there comes a snigger: Hibbert, I think, a nervous lad, but handy with a knife. On the stand Mr Poll weighs the brain in his hand, his eyes not leaving Marshall's.

'No doubt there is a gland somewhere, a fattened lymph or some such you have in mind. After all, were not toads said to have jewels set within their skulls in less enlightened times?'

Reddening, Marshall looks about, perhaps hoping for some support from his companions.

'I implore you, Mr Marshall, if you know where this gland might be, please do not hesitate in informing us.'

Now there comes a chuckle. Marshall lifts his chin defiantly.

'I cannot say,' he says.

'No,' says Mr Poll, 'I dare say you cannot.' At last, laughter breaks out, unrestrained and contemptuous. In deference to this appreciation Mr Poll inclines his head, then, knowing better than to let the scene outplay itself, he lifts a hand for silence. Almost at once the laughter dies away, leaving an uneasy quiet. Setting down the brain, Mr Poll wipes his hand upon his apron, then with a showman's poise produces a vial.

'See here,' he says, 'in this hand I hold an ounce of iron filings.' Next he takes his notebook and sets it down where the students may see.

'Emptied thus upon a sheet of paper they are inert, their arrangement determined by the accidents of chance. Physics, sir, no less, no more.

'But if a magnet is introduced, then something quite different can be observed,' he says, drawing a small metal rod from a drawer in the cabinet against the wall and placing it upon the page. With a sudden rush the filings shift and slide, their motion almost audible as they skitter across the paper, marking out the lines of force about the magnet's poles.

'No agency is visible, no atoms collide, yet the filings move. But how?'

'Magnetism!' calls one of the students from the rear.

'Your powers of diagnosis are as remarkable as ever, Mr Dawson,' Mr Poll replies, turning back to the body on the table.

'Consider, gentlemen, the man that lies before you here. Once . . . ' With a practised pause he looks down at the figure. In the light from the lamp that hangs overhead, the skin has already begun to mottle, as if fading bruises swam beneath the skin.

'. . . perhaps not quite as recently as we might prefer, he lived. His heart beat, blood coursed in his veins, his body was racked by all appetites carnal and sublime. Yet now he is as clay once more, the motion of his heart and blood gone still, his body cold. Already this shell of flesh begins to spoil, a week more and it will be foul, a year or two but tooth and bone. How can this be, you ask, what has changed? What force that once prevented this inevitable decline has failed, what secret charge has fled?'

'His soul?' quips Hibbert, and though a smile flickers across my master's face the others do not laugh.

'Look more closely at these filings here, and observe the image that they make. Though once inert they now have both shape and energy. Yet we need not invoke the cant of priests to understand how this might be.'

Pausing, he stares out across the silent room. None move, nor speak; they are his.

'We are men of science, gentlemen, students of nature. It is our purpose to tear down the veil of superstition, to pierce the very fabric of our living being and elucidate the nature of the force which animates these shells we call our bodies. And we will find it here, in this cold flesh. For these tissues we will divine the shadow of that force which drove the fuse within, which set his heart to flicker and beat. Call it a soul if you wish, yet I promise you it shall prove no more mysterious than this magnet's power to bend these filings to its will.'

———

With the lecture done the students make their way from the house into the street. Outside the afternoon has gone while we laboured here, and overhead the sky is already pale. Whether Marshall will be back or not I do not know: at a guinea a time it is an expensive way to be made a fool. But if not there will be others to take his place, for while there are many in London who give instruction in the science of anatomy, there are none who can exceed my master in quality of mind. Although the great work that will form the cornerstone of his enduring fame remains unfinished, and he is a man no longer young, in the grim theatre of the dissecting room he plays his role as none other can. With Charles beside him he is fast, merciless, a man in total command of his art, with a wit as sharp as his knife.

Yet in truth his is not an easy disposition. For all his talent, he taunts those who would admire him. A miller's son, sent to London to be made a clerk, who sought instead to be a surgeon – whose services now command a fee second only to that of Sir Astley of Guy's, and who has attended the bedside of dukes and earls. A man who does not seek to hide his origins, nor the way they linger in his voice, but rather flaunts them almost as a goad, who keeps a carriage and fine house on Cavendish Square and whose daughter would be a prize for any man, were she not already being paid court by Charles de Mandeville.

No doubt there are those with whom it rankles to be thus insulted, yet I do not think it is this alone which makes the students uneasy of him. For though as a surgeon and anatomist he has few peers, Mr Poll's true achievements are greater, and deeper. From morning until long after dark he works, his restless energy filling the house, his curiosity often seeming more like a hunger, a monstrous appetite which will not be sated, probing always deeper, seeking to understand not just the structures of the body but the very essence of life itself.

In this cause he has dissected all manner of creatures – crows and horses, fish and apes, insects, snakes, even a hippopotamus once, late of a menagerie in Chelsea – seeking to divine that which binds their being to the cage of their flesh. I have seen experiments too, things which amaze and horrify: a human tooth pulled still living from a harlot's mouth, which took root and grew in a cockerel's comb. The corpse of a newt given brief and slippery life by the application of electricity. A false womb, sewn from the bladder of a horse in which the blood-slathered foetus of a lamb swam briefly, struggling as if it were drowning in the air, before it grew still and died. In our work here, too, we seek out the monstrous and misshapen, those freaks in whom the script of Nature does not read true, for in the twisted mirror of their imperfections we might, he thinks, find the image of our own perfection.

Nor is it just the dead who must bend to our will. I have seen Mr Tyne catch cats in a wicker trap of his own making, and more than once bring men and women here, bought for a florin in the ginshops of St Giles so they might sample some medicine or other and their reactions be measured and recorded. And a week after I came here I lured a dog to the house with a piece of meat so Mr Poll and Charles might open its chest, feel its living heart jump like a fish against our inquiring hands.

———

As the lamps outside are lit the last of the students move away along the street, no doubt to some tavern, in which they will drink and laugh, and take their ease. Returning to the table I look down upon the opened corpse. It is a messy thing, to unstitch the dead, and it is my duty to ensure no trace is left in this room. Beside the basin which contains the heart, bisected to reveal its fat-clogged interior, the notebook Mr Poll used in his demonstration still sits where it was left. For all their theatricality his words have unsettled me, I think: it is a fearsome thing, this atheism of his; to put aside all belief which cannot be measured, to leave behind the strictures of what the world calls morality. Taking up the magnet I weigh it in my hand. Overhead the lamps hiss quietly, a steady sound, almost like rain. On the page the filings still mark out the ghost of the magnet's presence; reaching down, I brush my hand across the page. The filings rustle, a sound like dead leaves, the lines broken where it has passed, the elegant whorls erased. Without the magnet the filings do not move to repair the pattern, instead they lie upon the page inert, unresponsive. They are such thin things, these lives of ours; cheap got, cheap lost, mere flickers against the ever dark, brief shadows on a wall. This life no more substantial than breath, a light which fills the chambers of our bodies, and is gone.

IT WAS LATE that first night before I slept, summer heat giving way first to thunder, then to rain. High in my room I felt the night move by, my body restless in the dark. Outside the clocks chimed twelve, then one.

Then all at once I was awake again. Overhead a cobweb turned, slipping in and out of existence as it moved against a draught; on the roof the rain still moved.

I had been dreaming, though I did not know what of.

As first I did not move, uncertain what had woken me. And then there came a knock, a second one I knew at once, louder and more insistent. In the black I fumbled for my boots, groping my way towards the door.

The hall outside was empty, my movements loud in the unfamiliar space. About me everything silent, and still. The knocking coming again as I descended, making me jump.

Pushing the grille aside I peered out, and a face appeared, pressed so close I could smell the gin's sweet stink upon his breath.

'It's a great time you're taking for such a night,' said a

voice, its accent Irish, and thick. Instinctively I recoiled.

'Who are you?' I demanded, keeping my voice low. There was a moment then in which I felt him watching me. When he spoke again his voice was harder.

'Don't be a fool,' he said, 'just open it.'

'Not without a name,' I insisted.

'Get Tyne, or the prentice, they'll know.'

I hesitated, but as I did I heard a step behind me and, turning, saw Robert there, a lamp held in his hand.

'No, Gabriel,' he said, 'do as he says.'

The owner of the voice was small, and slight; behind him stood a cart, its shape outlined in the rain, another figure holding the horse's head cradled to his chest. Then Mr Tyne at my elbow, his voice sharp in my ear.

'Help them; there's been enough noise already.'

I pulled away, stepping out into the rain. In the doorway Mr Tyne watched, his eyes scanning the length of the sleeping street. Seeing me looking back he smiled, a thin thing of pleasure at my discomfort.

The rain spilled downwards, cold wires descending to strike our faces and cheeks. In the cart the Irishman was lifting something from the straw, a bundle shape, swinging it towards me, and then it was on my shoulder, heavier than I had expected, its bindings wet and thick with the scent of earth. Staggering, I felt the weight within begin to shift, a loose collapsing motion, as if it were soil it held, or stones, cold water running from the sacking and down my neck. And as it did I understood what it was I held, the shock sent me slipping on the oily cobbles. But then Mr Tyne was upon me.

'Sweet Jesus, boy,' he hissed, grabbing me by the arm and pulling me upright, 'would you have the beaks upon us?'

———

Their names were Caley, and Walker. In the dark one might have taken Caley for a boy of fifteen, so slight was he. But by the lights in the cellar he was clearly as old as Robert or I, his slightness not that of youth but of poverty – though with his kissing lips and too-pretty face, there was something of the child about him all the same, callow and cruel, an abruptness in the way he moved which made me uneasy of being close to him.

Once they were gone we unbound the bodies they had brought, began the washing. I should have been repulsed, I thought, as we worked, but I was not, nor was I afraid. Rather, I watched my hands upon their skin move as if they were not my own, as if I were outside myself, my body distant.

———

I did not sleep again that night, images of those faces and bodies rising unbidden in my mind. On my fingers the smell of the vinegar still lingered, and on my arms and neck I could feel the memory of their touch. With the first light of the dawn I rose, taking myself down, back into the yard, and there I ran the butt, watching the water break onto the stones. Slowly I drew up my sleeves, lathering higher, but still I felt them there, and so at last I pulled off my shirt, and leaning forward let the water run across my hair and down my back, knowing even as I did it would not wash their presence from my flesh.

21

M Y FATHER DIED when I was twelve. We found him half
a mile from the house, huddled in the wall's low lee.
His face turned away from the world, into the dark stones,
his body half covered by the snow. The sky overhead as fragile as an egg.

It was our neighbour, Tobias, who first noticed he was
gone. January, the new year scarcely begun. I saw Tobias coming, from where I sat in the window above the kitchen. As
he climbed he stared ahead, his head held stiff and straight;
only rounding the last bend did he seem to look up, his eyes
passing over the ruin of the yard, the broken gig and abandoned furniture.

I had opened the door before he knocked, and he peered
past me into the darkened room.

'How long has he been gone?' he asked. I bit my lip. For
as long as I could remember I had been forbidden to tell
any visitors who should come calling where my father
was.

'Three days,' I said at last. Tobias nodded, looking me over, no doubt considering whether he should take a starving boy with him on the hour's walk into the town.

'The dog is his?'

As if knowing it was she of whom we spoke she pressed her nose against my hand.

'Bring her,' he said.

Although the blizzard had passed, leaving the sky clear and empty, the air outside was cold, our breath rising in clouds. Tobias did not speak as we made our way down the high road, and so I was aware mostly of the silence that surrounded us, the way the lonely cries of the crows echoed out across the empty hills.

As we came about the bend in the road from which the town became visible, the dog lifted her head, her ears rising and tail quivering, as she would each time my father approached the house. Tobias glanced at her, perhaps thinking to tell me to catch hold of her, but she was too quick. For a hundred yards she hurried on, stopping at last before a low drift of snow which had gathered by the wall. For a few seconds she hesitated, emitting a plaintive, confused whine, then lifting her head she yapped twice. Tobias placed a hand upon my shoulder.

'Wait here,' he said, and still not altering his pace he continued on to where the dog stood, pawing at the snow. I watched him stop, and kneel. From the top of the drift a dark shape could be seen; reaching out a hand Tobias touched it, then he stood, and turned to me.

His body bore no sign of any violence. Indeed his face, rimed and blue with ice, seemed almost at peace. It is possible he was taken suddenly by a seizure of the brain or of the heart, but more likely he had grown tired and confused in the falling snow, and fuddled by the drink and the cold had decided to rest awhile. Save for where the dog had scratched at him, nuzzling his frozen flesh as if she

23

might warm it back into life, the snow was untouched, broken only by a long line of bird tracks, which ran across the road towards his form, then turned aside and ended, the bird having taken flight once more, lost to the air and the sky.

———

I remember my father as a restless, unpredictable force, a man possessed of a careless charm and great enthusiasms as well as fits of despondency and impotent rage. He was never violent with me, nor was the harm he did me done with any calculation, it was simply that he lived too much at the mercy of his own nature. Indeed, most often I seemed barely to exist to him, then, as if remembering me, he would seek to force upon me an intimacy we did not share. Had he lived even a few years longer I might have seen in him what I now guess he was, a man too fond of drink and cards, unhappy somewhere deep within himself, whether from some harm done him long before or by natural inclination, and possessed of the gambler's temperament, with its wild vacillations and capacity for self-deception. Yet to me he was simply my father, a figure I desired to be close to but had learned through experience not to trust.

Even from this distance though I can see something of the man he was when young. Handsome, charming, filled with wild energy and a sense of his own possibility. His father managed the manor farm, and yet it was his father's employer who took an interest in him and saw he got his letters, that his rough edges were smoothed away so he might find a place in the world. It was a fine figure he cut, I am sure, for he rode as if born to the saddle, and even near the end, when his looks had blurred and his clothes were ragged, he could still charm a maid or a passing lady with some show of gallantry.

Full of gin and regret, he would sometimes speak of those early years, not with the bitterness I might expect but with something like fondness. Disowned when he eloped with his benefactor's daughter, then left a widower with a child to raise before six months were up, he soon found the manners and the charm that had sustained him wore thin under the weight of his gambling, and so began the long, slow slipping down that was to be our life together. From London to Bath, from Bath to Liverpool, from Liverpool to York and finally to the road where he died, high in the hills above the city, only a few miles from the town in which he was born.

———

I waited by my father's corpse with the dog for company while Tobias walked the last mile or so into town. The day was still, and all about the snow glittered in the sunlight. I remember looking down at him, the dull presence of his silent form. No doubt it came as a shock, but I do not remember feeling surprise or even grief, only a kind of dull-ness, as if this discovery were somehow always waiting here to be made by me, in this moment. This is what the world is, I remember thinking, a place of absences, and leavings.

On the day of the funeral Tobias walked with me into the town. He was a Methodist, as many were already in those parts, and so would not join me by the grave, but he stood close enough for me to see him, his hands crossed before him, his hat held in them. I do not doubt my father would have liked to have been remembered as a popular man, yet his passage that day was marked by his son, the priest and two men who would not again see the money they had lent him.

Once the ceremony was over the rector took me aside. He was a small man, running to fat, and though I did not know him I had heard from one of the children of the town that he had had a son who died of a fever the summer past, a sickly child who had never prospered.

'Tobias says you can read,' he said.

I did not reply, just stood.

'I could use a boy in the classroom,' he said, 'to help me with my teaching.'

Sometimes I wonder what would have come of me had he not spoken that day. An orphanage perhaps, maybe some farm if I were lucky. But instead I ate with him in the Rectory, and studied in the school he kept. But though he treated me as if I were his own I felt no love for him, only failure, as if some vital part had died in me that day.

BY BARNARD'S INN I hear a shout, my name called loud amidst the racket of the street. Startled, I stop, and then it comes again, issuing from a coach on the road's other side. Its window open, Charles within.

'Is it not late for you to be about?' he calls.

'I have been with a friend of my guardian,' I begin, but he cuts me off with a grin.

'It was a joke, Gabriel,' he says. 'Where does this friend of yours reside?'

'Camden –' I begin again, only to be silenced by a shout from within the coach.

'Boring!'

I hesitate, but Charles is not to be deterred.

'And now where are you bound?'

'Home,' I say, then correct myself. 'Back to the house.'

Inside the coach there is a groan, as if its utterer has been pushed beyond all endurance. Charles hesitates, glances over his shoulder, then with a look I do not fully understand turns back to me.

'Come with us,' he says.

I shake my head.

'I do not think . . .' I say, but Charles waves me down.

'Why ever not? Your work is done for the week.' He opens the door so I may climb up. 'Do not fear,' he says. 'We will get you home again.'

The carriage is already full, Charles and another three I do not know seated two a side, so as I clamber in they must shift and squeeze to make room for me. The driver calls down a complaint that five is too many for his horses, but this only elicits a jeer from the one who sits opposite me. When the driver persists he rises to his feet and shouts a threat, and so the thing is ended and with a curse the driver cracks his whip. Falling back into his seat the man regards me scornfully.

'What manner of bird is this?' he asks of Charles, his face contemptuous. Though not tall he has a powerful frame and would be handsome, in a brutal sort of way, were it not for his nose, the line of which is broken, as if inexpertly set.

'Gabriel Swift,' I say, reaching out my hand. To my shame he does not do the same, just looks down at it incredulously. This insult seems to provoke his companion to great merriment, and all at once I realise that they are drunk.

'His name is Chifley,' Charles interrupts, 'and he is an insolent cur for not taking your hand.'

At this Chifley bellows with laughter. 'I'd not shake hands with you, de Mandeville, were you not paying for my drinks.'

Charles smiles at this, his eyes narrowing.

'This is Caswell,' he says, indicating the man who sits to Chifley's left. Although he can be little older than Charles or Chifley his pale brown hair is already thinning. No doubt in an attempt to remedy this deficiency he has affected a style in which the sides are grown longer and swept across the crown. His face too is that of an older man, weak and plumpish, but kind enough. Unlike Chifley he extends a hand, which I take.

Finally Charles turns to the figure beside me, who sits in silence. 'And this is May,' he says. May reaches out and takes my hand, clasping it in his and shaking it rather too vigorously. His face is gaunt, and has a strange pallor about it, but he smiles readily enough.

'Where was it you said you had been?' Charles asks. I had thought him drunk a moment ago, as Chifley and Caswell plainly are, but now he seems his usual self.

'The home of a friend of my guardian,' I say. 'Mr Wickham, who has the parish in Camden.'

'You go there often?'

'I have been his guest three times.' Thinking of the stultifying evenings I have spent there, listening to the droning voice of Mr Wickham and the tuneless warbling of his daughter, Georgiana, I hesitate. 'They have been most kind to me.'

Charles smiles gently. 'It seems a poor way for a young man to spend his evening.'

This is a talent of Charles, I have learned, to make those with whom he speaks feel he has understood the true meaning of their words. 'I have few alternatives,' I say, grinning. 'My friends in London are not numerous.'

'What of Robert?'

'He is with his family tonight.'

Perhaps bored by our conversation Chifley begins to sing, and almost at once Caswell and May join him. Charles looks at them, then back to me.

'Where are we going?' I ask.

Charles leans back, a secret smile playing on his lips. 'Does it matter?'

———

As the carriage jolts over the stones I look across at Charles. Three months I have worked alongside him and yet for all his humour and warmth I feel I have little grasp on who he is. A parson's son, he trained first with Sir Astley and later on the Continent, earning fame for the steadiness of his hand and the swiftness of his work. Robert says that Mr Poll believed no man his equal in the skills of their craft, until he met Charles. It was Mr Poll then who petitioned for Charles's admission into the College of Surgeons.

Since then Charles's reputation has grown to rival that of men twice his age, and his services are sought after by many of quality and influence. Yet a stranger might wonder at the closeness of the bond between Charles and Mr Poll, so different are their natures. Where Mr Poll holds himself always aloof, Charles has an ease which brings comfort to all he encounters, speaking not just as an equal but as a friend to those he treats, as at home in the rooms of the humblest as in the parlours of the powerful.

———

The carriage delivers us to a low-ceilinged tavern just off the Strand. Inside it is crowded with a great many men and women who sit pressed close one against the other or swirl between the tables. Everywhere is talking and laughter and hilarity. Charles and Chifley lead us to a table by the fire and, calling for the owner, order veal chops. I hear this nervously: my first months in London have been expensive ones, and have consumed almost all of the money my guardian provided me. Although I have written to him seeking an advance upon the money for the next half-year, I am worried I will be unable to pay, and even more alarmed that I may have to admit it. Charles though sees my discomfort, giving me a confidential look and telling me not to concern myself, I shall celebrate as they do tonight. Confused, I ask what the occasion is, which provokes great amusement, but before I can get to the bottom of this, wine is brought, and glasses filled and raised.

As we drink I try to divine what I can of my new companions. Chifley buys and sells horses, I learn, although he seems to treat his business as little more than an excuse to ridicule those who would use his services. By contrast Caswell, though amiable enough, appears to have no profession. And May calls himself an artist, although it is difficult to imagine him at the canvas, for he talks almost without stopping, breaking in and interrupting himself as he goes, as if humming with some mad energy. The effect of this is almost endearing, for he is utterly without malice, and laughs constantly, but there is something uncomfortably vulnerable in his guilelessness. He drums his fingers on the table in a rapid tattoo, and though I cannot feel annoyed, the habit angers Chifley, who several times demands that he stop, but each time he starts again, until at last he excuses himself and vanishes to the room Chifley insists on calling the thunderbox.

The chops are very fine, and although I have dined already this evening I eat them hungrily. Chifley waves a hank of bread in my direction.

'Do you starve this sparrow?' he demands of Charles, who looks at me with a quizzical smile.

'Do we starve you, Gabriel?' he asks.

I shake my head, telling him no, although this is not entirely true. At Mr Poll's ruling, Robert and I eat mostly tripe and gruel, our master holding excess of meat a source of melancholy. For a few moments Charles contemplates me, then he splashes more wine into my glass and bids me drink.

———

I am not sure when it dawns on me that I am drunk. Caswell is singing some song about a shepherd and a milkmaid, the detail of which I am having difficulty following, although I find it quite hilarious. On the crown of his head, what remains of his sandy brown hair has stood up in a kind of tuft, and his scalp shines pinkly beneath. But he sings in a fine tenor, eyes closed as if he is lost in his own voice, the rich sound incongruous from such a foolish, nervous-looking man. Charles has one of the women on his lap; for some time they have been engaged in a conversation in which he whispers things to her and she giggles, then whispers back. Where May has got to I am not sure, but Chifley is beating on the table, urging Caswell to sing again. A waiter is filling my glass, and I join in the cry that has gone up for Caswell to sing again, stamping my feet on the flags and pounding the table. Then, we are in the street and someone else is singing, not Caswell now but Chifley, I think; a face is pressed at the carriage window, leering, someone shouting from above us to be quiet. Sometime in this there is a moment when my gorge rises and, flinging open the door, I fall into the street, my stomach spilling its contents onto the cobbles like an upended wineskin, burning my throat and nose. When I am done being sick I feel myself lifted from behind, and my feet begin to move beneath me, then all at once I am on the doorstep of the house, and Charles and Chifley are thrusting me through the open door.

IN ITS WOMB of glass it hangs suspended, half-turned as if it sought to hide itself from the viewer's gaze. Though it has but one set of legs, above the waist a second, smaller body grows, a chest and arm which emerge from the chest of the first, and though this second body is but half-made, on its top there is a head, as perfect as the body is grotesque. Half-hidden by its larger twin this smaller head seems to sleep, nestled close against its protector, the tiny form cradled by the larger's arm.

But while the smaller sleeps the larger is awake, or so it appears, for by some trick of the preserver's art its eyes are rendered so they seem to follow the viewer to every corner of the room. The lids half-hooded over sightless orbs, their depths somehow malign, like those of a toad or some heavy, hateful thing, jealous of life and all its joys. But for the puckered stitches which run in a Y from their necks to their common nave, their skin is smooth, perfect as any child's, yet pale and chill as marble or alabaster.

On the shelves all about stand a hundred other jars, each

filled with their own monstrosity. In some the limbs and organs of the dead preserved, hands and eyes, ears and feet, their flesh turned grey and horrible by the alcohol; in others different things, less easily recognised: a blackened lung, a massive heart, an eyeball trailing its white thread of nerve like a jellyfish. In one stands the head of a man neatly bisected with a saw, the face on one side perfect and unblemished, eyes closed as if but for a moment, the other half pressed close against the glass to reveal the layers of bone and brain and muscle, the delicate chambers of the nose, the tongue's fat root. But here too are other things, less easy for the untutored eye to look upon, ones which draw their shapes from the shadowed realms of fevered sleep. Six-fingered hands, a scaled foot, the generative organs of an hermaphrodite, a half-grown cock and balls nestled in its vagina's anemone folds. And in their midst a line of larger jars, each holding a child deformed in some dreadful way: one's head an empty sac which billows on its neck; another made as a mermaid is, its back and legs disappearing into serpent coils; the head of the next turned inside out, the teeth growing in concentric rings through the exposed meat of the palate as if the inverted hole sought to consume the face in which it sits from chin to brow.

Each is preserved through the work of Mr Tyne, by whose cunning hands these creatures and their skeletons are given this semblance of life. Once, long ago, he was apprenticed to Gaunt, who makes teeth for the rich. From him he learned the art of setting teeth with wire and horn, of carving palates and clamps to hold them tight in their new owner's mouths. And from him as well he learned to find teeth, whether from the living or, more often, from the mouths of the dead. It was through this trade that he came to the attention of Mr Poll, who saw in him even then a talent for the craft, for the finding of the dead and the purloining of their riches. In time he bought Mr Tyne from his apprenticeship and took him as his own, setting him to work among the rookeries and slums, procuring the bodies of the dead as he once procured their teeth for Gaunt.

In every way he is my master's man, his faithful shadow, uncomplaining in his diligence, ruthless in Mr Poll's interests. Throughout the city he has men and places that he goes, sniffing out cases in which my master might find interest, arranging for the delivery of those we cannot save to the house. His is a secret nature, prying and watchful, and though he has no power over Robert and me, we have learned to watch him well, and trust him not at all. For there is no trace of kindness in him, however these creations that he makes seem to show the stifling hand of a mother's love, and he treats this house as if it were his own. But though he is my master's man in every outward way, I have sometimes glimpsed another thing within, a hatred harboured deep inside, as if he bridled to be so possessed.

A S THE DANCING PAUSES and she lowers her mask I feel myself tremble; in the hissing cast of the limelight her face shivers, as if she were at once real and insubstantial, a creature composed not of matter but of the substance of dreams. Marked out against the ghostly pale of the stage paint, her eyes look huge, liquid, her mouth wide as an ache.

Amidst the swirling colour of the ball upon the stage she stands like a point of stillness, and I stare at her, hungry, frightened she might somehow evaporate or I might wake, losing the sense of her lines in the urgency of this feeling. In the pit the orchestra is playing again, the audience laughs, then she replaces her mask and steps aside so her companion might speak once more.

The play is a drama, a thing of pirates and Turks set in a Venetian palace. She plays not the heroine, but a smaller role, a friend, and as the play proceeds she comes and goes, sometimes lingering with the heroine or the man who would be her lover, sometimes with the actor who plays the man that she herself desires. Her largest scene is the attempted seduction of her by the villain of the piece, which she plays with a strange kind of resignation, as if she has already lost herself to him in her mind, and her own lover's rescue of her, when it comes, is already too late. Each time she appears she takes the audience's attention, all of us, even the murmuring crowd in the stalls below falling quiet when she speaks. Why this should be is not clear, for she does not play to them as the others do, nor does she invest her lines with great drama. Indeed the part seems no more than a semblance, meant to disguise something else, something unrevealed and unsaid, an illusion within an illusion.

———

Later, in the rooms to which we repair, I see her pass through. Her face is clean of the paint, and she seems smaller, almost fragile. She walks with a pair of men and a young woman with blonde hair. She does not look our way as she moves through the room, but I cannot help but tense. May's mouth comes close to my ear.

'What is it you see, my little bird?'

'That woman, she was in the play,' I say, not sure whether it is a question or a statement.

'She was,' May says. His breath is hot. 'You think her beautiful?'

I nod, and May chuckles. Chifley too has seen me look-ing at her.

'Your prentice is learning your habits, de Mandeville,' he declares. There is laughter then, but also the look in Chifley's eye as he laughs, the chill of his appraisal.

THE KNOCK COMES unexpectedly, loud in the empty house. As the door opens, there is the noise of the street, a voice, the words inaudible. Then, sure and steady, the sound of a man's boots, overhead, moving closer.

Uneasily I rise, turning to face the figure who descends the stairs. He is tall, and powerful, and though no longer young moves with the tread of a man aware of his own strength and unafraid of it. By the fire he stops, opening his hands to warm them.

'A wet night,' he says. His voice is deep, its tones those of a gentleman.

'Indeed,' I say, glancing towards Mrs Gunn, who stands on the stairs behind him. She does not speak, just shakes her head, her face communicating some warning I cannot understand.

'They say a child was taken down a drain in Finsbury and drowned,' he says, looking at me as if to see how I will respond.

'What is your business here?' I ask. 'Whom do you seek?'

He smiles at this.

'Your name is Swift, is it not?' he asks, his eyes narrowing.

'It is,' I say carefully. He nods, his gaze straying to the books spread upon the table. On one page is a diagram, a picture of a child still huddled in its mother's womb, the image engraved with terrible precision. Reaching down he lets his fingers stray over it, then turns the page so he may see the next.

'You are apprenticed here, they say, bound by your guardian, your master's cousin.'

It makes me uneasy that he should know such things. In the silence he looks up again.

'Who are you?' I ask, and he laughs, a curiously silky sound.

'You mean they have not told you?' he asks, watching me. 'Lucan, my name is Lucan.'

I do not reply.

'Perhaps there are things they think it better you not know,' he says, and turns another page.

In the fire's light his wide mouth and hooded eyes lend something sensual to the too-brutal line of his jaw and his crooked nose. Not handsome, but something else, less easy to describe.

'Your master, Swift, where is he?' he asks, his voice lingering on my name as if tasting it.

'Not here.' The edge of the table is hard against my thigh.

'And de Mandeville?'

I shake my head. For a long moment he stands, unspeaking, his eyes not leaving mine. I feel the power of him, almost like a desire it trembles in me.

'If you have a message for my master or Mr de Mandeville I shall ensure they receive it.'

His eyes crease in amusement. Turning away he reaches into his jacket and produces a silver case. It is small, and carved in an Oriental fashion. With a practised gesture he

39

flicks it open, offering me one of the thin Turkish cigars within. I have smoked these cigars before – May is fond of them – but as I look down it is not the cigars I am struck by but the hand. Large, and long, its nails are chipped and grimy like those of a labourer, and though swollen with rheumatism the fingers are decorated with a profusion of rings such as a tinker or a Moslem might wear.

I shake my head. He waits, then with a small gesture of resignation withdraws one for himself and closes the case.

'I do not like your manner with me, Swift,' he says, taking a taper from the fire and lifting it to the cigar.

'I am sorry for that,' I reply. 'But this is my master's house, and you are a visitor.'

Drawing back on his cigar he lets the smoke coil slowly from his nostrils.

'Your master treats me as he might a servant. It would not hurt him to learn some courtesy.'

'Is that what you would have me tell him?'

He stares at me long enough for me to think better of my words. Then he chuckles, as if I have pleased him somehow.

'Yes,' he says, 'tell him that.' Then, moving slowly, with the steady, hypnotic motion of a snake, he lifts a hand and takes my face in it, turning it so he may look more closely upon me.

'You are a good-looking boy, Swift,' he says. 'The lady patients must enjoy your ministrations.'

The smell of his tobacco is heady and sweet, and though I know I should, I cannot break away, my body in the grip of some strange paralysis. Beneath heavy lids his eyes are so dark as to be almost black, and within them is a kind of fire.

From above there comes the sudden sound of the street door, the voice of Mr Poll and Oates, who drives his carriage. With a chuckle Lucan releases me and steps away.

'Perhaps I shall speak with your master after all,' he says, lifting his cigar to his lips.

———

In the hall upstairs Mr Poll falls still at the mention of Lucan's name.

'What?' he asks. His manner gives me the uncomfortable sense that he holds me somehow responsible for this breach. Behind him his driver Oates takes a step back, Mr Poll's coat clasped in his pudgy hand. 'On what business does he come here?'

'I do not know,' I say. 'Only that he would speak with you.'

Mr Poll considers this news. Then with a shake of his head he smiles, though not kindly.

'Tell him I will see him in my study.'

———

Mr Poll does not speak as Lucan enters. Instead he stands, observing him with poorly concealed contempt.

'You have business with us?' he asks.

'Perhaps,' Lucan says. 'I have heard things spoken you would do well to hear.'

'Indeed?' asks Mr Poll, mocking. 'What might these things be?'

'It is said Caley boasts he has made you and the others his fools. That he takes pleasure in taking money for bodies he does not deliver and cheats you wherever he can.'

'Caley says it is you who interferes with his work.'

Lucan smiles. 'Were I to interfere they would do more than complain of it.'

'You threaten me?' Mr Poll snaps. 'Remember whose

41

house you are in: I no longer have to submit to your extortions.'

'Extortion is a word I would use carefully if we are to remain friends,' says Lucan, his voice angry now. But Mr Poll only laughs.

'Do not flatter yourself that we are friends,' he says.

Lucan falls still. Suddenly I realise Mr Poll intended I bear witness to this insult. All at once Lucan laughs.

'There may come a time you wish you had not dismissed my friendship so lightly,' he says, and though he smiles his meaning cannot be mistaken.

Though it is my place to take my master's part, as I lead Lucan to the door I am ashamed for reasons that are not clear to me. Though he is proud Mr Poll is not a cruel man, nor a foolish one, yet I cannot help but feel he has acted ill. On the doorstep Lucan turns to me.

'All men are hostage to their natures, would you not say?' he asks, his eyes unreadable. In the street behind him the rain is falling, the lamps bleeding light into the misty air.

'You do not think our wills may master them?' I reply.

For a long moment he stands. Then at last he smiles, whether in amusement or contempt I do not know.

'No doubt we shall meet again,' he says, and inclining his head in a sort of bow he turns and steps out into the night.

I AM SEATED by the fire in the kitchen when Robert returns. He looks thin tonight, and tired too, but still he offers me some of the bread and stew Mrs Gunn has left so I may eat with him. When I refuse he looks at me curiously, but does not press. He has but little care for food, I think, and often will forget to eat. And even when he does so he eats slowly and methodically, as though each mouthful must be reflected on as it is chewed. At last he looks up, and with a smile asks what troubles me.

'Lucan was here,' I say. Robert does not pause with the mouthful that he chews, but once he has done he lays down his fork and looks at me.

'On what business?'

I shake my head. 'I am not sure,' I say. 'He sought to speak to Mr Poll.'

'And did he?'

'He did,' I say.

'And what did Mr Poll say to him?'

'That he flattered himself if he thought that they were friends.'

Robert nods, and taking up a piece of bread dips it in what remains of his stew.

'What is it?' I ask.

He shakes his head. 'There is no sense in this.'

'I do not understand.'

'To set ourselves against Lucan thus.'

'You would have us bow to his threats?'

'I would not make enemies of men who might cause us harm. He has reason enough to hate us as it is.'

He stops and looks at me. 'What do you know of him?'

'That he is a resurrectionist, as Caley is, and that he holds half the anatomists in London to ransom.'

Robert nods. 'You know too that he once worked for us, and for Sir Astley and the others, and that Caley and Walker were his men?'

He dips into the stew again, then continues. 'He sought to force us to pay more and more, and threatened to starve us if we did not. And so they determined they would humble him. By our master and Sir Astley's efforts Caley was broken from him, then as one the Club stood against him.'

'They were right to stand against him.'

'Perhaps. But the prices were driven by our own greed as much as by his. And besides, there is something that could be given far more cheaply, something Lucan seeks more than money.'

'And what is that?'

'Respect,' Robert says. 'He was a gentleman once.'

I make a sound of contempt, and Robert looks up from the plate, his eyes steady.

'You think their own pride does not interfere with their judgement? Then ask yourself: how is it that Lucan still works if they stand as one against him?'

'He sells to van Hooch, and Brookes and the others,' I say.

'Those anatomists who are not gentlemen and are not permitted membership of the Anatomical Club.'

Robert nods. 'No man will suffer his pride to be injured easily,' he says. 'And we have injured Lucan's in more ways than one.'

'And Caley?' I ask. 'How was he divided from Lucan?'

Robert gives a short, mirthless laugh. 'This is London, Gabriel – everything is for sale.'

———

Later tonight Caley will come, bearing bodies, and I will see the way that Robert and Mr Tyne are careful of him, as if they fear he shall learn Lucan was here. And though he makes no mention of it, as he turns to go he smiles, and asks what it is that we hide from him. And when we tell him nothing, then he just stands, examining us. He might be cruel but he sees lies well enough, and weakness too.

Now, though, upon the stairs, I find Mr Tyne, his body placed so as to block my path.

'How came he here?' he asks.

'I do not know,' I say. But Mr Tyne does not shift, and in his eyes is suspicion, a violence I have not seen before.

'You spoke to him alone?'

'I did,' I reply uneasily.

'And what did he say to you?'

'Nothing.' I shake my head.

For a long time he does not move. Then at last he steps aside so I may pass, his body close to mine, his eyes hard upon my face.

IN THE DAYS that follow the weather grows worse: first rain, then sleet, then a choking mist which settles on the streets and will not lift. Everywhere the air is thick with it, its fumes burning at the eyes and throat. Then as quickly as it came the mist is gone, the days as clean and clear as ice. No wind, just stillness, the freezing ache that comes before the snow. Upon the air the scent of burning coal and woodsmoke.

With the cold comes illness, blackened lung and pneumonia, all the afflictions of the poor, and so in the evenings we are often called to visit those who live in the narrow streets and tenements of St Giles and Saffron Hill. They have nothing to pay and yet we go to them, bringing what comfort we can, even if it is only a kind word or two.

It oppresses me, to be with these people, to see their naked need. There are so many of them, so few of us, the comfort that we bring is so small. I have no ease with them, no words to give, as Charles has, no sense of when I should be still and let them speak, as Robert does.

Afterwards, if we are alone, Charles will bid me come to

drink somewhere, or watch some show upon a stage. Sometimes the others will be there, sometimes not. In his company I begin to learn something of a city I would not otherwise have seen. That Robert knows where we go I am sure, though he never asks of it, nor does Charles often include him in the invitation.

Then, one evening early in December, I am woken after midnight by someone at the door below. Rising, I stand quietly at the top of the stairs, listening to the voice of Mr Tyne. We are alone tonight: Robert granted leave to visit his mother's home, his sister being ill; Charles and Mr Poll gone home. Hearing Mr Tyne's step coming up now, I begin to descend.

'There's a lady here,' he says when we meet on the stairs, 'asking for Mr de Mandeville.'

'I left him two hours since,' I say. 'He will not be back tonight.'

'You think I have not told her that?' Though his words are sharp he checks himself, as if seeking my confidence.

'What is her name?' I ask.

'She will not say,' he replies, 'only that she must speak with him.'

I step past him, down the stairs, not knowing what I will find. Some poor maid perhaps, sent running on her mistress's behalf and ordered to be discreet; maybe some wretch from the streets of St Giles or Saffron Hill bringing word of a relative's sudden worsening and too afraid of Mr Tyne to give a name. But what awaits me is neither. She stands by the fireplace, her coat still buttoned, and though I cannot see her face I know it is her immediately.

'You are the apprentice?' she asks. Her voice is deeper, less certain than it was upon the stage.

'I am,' I say. In the light of the fire her dark hair is the colour of burnished metal, and her face seems to shimmer as it did that night.

'And Mr de Mandeville?'

'He will not return tonight,' I say.

At this she turns her head, and all at once I see she is younger than I had thought, perhaps not much older than myself.

'Please,' I say, 'what is it you need?'

She looks undecided. Her eyes are that deep brown one rarely sees, more like those of a deer or some wild creature.

'A child,' she says at last. 'A dog has attacked him.'

'The child is your own?' I ask, feeling a sudden pang, but she shakes her head.

'A friend's.'

'His injuries are serious?' I ask.

She nods. I think for a moment, then gesture for her to accompany me.

'Then I will take you to him,' I say.

———

Outside Charles's rooms I strike the roof of the cab, and telling her to wait I climb out. A light is visible in Charles's window three floors above; lifting my hand to the door I strike at it, then step back and urgently call his name upwards. Almost at once a figure appears behind the glass, drawing back the drapes before vanishing again. A few seconds pass, and then the street door opens, revealing not Charles's valet, Holroyd, but Charles himself, a lamp held in his hand.

'Gabriel,' he says, holding the lamp higher, 'is there some emergency?' Before I can answer there is a step upon the stones.

'Arabella?' he asks. 'What is this? What are you doing here?'

Though he seeks to hide it there is something in his voice, some fear, and it is in her face as well, that sad, wary look we reserve for those with whom we have shared an intimacy which is now gone.

'Is it Kitty? Has something happened to her?'

'Not Kitty,' Arabella says. 'Oliver.'

At this Charles falls still. When he speaks again his voice is softer.

'Dead?'

She shakes her head. 'Hurt, most grievously.' Her words are spoken in a flat voice which seems to speak of private meanings.

Charles hesitates. 'Let me fetch my coat,' he says then.

It is some moments before he returns, moments we spend standing in silence in the darkened street. Now we are here Arabella does not look at me. When Charles returns he places a hand upon my shoulder.

'Thank you, Gabriel,' he says. 'I will speak to you tomorrow.'

'I will ride with the driver,' I volunteer, the cab only being large enough for two. Something in my manner must give Charles pause.

'Very well,' he says.

———

The cab delivers us to a street near Drury Lane. Although it is not the worst street in the district, it is a dilapidated place, the buildings stained almost black by the soot, broken windows gaping here and there, some left unrepaired, others boarded shut. Underfoot the road is rutted and muddy, and even in the cold a foul smell hangs over the place, as if a privy has overflowed.

The house Arabella leads us into was once a better place than it is now. Pale shapes on the wall still show where paintings hung, but any trace of luxury is long vanished, its rooms divided into a warren of individual lodgings, the paper on the walls peeling and spotted with mildew. Charles says nothing as we ascend the stairs; his mouth set, face closed.

On the third floor we come to a room which must have been a study once, or perhaps a bedroom, for its walls are decorated with frescoes, much damaged by the damp, and heavy curtains musty with age hang across the windows. Now it is a parlour of some sort, furnished with a faded divan and two chairs. At the sound of our arrival a maid appears at a door on one side; she is thin and poorly dressed. Seeing Arabella, she motions to us to enter the further room quietly.

Inside a woman lies upon a bed, the child's form cradled in her arms. As we enter she looks up, and though her eyes are swollen with tears there is no mistaking the anger in the gaze she fixes upon Charles.

For a moment Charles stands, staring back at her. Once, perhaps not long ago, she was beautiful, but now her face has the hard cast of poverty, its look of desperation. Without speaking Charles extends a hand towards the child. The woman watches his hand, then, as if it revolts her, she draws back. Charles lets the hand fall to his side.

'Please, Kitty,' he says. 'I must see him.'

For a long moment she stares at him, then with a sudden, convulsive movement she passes the boy to Charles, who takes him in his arms and, bearing him to the divan under the window, lays him down. As he draws back the blanket he does not flinch, but I feel the way the sight of what lies beneath runs through his frame. The boy is barely conscious, his breath coming in shallow gasps, and at first it is hard to make out the extent of the injuries, for all that is visible is blood and ruined flesh.

'A dog did this?' I ask, regretting the vehemence of my words even as I speak them.

'Its master said it was a country dog, that the carriages had startled it,' Arabella says softly.

By the door the maid cuts in. 'There were no carriages, the dog was wild.'

Charles is listening, his eyes not leaving the boy. His face is expressionless, as if all feeling has drained out of it.

'Bring me water,' he says when the women are done, 'and rags. We must clean him.'

In the kitchen Arabella takes down a pot from above the fireplace, and begins to fill it, her arms cradling the pitcher as she pours. She is smaller than I had thought at first, and slighter, and as she stands lost in this task there is a fragility in her presence I had not glimpsed before. As the last of the water falls, and the pitcher rises in her hand, she looks up, and I see again the way she seems to exist within herself.

'Were you there?'

She pauses, then shakes her head. 'Tetty was with him.'

'The maid?'

'He gave her a sovereign; such a fine gentleman.'

For a moment we stand united thus, caught in the knowledge of this thing. Then she lifts the pot, heavy now with water, and places it in my hands.

'Here,' she says, 'take this in. I will fetch some rags,' her eyes level and clear.

———

Charles sends the women away before we begin, Arabella and the maid helping Kitty from the bed and leading her to the room outside. Then we take the water and sponge the blood from the boy's skin, wary lest we set those of his wounds which have already skinned bleeding again. Several times he regains consciousness, whimpering and moaning, and once looking up with sudden clarity, but for the most part he is quiet. As the extent of his injuries is revealed a heaviness descends upon Charles, as if he knows already that the battle is lost. The right arm is ruined, two fingers missing from the hand, the flesh on the forearm and elbow so lacerated and torn in places that bone and sinew are visible, shocking white against the oozing blood, while across the shoulder and neck and chest bruises and puncture wounds are everywhere. But it is the face and head which are the worst, his scalp torn clean away from the skull, the hair and meat hanging on a grisly flap where the ear protrudes. Perhaps once he was a handsome boy, but now the face has been almost destroyed as well, the nose and cheeks mauled, the right eye staring blindly from a mass of oozing flesh, its lid ripped away altogether.

When the wounds are clean we begin work. Carefully Charles stitches and sews, folding the scalp back onto the skull, closing those of the wounds he can. An hour passes, then two, and more, time slipping away as we are lost into the careful business of our craft. The boy by now is delirious, moaning and murmuring as dreams chase through his mind, mercifully oblivious to what is being done to him. The hand is beyond help, and we must remove part of it before the injuries can be repaired. As the saw bites through the tiny bones I see a look of revulsion mar Charles's handsome face, but he continues nonetheless. And when we are done we bandage him carefully, and bear him to the bed, where we lay him in its centre, his breathing shallow, and slow.

———

Kitty and Arabella are seated on the divan, Kitty's head laid across Arabella's lap. As we enter, Kitty rises, her face searching Charles's for some sign. Charles goes to her, and to my surprise Kitty grasps him about the neck and presses him to herself, her body expelling a long, wrenching sound. Arabella places a hand on Kitty's shoulder.

'We have done what we can,' Charles says to Arabella.

Arabella stays quiet, and for a long time the three of them stand like this, until at last Charles unknots Kitty's arms from his neck and passes her back to Arabella.

'May we see him now?' Arabella asks.

Charles nods. 'Send word if he grows worse.'

With Kitty, Arabella goes to the bedroom door. The maid starts to follow, but does not cross the threshold, lingering instead in the doorway, her back to us.

From within there is a murmuring, and then the maid turns away, looking at the floor. The gesture is so eloquent. Anyone would know without being told that it was she who had charge of the boy when he was mauled.

'Come,' says Charles. 'There is nothing more we can do here.'

Outside the dawn has come and gone. Picking our way through the mud which sucks at our boots we walk slowly westwards. Here and there the business of the day has begun – a driver brushing the gleaming coat of his horses, a maid emptying a bucket into the roadway, the first sweepers of the day patrolling their corners – but for the most part the streets are still empty of life. Charles does not speak, his silence forbidding my questions.

By Drummond's Bank, where we must part, one of the barrows bound for the market has overturned, spilling its load of turnips across the cobbles and attracting the attention of a pig, which roots and snuffles after them. Desperate to save his stock, the barrow's owner, a shabby man with a twisted walk, is trying to drive the pig away with a stick. He is a small man though, and not strong, while the pig is a monster of a thing, all swinging belly and yellow tusks, and is little deterred, each blow merely evincing a squeal and sending it tottering sideways on its absurdly dainty feet, without slowing its gobbling. Who the pig belongs to is not clear, but the scene has attracted the attention of a trio of urchins, who now dart about the barrow, eagerly filling their shirts and pockets with the turnips, while the frantic owner puffs and grabs at them, even as he battles with the pig.

'What can be done for people who live like this?' Charles asks at last. His words are spoken as much to himself as to me.

'The child will die, will he not?' I reply.

Charles nods, not looking round. 'Most likely.'

Now the barrow's owner strikes the pig across the snout. The blow is quick and hard, and it clearly stings, for the pig raises its head and bellows with rage, its hot breath clouding the freezing air as it turns to focus on its attacker. Apprehensive, the barrow's owner takes a step back, but then he is struck in the head by a turnip thrown by one of the children. The pig forgotten, he wheels about, waving the stick and grabbing at his assailant.

'Is Kitty an actress as Arabella is?' I ask. Charles turns as if noticing me for the first time.

'Once,' he says. 'Not now.' The barrow-owner has grabbed one of the children by the collar, sending her spinning away, only to lose his footing and fall hard upon the stones.

'I see no reason for Mr Poll or Robert to know of what happened tonight,' Charles says suddenly, his words careful but deliberate.

'Of course,' I say. For a long moment we stand, then without a word he turns and walks away, across the almost empty space of Charing Cross, his body fading into the mist that lies upon the ground, until at last his shape is lost within it.

M R POLL SHAKES the letter open, scanning it quickly.
'What is it?' Charles asks. As if it were but a little
thing Mr Poll hands it to Charles for us to read. It is from Sir
Astley, informing Mr Poll of the results of an autopsy con-
ducted on a woman who was, until two days past, a patient
of ours.

'Caley was to bring *us* her body,' Charles says, and Mr Poll
nods. No love is lost between him and his rival, whose fine
manners and vanity play ill with Mr Poll; there can be little
doubt Sir Astley's letter is intended to provoke, despite its air
of generosity. For a second or two Mr Poll considers, then he
looks to me.

'Fetch Mr Tyne,' he says. 'Tell him I would speak with
him.'

Mr Tyne is in the room below. He looks up as I enter.
Though with Mr Poll his manner is unchanged, in regard to
me I have felt a change in him since the night of Lucan's
visit, a hardening of some suspicion. Told of Sir Astley's letter and asked how this might be, when the body was

requested of Caley only two nights ago, he says he knows naught of it.

Tight-lipped Mr Poll dispatches him to find Caley and seek some explanation, but he returns with little more than we might have guessed. By Caley's account the grave in which the woman lay was empty, the body already taken by another. When Mr Poll asks Mr Tyne if Caley might have lied to him, that it might have been Caley himself who sold the body on to Sir Astley's men, Mr Tyne's face hardens, the charge dismissed.

'He is too close to them,' Charles says, once Mr Tyne has gone.

'You think he lies for them?' Mr Poll's voice is sharp. When none of us replies he lifts his hand.

'Go,' he says. 'I will have no more of this.'

———

That night, alone in my room, I listen to Mr Poll and Charles speaking below, their voices low and urgent. It is Charles's view we should raise this thing with Sir Astley, learn how the body came to him, but Mr Poll will not. Against my back the wall is cold, yet it is not the chill of the air that is most keen, but the remembered image of Arabella, the sense of possibilities contained within her as she stood pouring over that bowl. Though I have not chanced on her again she has occupied my thoughts almost constantly. I would ask Charles of her, but his silence on the events of that night seems to forbid it, and my promise to keep the events a secret between ourselves prevents me from inquiring of her with Chifley or Caswell or the others. More than once I have thought I glimpsed her in the streets, moving ahead in a crowd or passing in a carriage, but each time the likeness vanished as I approached. Once, alone with Charles in a tavern near Drury Lane, I thought I saw her in conversation with another woman in the street outside, her face distorted by the flaws of the panes, but as she came close she turned away, and although I strained to see her once more I could not, and she was gone.

OUTSIDE DRYDEN'S BOOKSHOP, I come upon May. It is a low, cold day, the streets thick with a freezing mist which seems to grow heavier with the approaching evening. The snow of a week before has melted, the straw that was laid to cover it turned black and slippery with soot and ice.

Though a single misstep would send one sprawling May hurries carelessly, head down and one hand held out, his first finger half-uncurled and waggling slightly as if in preparation for some admonishment or explanation he rehearses in his mind for any who might seek to delay him. Stopping by a door next to the bookshop, he fumbles in his pocket for a key. Without thinking I call out his name. At once he looks up.

'Gabriel,' he cries, shaking my hand delightedly.

I grin, disarmed by his enthusiasm. Several weeks have passed since he last accompanied us on one of our adventures and I am surprised to realise I have missed him.

'What brings you here?'

'An errand for my master,' I reply. 'And you? Where are you bound?'

'Home,' he says. 'Here.' He points to the door.

'In such a hurry?' I ask, laughing.

At this he is suddenly less certain. 'I have been to see old Ruthven the apothecary,' he says in a rush, then laughs nervously, a high-pitched, whistling giggle. He looks round at the door then back at me.

'Come,' he says, already backing up, 'I will show you my rooms.' Behind the door the stairs are cluttered with a strange assortment of refuse and abandoned things: chairs and carpets, cages for birds, an escritoire. As May closes the door he tells me they are the property of his landlord, a man with an aptitude for the accumulation of things of dubious value – then May is pointing first to one and then to another, giving an account of each, his words flowing in a spilling rush, each story beginning before the last has ended, before looping back to try to resume itself, until at last I laugh, and for a moment he stares at me in bewilderment, before he too laughs.

'Here,' he says, leading me up. The staircase is so steep it is almost a ladder. Still chuckling I follow him, up and in through the door at the top. The room is dark, a low-beamed space lit only through the panes of the dormers. Although a stove stands in one corner, the air is freezing, and as May strikes a match to light a candle I draw my coat closer. The place looks to have been furnished from the collection on the stairs, everything worn and broken, nothing matching. By the stove stands an armchair draped with a blanket, stuffing leaking out at the back; opposite is an old divan, one leg gone and propped up on a stack of books; beneath the window a chair on which a sketchbook lies. But the pieces of furniture are crowded out by the canvases which stand deep against the walls, and the boards and sheets stacked and piled on every conceivable surface.

The candle lit, May draws a flat bottle from his coat, and pours a measure into a wineglass on the floor. Though it is done openly I turn away, something in the manner of its execution making observation seem an intrusion.

On the chair the boards of the sketch book are open, and on the uppermost page a face is visible, the first outlines of a body. Setting down his glass May approaches.

'You draw?' he asks.

'A little,' I say.

'Perhaps I might give you a lesson some day?'

His face is earnest. 'Perhaps.' For a few moments we contemplate the drawing.

'So, where is your master this evening?' he asks then, his voice slower somehow, looser.

'With his daughter,' I reply. 'And Charles.'

He pauses. Then, 'How is Charles?'

I look at him in surprise. 'You have not seen him?'

May shakes his head, jiggling the glass in his hand.

'One does not quarrel with Charles,' he says. 'Surely you have realised that by now.' For a moment May simply stands, then he laughs, as if to deny what he has just said. Then he pauses again.

'He has made you his friend, has he not?'

For a long time I do not answer. Looking down I indicate the sketchbook on the chair.

Then I ask, 'Who is the girl?'

May looks up from the sketch.

'Come,' he says.

A low door is partway open at the room's end. May presses on it and quietly ushers me in. On a bed a girl lies sleeping, the blankets cast off so her breasts and shoulders are exposed to the icy air. She has the translucent skin of the redhead, her nipples as pink and small and hard as those of a child. Her head is cast back, the mouth slightly open, her face that of a dreamer, lost in some hidden place within. From outside comes the clatter of a carriage, the sounds of a coster's cries, but here it is so still her breathing can be heard, gentle and steady. I feel myself colouring. This is some private thing – not her nakedness, but her vulnerability.

'You think her beautiful?' May asks, as we step out again, his face eager.

'Who is she?'

'Her name is Molly.'

'She is a whore?' I ask, my tone harder than it might have been. A look of hurt passes across May's face.

Behind us there comes a sound. The girl has risen, and stands in the door behind us, a blanket wound about herself.

'Who's this?' she asks.

'Gabriel,' says May. 'A friend.'

She gives me a hard, assessing look, a warning of the perils of encroaching on her domain. Seeing then that I have understood she smiles, and crosses to the chair beside the stove and seats herself. Her legs protrude from the blanket and her feet are bare, their soles stained and roughened by a lifetime without shoes.

'Light me a fire,' she says, and though she still smiles there is no softness in her face. May takes a few lumps of coal and places them in the stove.

'What manner of man is he?' she asks, looking at me. 'Another of your painter friends? Or is he a gentleman?'

'One cannot be both?' May asks, smiling. As he speaks I am struck with pity for him, for I see he loves this girl with all that is good in him.

She makes a sound of derision. For a long moment May stands watching her, then, smiling nervously, he turns away, and taking up the flat bottle from before he pours two more glasses. In her chair Molly follows the movement of his hands, and though she seeks to hide it I see the way she hungers for the contents of the bottle. May brings a glass to her, and as she reaches for it she grasps at it. Taking the glass

61

in both hands she drinks it quickly, an urgent motion of the throat. And then, when the glass is done, she sets it aside, ignoring May's outstretched hand. Looking at me now she laughs, a slow, dreamy sound, absorbed in itself.

'You would have some?' May asks, watching me.

I hesitate, my eyes on Molly, then slowly nod.

———

Even through the sweet burn of the alcohol the opium is bitter, a sharp taste which coats the tongue and lingers in the mouth. At first I feel naught but the brandy's heat, but then it comes, a stealing ease that flows through me like a tide. At first the world seems unaltered, the only change the weight of something in its textures. At rest in his chair May is talking, his voice both huge and far away, while Molly lies with her head spilled back. I feel a presence press against the surrounding air, another world, as if this room, these lives of ours, this very world were a dream that moves upon some deeper place, like the crossing patterns of ripples on the surface of a lake disturbed by rain, pierced here and there and set to motion only to pass, and fade, its knowledge coming like the memory of something I had not known forgotten, with a rightness that goes deeper with words, as if I understand at last the nature if not the name of the void that lies at my centre.

How long it has been when I leave I am not sure, yet outside the streets are long quiet. Overhead the fog turns the lamps to hissing gold and falling flame, as metal in a blacksmith's forge. No heat, nor even noise, though on every side the world ticks and shivers. On Old Compton Street I hear a hoot, then overhead an owl swoops by, the pale feathers of its belly and its banded wings beating slow upon the heavy air, its ghostly form so close I might lift a hand and touch it there. Somewhere later in my bed I sleep, a shifting dream-less thing, until I am woken by the dirty light of dawn, my body filled with memory of what has passed, and feeling now only its absence, the knowledge of its loss.

CHRISTMAS COMES, bringing snow and a sort of quiet to the city's streets. Across the roofs bells ring out, their sound as clear as glass in the frozen air, carriages jangling on the stones. Though I have no family to call my own, by Robert's invitation I spend Christmas night with his mother and sister, who have a house in Kentish Town. It is strange to see Robert thus, laughing and careless with his family, for he seems not at all the serious young man I have grown to know, and instead he clowns and jokes, teasing his sister until she laughs and pulls his hair, and dancing with his mother by the fire. The house is nothing grand: one floor of a building beside a field where donkeys graze, and its furnishings are threadbare at best, circumstances quite unlike those they must once have known, but tonight at least these things seem not to worry them, and they are to all appearances happy in themselves and in each other.

Though they would have me stay as Robert means to do, I decline their invitation. From his uncle, Robert has a case of cigars, and he presses one on me as the two of us walk across the frozen midnight fields, made a little drunk and foolish by the smoke. Overhead the sky is clear, the massing light of the stars moving silently against the earth's darkened curve, the only sound the lowing of the cows as they shift in their sleep. Something in the stillness of the night soon quiets us, and then I feel a sort of emptiness descend. All evening I have felt it there, as if I watched their happiness from without and even my laughter and our songs were illusory. Perhaps Robert sees something of this, for as we stop by the stone gate where he takes his leave of me he grips my hand and holds it, once more urging me to stay. But I shake my head and tell him I would not intrude further, and so we part for the night.

Beneath the open sky I make my way slowly back through the fields and gardens into Camden Town, and thence past the last inns and houses of the country roads into the city streets. From a cart some local lads call out to me, and I wave, but truly my thoughts are not with them. A fortnight has passed since the night of the child, and in that time Charles has not spoken of it again. Outwardly he seems unaltered, but something has changed: in the Cock not two nights past he snapped at Chifley, his temper quick and hot upon him for some little thing. And yet afterwards he urged us on, his mood exuberant and uncontrolled, until even Chifley was afraid of him and our celebrations were abandoned for the evening.

———

Before the fire in the kitchen Mrs Gunn is asleep, slumped low upon her chair, the ruins of her dinner on the table, a flagon of porter in her lap. The house above silent as the grave. Of Mr Tyne there is no hint, so carefully I help her up, and with my arm about her guide her to the room beside the

65

kitchen where she sleeps. As I set her down she grabs at me and tries to plant a kiss upon my mouth, her wrinkled lips murmuring something I would rather not have heard, and ashamed for her I pull away. My room upstairs will be cold, so I sit before the fire, losing myself within the pictures in the flames.

EVEN HERE IN THIS HOUSE, where we live pressed so close against each other, it is possible to feel alone. I have learned to mind my master's temper, just as I have come to respect Robert's silences. There is much of which we do not speak, and much I keep to myself. But these secrets can lie heavy on us when it is quiet, as it is in the days that follow. I have little to do, little work but my study, so I am idle, drifting through the empty rooms. With Christmas we have no classes to teach, few patients, and so, little need of bodies.

This may be a blessing of sorts, for in these last weeks Caley has seemed altered. Though we have been careful not to speak of Lucan's visit, he has other ways of uncovering things. But whether he knows or not, he has been more erratic of late, less reliable, and when questioned responds with anger and suspicion.

And so I am surprised to be woken two days before the New Year by Robert telling me Caley is here. Rising, I button my jacket and follow him down to the cellar, where

Caley and Walker are waiting with Mr Tyne. Caley looks agitated, moving nervously.

The two bundles they have brought lie on the floor. With Caley watching, we kneel down to examine them, Robert unbinding the larger first. It is oddly shaped, and as he sits back on his heels I understand the reason. Within, there lie two children, their bodies wound together as if they lay tumbled close in careless sleep. For a moment Robert does not move or speak: we none of us have any love for purchasing the bodies of the young, though we do it from time to time.

'They are twins,' Caley says. Indeed, though one is male and the other female, the two of them are so similar they might be each other's images. Robert reaches down and, moving carefully, touches their faces and necks, looking for any sign that they are damaged.

As Robert's hands move over the children's skin, I feel Mr Tyne grow oddly still beside me. Glancing up, I see the way he stares, the way his whole attention is focused on their tiny forms. And opposite me Caley is watching him as well. Without a word he shifts his eyes to mine, a smile playing on his lips, and I realise he watches Mr Tyne not as one might an accomplice or a friend, but as a man whose weakness he understands.

At a sign from Robert we lift the two of them onto the tabletop. Then, drawing my knife, I crouch down again to cut the cords which bind the other, smaller bundle. I feel a sort of wretchedness: there is still something horrible to me in this, something pointless and deadening in these voided shells. And then, as I draw the body forth, I see the stitching, this child's ruined face.

'What is it?' Robert asks. At first I cannot speak, only sit, my hand held just above his little chest.

'Gabriel?'

'We cannot take this one,' I say, leaning back.

'Why not?' He kneels beside me.

I just shake my head, unsure of what to say. The child is Oliver, Kitty's son. Robert extends a hand and touches him.

'He is marked,' I say, gesturing towards the ruined scalp and hand, Charles's stitching, a ghastly patchwork.

'We no longer have the luxury to pick and choose,' Robert says.

Behind us Caley is watching.

'He is too long dead,' I say.

'Two weeks perhaps,' says Robert. 'Not so long in this weather.'

I shake my head. 'We cannot take him,' I insist.

Glancing back at Caley, Robert leans close. 'You say we may not take him yet you give me no good reason.' He keeps his voice low but I hear the frustration in it.

'I have given you two,' I say.

'And I have said neither is enough.'

Looking down again at poor Oliver, I shake my head. 'Please,' I say, 'do not take him.'

Caley draws closer, his eyes moving from the child to me.

'What is this?' Though he holds himself still the threat of his mood is visible. Robert stares at me one more time. Then, as if I have failed him somehow, he turns back to Caley.

'We cannot take this one,' he says.

Caley's face clouds, but before he may speak Mr Tyne is there, one hand raised to settle him.

'Why not?' he asks.

There is a silence, then Robert shakes his head.

'His injuries are foul,' he says, his tone level, as if there is no more to be said than this. But Mr Tyne is not put off so easily and, kneeling down, he lets one hand touch the poor child's cheek. The gesture is unpleasant in its intimacy, and I wish as his hard fingers brush that naked flesh that I might avert my gaze.

'We have taken worse,' he says, exploring the chest and the hidden spaces beneath the arms. 'What is it you object to in this one?' When we do not answer he looks up, first at Robert.

'I see,' he says. 'It is not you that objects but him.' Next he looks at me. 'You know something of this child, I think.' His face is suddenly so close I can smell the sour reek of his breath. 'That is it, is it not?'

I shake my head, although my eyes will betray me.

'It is my decision,' Robert says, his body guarding mine. Mr Tyne does not move, but slowly he lets his eyes shift to Robert's face. At last he makes a sound of disgust and turns away.

———

Though Caley is ill pleased, he binds the child up again and with Walker goes back into the night. Mr Tyne lingers in the room, watching as we wash the twins' tiny bodies. With him there I cannot speak, and it pains me that this should be, for in the silence I feel a reproach which shames me. Only when we are done, and Robert and I are alone, do I manage to speak.

'Thank you,' I say.

At the stairs Robert turns, and for several seconds stands watching me.

'I do not know what happened tonight, Gabriel,' he says, 'nor do I care. If you choose to have secrets that is your own affair.'

'The secret is not mine,' I say, but he shakes his head.

'That is as may be.' His voice is level, but I hear the anger in it. 'I care only that these secrets not follow you home again.'

I nod, but he has not finished.

'That was badly done. Caley is Tyne's creature and there was profit in it for him.'

'I am sorry you quarrelled with him on my account.'

'It is not for me I am concerned,' he replies. 'Tyne is a man to be cautious of and you have cost him money tonight.'

WITH THE YEAR'S TURNING the weather grows worse, freezing rain giving way to black sleet and howling wind. In the cellar icicles form on the rafters; ice veins the water in the pails, in every room the cold growing deeper by the day. Then, without warning, the wind turns to the north, and overnight comes snow, clean and white, drifting silently earthwards, carpeting the dark roofs and transforming the city into a place of stark beauty, the spires of the churches rising like white-capped peaks, the trees stretching their branches into the freezing air, slivered with gleaming ice.

And with the snow a kind of silence, as if the city were stilled by its weight. In the churchyards and the parks huddled figures move across the frozen ground, gathering sticks to burn, to warm themselves, and on the streets the carriages and people do still move, but their numbers are thinned, their motion less urgent.

Of my refusal of the child there is no mention. But Mr Tyne has not forgotten: he watches me more closely now, and twice I am sure I see him from the corner of my eye in the street. Perhaps it would be easier if he were to speak of it to Mr Poll; his silence seems somehow more ominous, and I am uneasy.

———

Upon Prince's Street, before St Anne's, a handful of crows move upon the cobbles, picking at the lines that trace the passage of the carriages across the snow – black against white. Overhead the sky is low, heavy and bruised. In the tower the bell tolls, the sound loud in the stillness of the freezing morning, and at its call I halt, staring back towards the church's looming mass. Through the churchyard rails I glimpse the heads of mourners, the high hats of the bearers and the coffin on their shoulders just visible as it is borne across the ground.

For several seconds I stand thus, gazing up, then slowly I turn and cross the rutted surface of the road to the gate. The iron cold beneath my hand. White here too, the crowded stones jumbled together. In places graves gape, dark against the snow, almost like doors opening emptily in the earth. Now the mourners come to a halt beneath the bare form of an oak, the coffin is lowered, then comes the voice of the priest.

A stillness lingers in the yard, that silent space of grave-yards everywhere. By the grave a woman weeps, her head cast down; a man beside her, a son perhaps, for he is younger than she, reaches out to steady her, but she will not have it, and shakes him off with an abruptness that is almost violent, the motion stilling even the voice of the priest. The young man stands, his hand outstretched, the woman staring fiercely ahead, and the small congregation shifts uneasily.

Struck all at once with the sense of intruding, I turn away to leave – and as I do I see her in the street outside the gate.

As our eyes meet she hesitates, as if she had meant to slip away but stayed despite herself and now is caught.

'I fear I shall not like your reason for being here,' she says as we meet.

I shake my head. 'I saw the funeral, nothing more.'

She examines my face. Then, with a small movement she glances over her shoulder at the buildings that rise on the opposite side of Prince's Street. Their windows gape emptily.

'Walk with me,' she says.

Her pace is quick, as if seeking to be quit of this place.

'It is a bitter day to be about on foot,' I say at last. 'Where are you bound?'

'A friend's,' she says. I hear the evasion but do not press her. She is shivering, pressing her arms closer to herself; although her hat and collar are of fur, the coat she wears is thin, and her face is flushed with the cold.

'I was very sorry to learn of Kitty's loss,' I say, the words sounding so clumsy I regret them immediately. But if I have trespassed she gives no sign. Instead she looks as if something in what I have said surprises her somehow.

'A child dying is always sad,' she says then, turning away. Her words seem hard, but something else is in the tone.

'How is Kitty?' I ask.

'It was a grievous blow. And she was not strong before.'

This last brings silence between us for a time.

'I had hoped to see you again,' I say then, my body trembling, again regretting my words even as they are spoken. Yet she does not laugh or sneer.

'Does it bring you happiness, your work?' she asks.

I hesitate. 'It was my guardian's intention that I have a profession so I might provide for myself.'

'What of your parents?'

'They are dead,' I say.

She nods, gazing both at and through me, as if I were not quite real, or as if she saw in me something long forgotten.

'And yours?' I venture.

For a fraction of a second she pauses, then she looks away. 'Dead too,' she says. 'Long ago.'

I wait, thinking she will continue, but instead she comes to a halt.

'I have business here, Mr Swift,' she says. 'You must excuse me.'

I bow. For a long moment she stands watching me. 'I do not think we shall meet again,' she says at last, then, her coat still wrapped tight about herself, she turns away, leaving me to watch her form as it recedes along the lane. At last I feel something upon my cheek, and looking up I see it has begun to snow once more, the white flakes drifting and spinning in the frigid air.

———

In the dispensary I watch Charles measure a dose of belladonna into a bottle.

'There is something I must tell you,' I say, knowing he has noticed my silence.

He smiles. 'Oh yes?'

'Three nights ago, when Caley came, I caused one of the bodies he brought to be refused.'

'Was it spoiled?'

I shake my head. 'No, not spoiled.'

'Then why?' he asks, his voice flat.

'It was Kitty's child.'

He does not answer.

'You knew?'

'Not that they had brought him.'

'I am sorry,' I say, but even as I speak I know the words are wrong, and I have offended somehow. Corking the bottle he checks the dosage once more, then places it inside his coat.

At the door he pauses, turning back to me. 'I have not thanked you properly for your discretion in this matter. I will remember it.'

T HE WEEKS THAT FOLLOW bring little cheer. Though
Caley and Walker bring us subjects, their deliveries are
erratic, their promises often unfulfilled. They give no reason
for their failings, though Mr Poll has little doubt Lucan is
responsible. This would be trouble enough on its own, but
with so few bodies Mr Poll and Charles are forced for want
of subjects to cancel lectures more than once. To lose the
money is galling enough, but to suffer the ignominy of seeing others teach when we may not is a bitter thing. Nor is
this the only sting these weeks provide: from here and there
come rumours that others take pleasure in Mr Poll's predica-
ment, and worse still, it is said the Duke of Kent has declined
Mr Poll's services in favour of those of Sir Astley. Without
evidence we cannot know why this should be, but Mr Poll
is not to be dissuaded from the belief the cause lies with his
rival, who, for all his letters of sympathy, is said to have been
working tirelessly to cast aspersions on Mr Poll's abilities.

Of Arabella there is no glimpse; indeed, as the days turn
into weeks her parting words seem more and more likely to

come true. Twice I take myself to the theatre where she plays and, seating myself among the cheapest seats, watch her moving on the stage. Though she is beautiful, there she seems impossibly distant, as if the woman that night in Kitty's house were made less real by seeing her thus, which saddens me, and so after the second time I do not go back.

In Charles too I have felt the change grow, the shift in his manner. Perhaps to another it would not be visible. There is much to Charles which is hidden, for all his apparent openness, much he holds close. But as these weeks have passed he has been less himself, his temper quicker, and though he still laughs and sings, he often seems distracted and harder somehow, as if some vital part of him is broken.

I am sure Chifley senses it too, though I would not ask to know. What it is that binds the two of them I have never understood. Oftentimes they appear not friends at all, but as if they are connected by some deeper need for each other's company, some unspoken bond of mind and temperament, against which each of them strains and pulls, this strain expressing itself sometimes in wild energy – that intoxicating exuberance they seem able to engender in each other – other times in sniping, silence and something closer to dislike.

THOUGH FLEET STREET lies but a hundred yards away, here silence ticks, the rags hung on the lines overhead moving like wraiths upon the occluded air. Not for the first time in these last few minutes I glance back, thinking I hear a sound, straining to make out something through the fog. For a moment I think I see a shape revealed, but almost at once it is gone. With thoughts of thieves I draw my coat closer and turn aside, slipping down a covered passageway. And then all at once he is there, leaning in a doorway.

'These are unfriendly streets,' he says, straightening to block my path.

'Do you follow me?' I demand.

'Why should I follow you?' he asks with his silky laugh.

'That is something I would not know,' I say.

'How goes the business of your master's house?'

'The worse for your attentions,' I reply.

'I am sorry to hear that.' He smiles, and I feel a twitch of complicity. Shaking my head, I make a noise of disbelief.

'Yet it is said you refused a child.'

I hesitate, realising as I do my reaction has given him whatever answer it was he sought. For a moment he is silent.

'It ended up on van Hooch's table,' he says. When I do not reply he takes a cigar from his case and, striking a match upon his boot, lights it carefully.

'Tyne is not a man to anger lightly. Why take such a risk?' The smell of the cigar mingles with the sulphur from the match as he draws back on the smoke and lets it coil from his lips. Then with a lazy movement of his wrist he flicks the match away.

'Your master did me a disservice, you know. I came to him as a friend and he insulted me.'

'You threatened him.'

He shakes his head. 'No,' he says. 'It was he who took what was mine and sought to do me harm.' I am uncomfortably aware of the passage walls close against us, the low roof overhead stained with soot.

'These troubles of his, they are in his power to prevent. Remind him of that.'

I nod, and he comes closer, the sweet, throat-searing smoke surrounding us.

'It is said de Mandeville has made a project of you, that he takes you drinking, and to see his women.'

I do not answer, and slowly he moves past me, until he stands at my back.

'I could help you.' His voice is lower now, more intimate.

'I cannot imagine how,' I reply, and he chuckles.

'Come, think upon it. You are an orphan, without property or a name, and already it is said you owe money to the Jews.'

'I am a gentleman,' I say, the words coming stiff and broken from my mouth.

'You are proud. That is good. But do not let that pride make you blind.'

I stand, unspeaking.

'We all of us have need of friends in this world, Gabriel.'

'I have friends enough already,' I reply.

For a long moment there is silence, then at last he steps away. 'Tell your master that we met.'

———

Once he has gone, I stand looking into the space he has left. My hand, I find, is clutched tight around the package my master has entrusted to me. Under the fog the city seems to breathe. Upon my neck a weight, as if I were watched somewhere.

Nervous, I turn and walk, faster than I should.

I understand full well the import of Lucan's words. Just last night Caley and Walker arrived late, dawn only half an hour away, Caley beating upon the door over and over like a man possessed. Robert went down.

'Silence, man,' Robert hissed as he opened it, but Caley only pushed past him, Walker following with a bundle across his shoulder.

In the cellar Caley gestured to Walker to lay the bundle on the floor. I stood back, uncomfortably aware of his temperament. As Robert drew his knife to cut the ropes, Mr Tyne appeared on the stairs, watching the scene from above.

Even before Robert drew back the bindings the smell told us what we would find. But the truth was worse – the body blistered and bruised and foul. Letting the bindings fall, Robert rose, turned to Caley.

'You will take it?' Caley asked.

Robert looked at me, and then up at Mr Tyne.

'We cannot, you know that.'

Caley hesitated. Behind him I could see Walker watching, his ruined face pale.

'No,' he said, 'you will give us eight guineas for it.'

Robert did not speak, just shook his head, his expression firm. Less certain now, Caley glanced at Mr Tyne and then back at Robert.

'Six,' he said, too quickly.

'No,' Robert replied. 'The body is spoiled, we will not take it.'

'Then what of us?' Caley demanded. 'Would you have us starve?' But before Robert could answer, Walker's voice broke in.

'It is L-l-lucan,' he stammered, 'he incites the keepers of the yards against us.' Caley shot him a look of fury.

'I am sorry,' Robert said, 'but these matters are not my master's concern.'

'It is your master and his schemes which brought this retribution upon us!' Caley said, his voice trembling. 'And now he abandons us.' As he spoke he rose high on the balls of his feet, his body tensed as if to strike.

'A scheme you were party to,' Robert said carefully. Caley hesitated again, the moment seeming to stretch on endlessly. Then, with a sudden movement, he dragged the bundle up.

'Come,' he spat at Walker, 'we'll not tarry here.'

————

Back at the house Mr Tyne follows me as I climb the stairs towards my master's room. He is close behind, unspeaking, but I do not turn. A month has passed since my refusal of the child, and still he keeps the fact of it close to himself, as if he thinks in time to divine its cause.

As I enter, Mr Poll looks up.

'What is it?' he asks.

'I have a message,' I say, shifting uneasily. Behind me there is a foot upon the boards; glancing back I see Robert, Charles beside him.

'From whom?' asks Mr Poll.

'Lucan,' I say.

'You spoke to him?'

I nod. 'He wished me to remind you this thing is in your power to end.'

'How so?' he asks.

'He says you have insulted him.'

'And now he would have me beg forgiveness of him? Never.'

'Surely there is no harm in it,' Robert says. 'Why not end this matter if we can?'

Mr Poll looks at him with undisguised annoyance.

'Be careful, sir,' he snaps.

Robert hesitates, but does not relent. 'And what if he keeps Caley and Walker from us as well? What then?'

'Silence!' Mr Poll snaps. 'I will not be lectured by my own apprentice.' In his fury his voice grows coarse, a tradesman's voice, and I fancy Charles flinches.

Robert waits then, while Mr Poll considers.

'Damn him,' he says finally. 'He will not have the pleasure of seeing me beg.'

I HAVE WANDERED AWAY from Charles and the others at the theatre when I come upon her without warning. At first I think she means to turn away, but she hesitates, and I have time to speak her name.

'I had not thought to see you here,' she says. Her face is painted and rouged, and though up close it gives her a hardness which I had not seen before it also makes her seem younger, more fragile.

'A friend of Charles's has taken a box,' I say. 'I am his guest.'

She nods, but does not reply, her silence making me afraid I have angered her, or that she fears I mean her harm.

'I came to your plays,' I say awkwardly. 'I saw you upon the stage.'

'In company?'

'Alone,' I say. Then, 'I am sorry for the way we met,' and she looks at me, her eyes softening. For a moment it is as if there is something she means to say – then she lowers her head.

'I must go,' she says, 'I am expected.' But suddenly another woman appears beside her. She is a pretty thing, and glancing first at Arabella and then at me she grins cheekily, with the air of one who has stumbled upon a tryst.

'Who's this?' she asks, looking me up and down, her gaze unabashed and amused beneath her blonde curls.

'This is Mr Swift,' says Arabella, a sort of panic in her eyes. Her companion nods, still with that expression of lively amusement.

'Isn't he the handsome one?'

'I am sorry,' I say, 'but . . .'

'This is Miss Amy Stanton,' Arabella says. 'Mr Swift is an associate of Mr de Mandeville's.'

'You are a surgeon?' she asks, quivering with an irresistibly mercenary glee.

'No,' I laugh. 'I am but an apprentice.'

Lifting her fan to her face she looks away. 'That's a pity,' she says, although she shows no sign of any regret.

'Perhaps you might join us?' I gesture towards the staircase and the box, but Arabella shakes her head.

'No,' she says, 'that is not possible. We must go.'

Amy sighs in mock exasperation.

'Perhaps you might call upon us, then?' Now she is all teasing wickedness.

Arabella begins to speak, no doubt meaning to contradict her friend, but Amy cuts her off with a hand upon her sleeve.

'Mr Swift?'

I look to Arabella, who is caught.

'I would be honoured,' I say.

'Good!' Amy's eyes flash with delight. 'We have too few handsome men about the place.' Her eyes hold mine, then, as if we have reached some kind of understanding, she lets Arabella draw her away into the crowd.

Only when I turn do I see Charles above me, paused at the

entrance to the corridor which leads to our box, one of the women who has accompanied us beside him. Five minutes past, when I left them, she had been shrieking with laughter at something or other. Though Charles seems unaffected, she is drunk, her cheeks flushed, and as I watch she turns to him, her face pressing against his neck, nuzzling. We stand like this, staring one at the other. Then, letting one arm encircle her, he draws her close, his eyes not leaving mine.

———

That night Charles's mood seems to burn too bright, the air around him dangerous, fickle as as quicksilver. What part in it is mine I do not know, only that tonight I am afraid of him, afraid of what he might do. That there is some change in him these last weeks all of us now see. When he is alone with me he is still friendly, and even, when he forgets himself, careless. To be asked to accompany him on a visit or to assist in an operation remains a pleasure I never fail to enjoy. But in company, particularly Chifley's, his manner is different, harder and less predictable, the two of them urging each other ever further as they do tonight.

Only May seems still able to resist when this madness is upon them. He comes with us again these days, and whether chivvied and coaxed by Charles, or ridiculed by Chifley, who seems to regard May with something close to scorn, he stays always removed, laughing with them but never quite part of whatever revel we are engaged in. Even Charles is different when he is there, something peculiar in his manner towards him, an exaggerated politeness, almost as if he does not wish to come too close to him. And though I could not say why, for her name is never mentioned, I see that the cause for this is Molly, and the hold May has allowed her over himself.

What it is that binds those two I cannot see, for their

natures have little in common. Where May is kind, in Molly there is something jealous and spiteful that cannot be won. With May her moods change without warning: one moment they are tender as lambs with each other, the next she taunts him cruelly. The hurt this causes him is clear enough, but worse still are those moments when he answers her in kind.

Nevertheless as the weeks pass I have found myself more and more in May's company. In those hours when I am free I climb the stairs to his room, sometimes to talk, other times to sit and watch him work. He has an openness about him, a quality of kindness, which makes it near impossible not to like him, for all his peculiarity. More than once I have come upon him engaged in conversation with a shopkeeper or crossing-boy or gentlewoman, their faces frozen in an expression of bewilderment as he talks at them uncontrollably, hands moving all the while, gesticulating right or left. He has no quality of discretion either, once a thought is in his head it is upon his tongue, regardless of its nature or tone. And every time, he moans and tries to catch himself, sinking into a state of despondency for having so betrayed whichever friend or acquaintance it is he has mentioned, before beginning in ardent terms to try to extricate himself with explanation and excuses, a process so predictable in its course that it is all one can do not to laugh as he proceeds.

Only in his work does he find some measure of stillness. When he takes up brush or pen he seems able to work for hours at a stretch without a word, pausing now and then to stare into space or move about the room in thought, his movements as steady and deliberate as, at other times, they are awkward and rushed. Little is able to disturb this mood once it is upon him, and I have seen him work on as the light fades from the room, until he draws almost in darkness, as if he need not see elsewhere but in his mind. There is great peace to be found in watching him work thus, not just for me but for Molly, and it is not uncommon for the two of us to sit together and watch him as he works, close then as we never are at other times. What thoughts she harbours in these hours I could not say, but she appears gentler, less angry.

This peace persists too, into the hours that come after his work. With the wind pressing upon the roof, we gather fondly close around the stove and talk. And May takes forth the opium and with wine we drink it. A few grains are enough at first to slip into its embrace, the black-eyed dreams it provides. Time then has no meaning, all that matters is the sound of our voices, the small space of light in which the three of us sit, May, and Molly, and me, adrift upon the night.

———

By the door I pause. Robert is within, intent upon his work. On the bench before Robert a woman's foot, already blackened with the taint of its own corruption. Divided from its body it is anonymous, the gracile toes twisted and burred by years of shoes worn too tight. Yet as Robert works it reveals itself, his steady knife pressing into the flesh's soft resistance, the slipping meat slowly exposing the sinewed bone and cartilage. From the window pale light falls on Robert's face, smoothing the lines of care away. He pauses now and then to make a mark upon the page beside him. As a draughtsman he has an awkward hand, yet in this sketch, its very clumsiness, there is something I have not glimpsed before. A quality of grace, as if these simple lines of light and shade marked out a plainsong for this strange temple, its small cathedral of bone and flesh an obscured divinity.

IT IS A WEEK before I go to her. Though noon has already passed, the drapes are drawn. Through the door my knock rings out, and soon the door is opened by a sallow-faced maid. She regards me coolly as I give my name and business. Though she is little more than a child, there is an unsettling frankness to her gaze. Perhaps to another man it might seem an invitation, but it seems to me it's something closer to a bruise, for I have seen this look too many times upon the city's streets, and know it for the look of girls who are women before their time and do not love the world for it.

Bidding me wait in the parlour she disappears upstairs. I am nervous, unsettled, and as Arabella enters, I start. She too pauses upon seeing me, her eyes meeting mine with that look of vulnerability I have glimpsed in her each time we have spoken, before she hardens herself and extends her hand for me to hold.

'Mr Swift, you have caught us unawares.'

'I had not thought to disturb you . . . If you would prefer me to leave –'

'No,' she says, then as if embarrassed by the urgency of her reply she corrects herself. 'Please, stay. I will have Mary bring us some tea. Or would you rather brandy?'

'Tea,' I reply, and she nods, drawing the maid close as she gives some instruction. Straightening, Mary regards me with a look which is at once contemptuous and cautious, then is gone.

'I am sorry if I have intruded,' I say.

'Please,' she says, 'do not apologise again.' The terseness of this sets me off-balance, and lost now for words I wish I had not come.

She seats herself, stroking her gown to settle it. For several seconds we remain thus, then all at once we both begin to speak, she asking how I have been these last weeks, I for news of the play in which she is cast. I stop, asking her to continue, and she does the same, both of us speaking over the other before falling silent once more, this awkwardness between us overwhelming all.

And this is how we are when Amy comes bustling in. Unlike Arabella she seems to have only this minute risen, her curls loose and disarrayed, an effect which is at once girlish and curiously pleasing. Her face is filled with expectant glee, and as she enters her eyes alight on me. Thankful for her interruption I rise.

'Have you come to take us somewhere in your carriage, Mr Swift?' she asks as I take her proffered hand. 'An outing would make a dull day so much more bearable.' She gives me a teasing grin, and unable to help myself I smile.

'Would that I could,' I say. 'But I am afraid I do not have a carriage.'

'But you are a surgeon!' she replies delightedly. 'Surely you have a carriage.'

'As a rule we apprentices do not tend to have carriages of our own.'

Behind her Arabella smiles, her face filled with indulgent love. Catching her eye I smile back, conspiratorially.

'Perhaps we might walk then,' Amy says. 'It looks to be a fine day without.' Turning to Arabella she gives her a pointed look.

'You did say only yesterday it had been too long since you visited the park.'

Arabella shakes her head, but I see her resistance is already failing.

'What of your performance?' she asks Amy.

'It is not until tonight.'

Arabella shakes her head, conceding. 'Then let us go out,' she says, 'if you are so set on it.'

———

I am left alone while they dress, though they are not long, and it is with a sense of elation that I step into the street with them not half an hour later. Although the air is cold the day is fine, the sky a high, fragile blue. Amy is the first outside, turning back to face the two of us as she reaches the street, one hand raised to hold her hat upon her head. In the daylight she is little more than a girl, seventeen perhaps. By the corner a cab stands, an ageing hackney with two roan horses. I step forward to catch the attention of its driver but Arabella catches my arm.

'Let us walk,' she says. In her eyes there is a new solici-tousness – she must know I could hardly afford the ride. Awkwardly I nod, thanking her, grateful for this small kind-ness, even as its shame makes me smart.

We wind our way towards the park observing how the weather has brought the city back to life. Everywhere are people released by the sudden sun into a sort of ease. Men and women stand conversing, servants go about their work, children chase and run along the streets – a sort of gladness rising. Amy speaks for all of us, laughing and teasing, commenting loudly and unashamedly upon whatever takes her eye. Between Arabella and me there seems to grow something almost conspiratorial, as if to be cast thus as Amy's foils presses us together. Whether this is Amy's intention or not, I could not say, but outside a bookseller's on Portland Street, I offer Arabella my arm. Whether she might accept it I am not to know, for it is Amy who takes it, laughing a wild, happy laugh. Nervously I glance at Arabella, but she smiles and shakes her head, not in reprimand but affectionately, and a glow starts within me, for I understand that though it is Amy who clings close to me, it is not she who walks beside me but Arabella.

Across the park the trees' boughs rise naked against the sky, their trunks pale against the returning grass. The paths are crowded, a press of people, all primped and powdered for each other. In my sober suit I might have felt out of place, yet the admiring stares of passing men and jealous glances of the women banish such thoughts from my mind quickly enough.

The sun is bright upon the surface of the lake, the water throwing light into the air. Here and there swans move; as we reach the edge Amy kneels, whispering something as if to attract them to her. Arabella watches her lovingly, and I watch Arabella in turn, glad to see her so at ease. When the swans have come, and Amy has cupped her hands before their inquiring heads, she stands again, content, and her eye settles on a gentleman who has paused further along the path, staring back at the three of us. Arabella tenses, but if she means to avoid him Amy has no such intentions, for she greets him happily, curtsying and ushering him over, one arm thrust through his as it was through mine not half an hour since.

Brought before us, his greetings are amiable enough, although something in the way he presses his lips together shows that despite his manners he is not well pleased to have found Arabella and Amy here with me. He is thin-faced, only a few years older than myself, with a sour cast to his features, and though he is at once familiar it is not until I am told his name is Ash that I remember him as a friend of Chifley. That he remembers me as well is plain, but we say nothing of it.

Once the business of introductions is done we wander on, Ash and Amy walking ahead. At the lake's end Arabella and I pause: high overhead, in the space above the lake, a flock of starlings has begun to mass, their tiny bodies streaming in like sand. A common sight, yet nonetheless we gaze up at this small wonder, as they wheel and turn as if directed by a single mind, a shifting cloud which pulls and grows, only to disperse again, all at once into the air.

Amy has paused meanwhile, with Ash, beside a fiddler. Ash takes a coin from his coat and hands it to Amy, who turns, holding it aloft for us to see before casting it into the musician's hat.

'You are a good friend to her,' I say, but Arabella shakes her head.

'Would that I were better.'

'How so?' I ask. Arabella hesitates. When she speaks again her voice is soft.

'She was no more than a child when we met. She was a seamstress and I an actress already, playing little parts. Yet her heart is twice the size of mine.' Together we watch Amy grip Ash's arm tighter, pressing herself against him. I cannot imagine her upon the stage, for unlike Arabella she seems so utterly herself. To become another is to hide oneself, perhaps even to lose oneself, and it is a terrible thing, and the easiest.

'He is kind to her?' I ask.

'He is a man,' she says, her tone sharp. But then she continues, her voice softer again.

'You know him, do you not?'

I look at her in surprise. 'Not well,' I say.

She nods. 'Then you know the sort of man he is.'

'You think he does not mean to marry her?'

'He is a gentleman, and gentlemen do not want girls like Amy for marrying.'

Although there is no anger in her voice, I am ashamed at this, but for which of us I am not sure.

'Why did you wish to avoid me at the theatre?' I ask after a time. She lets go my arm and turns on the bank. Two drakes are fighting, their wings throwing clouds of water all about them.

'Arabella?'

She does not look at me. 'You must not do this, Gabriel.'

'I do not understand,' I say.

Her arms are crossed before her when she turns, and again it is as if she thought I might mean her harm.

'Look at Amy,' she says, 'and your Mr Ash. He is a gentleman, and for that reason will never marry her. Of course if the truth be known that is no great matter in itself, for Amy does not much care for Mr Ash. But what of the other Mr Ashes? She will not be young forever, nor so pretty either.'

'And you?' I ask.

She fixes her gaze on me, caught between anger and something else. 'Do not be obtuse, Gabriel,' she says at last, turning to walk on. 'It does not suit you.'

————

At the gates Amy and Ash are waiting amongst the passing crowd. As we approach I cannot help but see his sourness, the space in him her youth will fill, and never be enough.

'We would take lunch,' he says, smiling at me as he speaks.

Knowing that he hopes I will decline I nod and we make our way out into Mayfair, where in a tavern we take a table and are fed. Amy, no doubt sensing something between us, speaks enough for everyone, eating all the while, oysters and bread and beer, her hand moving to cover her mouth each time she laughs. Arabella eats more slowly, joining in Amy's laughter sometimes as an elder sister might. Ash though is silent, his body hard against Amy's. Several times I catch him watching me, his dark eyes steady and unwelcoming.

By the time we are done the afternoon is fading, the sky overhead almost colourless, a sliver of moon visible above the rooftops. Amy is due at the theatre in an hour, and so she departs with Ash in a cab, leaving Arabella and me to make our way back on our own. We walk side by side, untouching, our conversation now we are alone together careful, guarded, although with a closeness that was not there before.

'I do not think I like this Ash,' I say.

Arabella looks at me. 'No?' she asks, then shakes her head and looks away once more. 'He is not the worst of his kind.'

'That is not what I mean,' I say.

'No,' she says, 'I know.' Taking my arms she draws me closer, lets her small weight lean into me.

I KNOW AT ONCE something is wrong, for there is murder in the eyes of Mr Tyne. Behind him Oates, the coachman, shifts uneasily, his fat face caught somewhere between fear and self-righteousness. The two of them have been at St Bart's to collect a corpse from old Crowley who teaches there.

'Where is the body?' Mr Poll asks, and Mr Tyne shoots a look at Oates whose mouth is opening and closing like a fish.

'Stolen,' replies Mr Tyne.

The room falls still.

'Before or after you paid for it?' asks Mr Poll.

'After,' Mr Tyne replies.

Mr Poll turns towards him.

'How?' he begins, then shakes his head. 'No, do not tell me, let me guess. You left this prattling fool there to watch for you.'

Oates hangs his head in shame, but not before Mr Poll looks at him in a manner that makes it clear he has not heard the last of this.

Mr Tyne nods slowly and, though he holds himself carefully, the anger that eats at him to be so upbraided is plainly visible. I try to look away, but he catches me, and in that moment I see his hatred plain as day.

'You thought he would not take every chance to torment us?' asks Mr Poll angrily, and for an instant I think Mr Tyne will speak back, so violent is his rage. Then Mr Poll shakes his head, a look of disgust on his face.

'Get out,' he says. 'I would not have to look upon you.'

Mr Tyne clatters away down the stairs and out into the street. No doubt he means to find Caley and have it out with him. In the hall Oates trembles, his fat face flushed with shame and indignation. Having no words of comfort I might offer I leave him there.

———

Though the afternoon is already half gone the house is quiet, Robert away and Charles not yet arrived. I am thankful for the quiet; these last weeks Mr Poll's temper has grown worse with each passing day, and I have too often been on the receiving end of it. That we were forced to buy the body from St Bart's is only the latest indignity Lucan has brought upon us. Again and again over the last weeks bodies sought by Caley and Walker on our behalf have vanished before they could retrieve them, their graves already pillaged or the coffins filled with stones, their contents stolen before they were even committed to the earth.

This would be bad enough, but a half a dozen times these bodies have reappeared almost at once upon the table of some other surgeon, delivered there by Lucan's hand. Twice we have bought ones particularly needed back, once from van Hooch, once from Guy's, paying a premium for the privilege. The body stolen from Mr Tyne and Oates was another thus, a man called Polkinghorne dead of a swelling of the brain, on whose examination Mr Poll was placing great stock, and yet this time Lucan has contrived to make us pay a premium and then spirited it away once more, so both the subject and the money are lost to us, fifteen guineas gone on a body we no longer have.

I close the door of the library behind me, arranging my books upon the table. Outside the day is still, cloud lying flat and low and featureless, diffusing the light, soft grey without register or source. On the table lies the arm of a woman Caley brought two nights ago, its skin pinned back so I may draw it, and taking up my pen I begin. A few minutes pass, then on the sill a sparrow alights, its body stilled for an instant or two. In my hand my pen stops, poised above the paper. Careful lest it see my movement and flit away once more, I turn the page of my book, letting my hand run over it, tracing out the shape of its head, its back's fat line, drawing as quickly as I can, my eyes shifting between page and subject, trying to fix it in my mind, to catch the essence of it. It can only be a matter of seconds, but it feels more like an hour or a day, my heart beating fast, my body lost to this moment. And then I lift my eyes again to find it has turned and is looking in. In my hand the pen falls still, the black eyes meeting mine, full of being, aware in some unknowable way. The moment stretches on, my heart seeming to slow, and then as suddenly as it came it turns its head and is gone, its body thrown in a blur of wings into the air.

In the space of its leaving I sit, staring outwards, into the light, and so I do not hear him enter. It is only when he stops behind me that I realise I am no longer alone and turn, one hand falling across the page, the other raised towards my face as if I might wipe away the light.

'That does not look like the task that you were set,' he says, and though his tone is stern the anger of before seems to have gone. Something awkward too, as if he sought to be friendly, and the manner of it came not easily.

'No, sir,' I say, standing clumsily.

'No,' he says, 'sit.' He places a hand upon the drawing. Knowing I must, I lift my arm, relinquish it.

'It is a sparrow,' I say weakly, and he darts a look across the page's top at me.

'You think me blind?' he asks.

He is not an easy man, and I am afraid of him. Reaching out again he shifts the papers that lie upon the desk. This reveals not notes and drawings of my work, but sketches I have made, day by day: a profile of Charles, a washerwoman, two cats, Blackfriars Bridge. One by one he examines them, studying carefully, until eventually the last is reached.

'You have some skill with a pen,' he says, as if surprised. I nod uncertainly: it is his belief that drawing is a vital part of our education, for only through the reproduction of a thing will its image be truly fixed within the mind, and so at his direction we are made to draw, but I know, as he must know, that it is the only part of my training I have any aptitude for.

'Thank you,' I say. All at once he turns away, leafing through the pages of a book that lies upon the bench nearby.

'Charles tells me you have seen a little of the city in his company.'

I shift, uneasy. These last weeks have seen a change in the relations between him and Charles, as Mr Poll's temper has grown more troublesome Charles has become more solicitous towards the older man, but with a solicitousness that seems designed to disguise a growing distance between the two of them. Perhaps an outsider would not see it, and indeed it is not always there: when they are engaged in the business of dissection and surgery, they are as they ever were, two bodies possessed of one mind, lost to the work. But it is there nonetheless.

'A little,' I say.

'And how do you find him?'

I do not answer. Mr Poll watches me, then nods slowly.

'You are loyal, I see. And he is a man who inspires loyalty, is he not?'

'He is,' I say.

'Would you call him a friend?'

'I hope he would see me as such.'

Mr Poll considers, then, quite suddenly, he thrusts a drawing into my grasp.

'What gives strength to the muscle?' he asks, prodding the woman's arm.

'Exercise,' I say cautiously.

'Then do not let this facility of yours become an end in itself. To do what is easy does not exercise the moral faculties of the brain. There is a weakness inherent in those who are easy with themselves, a weakness you would do well to avoid.'

THE END WHEN IT COMES is swift. On the doorstep a man I do not know. One eye staring pale and blind, the colour in it seemingly scoured away, its emptiness making me recoil. At first I take him for a sexton, or an undertaker perhaps, for he wears a dark suit and hat, and there is something about his long face and manner, his air of false sympathy which somehow fits the part. But his suit is too ragged, and his smile at the way his eye startles me betrays a different sort of nature.

'Here, boy,' he says, 'this is for your master.'

I take the letter he holds outstretched.

'Who is it from?' – but as I ask, the door behind me opens. Mr Tyne. His eyes move from one of us to the other, and then his expression changes.

'You?' he spits. But our visitor only smiles, as if Mr Tyne's temper pleases him. Seeing the letter in my hand Mr Tyne snatches it.

'This is yours?' he demands. The other man simply touches his hat and bows exaggeratedly –

'Give your master my blessings.'

———

Left alone with me Mr Tyne lifts the letter to my face.

'Did you bring him here?' he demands.

Shaking my head I tell him I have never seen him before today. With a sudden motion he casts the letter at my chest.

'Your master is inside, boy. Do as you were bid.'

He follows me up to Mr Poll's study. Charles is there, and Robert too, and as we enter the three of them turn.

'Yes?' asks Mr Poll, and I step forward, placing the letter in his hand. Seeing the script on its front, a flicker passes across his face, but otherwise his expression is impassive as he opens and reads it.

'Who brought this?' he asks then, looking up at me. Mr Tyne takes a step forward.

'Craven,' he says, and at this the room grows quiet. Even I know it as the name of Lucan's man, the most trusted of his gang.

'What does it say?' Charles asks, rising from the chair. Mr Poll makes no move to put the letter in his hand; indeed, he does not even look at Charles.

'It is from Lucan,' he says. 'Caley and Walker are taken by the law.'

Beside me Mr Tyne makes a hissing sound, but it is Charles who speaks.

'Would he have us beg?'

'That is precisely what he means to have,' says Mr Poll, his voice dismissing Charles's words as if they were those of a foolish child. Charles's face darkens, but if Mr Poll sees it he gives no sign. Instead he rounds on Mr Tyne, holding the letter out at him.

'And you, man. How is it I must learn of it thus? Is it

true?' – though it is plain from the fury of Mr Tyne's expression that he knew no more than any of us. 'Well? Answer me!'

'I do not know.'

Mr Poll stares at him for a long moment.

'Go then, find out.' And then he turns away, dismissing us. Only Charles remains, looking at his back, his eyes cold.

———

It is dark before Mr Tyne returns, the house silent and still. We follow him to Mr Poll's study, where he makes his report: Caley and Walker are indeed taken, and at this very moment sit in the cells of Bow Street where they were brought after a struggle in the yard of St Bartholomew's.

Outside in the street the night is mild, the cries of children and the scent of smoke rising through the windows, but in the house it is cold.

'Very well, then,' says Mr Poll. 'It is done.'

ONCE MR POLL HAS GONE I follow Charles and the others to a place in the Haymarket. Inside the air is hot, and close, the rooms crowded with men and women all talking and drinking. Chifley would play at cards, and almost immediately takes himself and Caswell away to find a table, leaving me alone with Charles. Charles moves restlessly, looking through the rooms as if for something which remains ever out of reach.

'What will happen to Caley and Walker?' I ask as we go, and he gazes at me though I speak of something from long ago, another time, another place.

'They will be tried, and no doubt convicted.'

'Of what?'

'Theft, trespass, public affray. Some charge will be found.'

'And us?'

He shrugs. 'We will be Lucan's again.'

Surprised by the carelessness of his tone I begin to object – but he reminds me that these are not subjects for company such as this. On the room's other side Chifley and Caswell have found a game and are seating themselves. Chifley motions us to join them, but Charles declines, excusing himself and leaving me there.

And so left alone I wander back through the house, looking at the faces, the dresses and the jewels and the beauty of the women whose bodies fill its rooms. Down the stairs in the hall, there are palms in massive pots, and by the door Negroes in uniforms, and in the ballroom the band plays.

And then quite suddenly I see her, half-turned away. She wears a dress of the deepest blue, her hair piled high upon her head. I begin to walk towards her, delighted to find her here, but then I realise she is not alone, that she is on the arm of a man I do not recognise.

He is older than her, moustachioed, his frame broad, and powerful. I stop, a kind of space opening within me, and then she turns. That she sees me, I know – for our eyes meet and for a long instant she freezes, gazing back, her eyes dark with the look of warning she gave me that night, months ago, in Kitty's room. Then she looks away, showing no sign of recognition.

'You know her then?' Chifley's voice.

'Who is that man with her?'

'Her lover, Sparrow, a man of property.'

I will not flinch.

'What? You thought she might love you alone?' Chifley asks.

I step away, not prepared to let him see how his words have cut me, the room moving as if I am drunk, my legs weak, and his face lit with his crooked smile.

LATE, AND IN THE STREET rain has begun to fall, a mist which moves in clouds through the glow of the lamps. Alone and drunk, in front of the house I draw out my key, push the door as quietly as I can. Inside it is dark, the events of the day lingering in the stillness. Tomorrow Lucan will come, we know. He will offer terms we have no choice but to accept along with the knowledge of our defeat at his hands.

Beneath my feet the boards creak, the sound loud in the space of the hall, and then I feel it – a presence in the air.

'Robert?' I ask, swaying slightly. 'Mrs Gunn?'

Something, barely more than a rustle.

'Hello?' I call, pressing open the door which leads to the dissection room at the house's rear. A suggestion of light falls from the glass roof. Otherwise darkness. Taking a step inwards I peer into the silent space. In my chest my breath is stopped, my blood moving in the silence. Then behind me I hear the hastening creak of the door as it shuts, the rising light of a lamp filling the room, and turning I see Mr Tyne.

'What are you doing here?' I ask.

He does not reply, just takes a step towards me.

'Have you some need of me?'

In the light of the lamp his eyes seem without white, small and hard as those of the shark that sleeps in a tank next door. The way he moves frightens me, and without thinking I step back and aside as he approaches. Only when he is almost on me does he speak.

'I know what you are, boy,' he says, his voice low.

Turning slowly I follow him with my eyes as he moves past me into the room, unwilling to let him out of my sight or to let him come too close. It is not me he reaches for though, but the dissection table, its surface hidden by the sheet which covers Caley's last body, delivered the night before last. Mr Tyne pauses beside it, watching me, one hand extended to grip the sheet.

'What is it?' I ask again, but Mr Tyne only laughs, one hand drawing the sheet down, and away, so it slides and falls to the floor below, exposing a woman's body. I look at her numbly for a moment, and then Mr Tyne lets the hand which drew the sheet aside stray to her face, moving as he does about the table's end, so he stands at her head. There is something unpleasantly intimate in the touch of his hand, the way it lies upon her naked skin.

'She is for dissection tomorrow,' I say. He nods, his eyes moving up and down her naked form. I am ashamed for her suddenly, lying exposed before this man. I am uncomfortable with him even this close to me too, and gingerly I take another step back, but as I do his hand slips into his jacket, and emerges with a knife. With one fluid movement he steps forward, the tip of it coming to rest against my neck.

'What are you doing?' I ask, willing my voice not to tremble. In my chest I can feel my heart now tapping a quick, shivering beat. This close I see the powder on his face, smell the gin that lingers in his breath. Then with a slow movement he lets the knife slide over my collar and down my chest. As it drops he moves closer still, until we are almost face against face, the blade coming to rest beneath my ribs, the point pressed into my skin.

'You have the airs of a gentleman, yet your father died a beggar.'

'Have I offended you somehow?' I ask, my voice trembling. Mr Tyne's eyes narrow.

'You want for manners, boy,' he says. The knife slips away from my belly, and almost convulsively my breath escapes. Mr Tyne takes a step back, the knife hanging in his hand almost casually. It is a short, ugly thing, its sharpened sides tapering to a point. A knife for killing, nothing else.

'I am sorry you think that.'

'Perhaps it is time you had a lesson,' he says. For a few seconds more he watches me, then he turns to the corpse again, lifting her head, and pressing the knife against her cheek. The skin gives, but does not break.

'You must not mark her,' I say, willing my voice to sound authoritative.

'No?' he asks. 'What would you do if I did?'

'I should be forced to tell our master.'

'And if I were to deny it, who do you think he would believe?'

I hesitate. 'Why are you doing this?'

A terrible stillness seems to have gripped him, all save his eyes, which he raises to mine.

'Do not play me for a gull,' he says. 'For I am not.' As he speaks he lets the knife snake across her face.

'Mr Poll will want to know who is responsible if she is marked. He may not believe I did it without reason.'

He nods, smiling, the knife loosening in his grasp. Relieved, I relax, my breath escaping again in a rush. Then in one quick movement he lifts his hand, takes her nose between his thumb and forefinger and cuts at it with a hard, hacking motion until it comes away in his grasp. Opening his hand he displays the severed nose to me, nestled in his palm. I stare back, unspeaking. Then, with a quick flick of his wrist he flings the ghastly thing at my feet.

'Tell him it was me and I will kill you in your sleep.'

IT IS MRS GUNN'S VOICE I hear first, laughing delightedly. Then Oates, and laughter once more, although this time stifled, as if they fear being overheard. To hear laughter from the kitchen in the day is not unusual. It is the habit of Oates to settle there when Mr Poll is in the house, and although I have heard Mrs Gunn complain of him, in truth I do not think she minds, for Oates is amusing in his way, and much given to all sorts of gossip.

Wiping my hands upon a cloth I make my way towards the door. Both fall silent, turning their faces to me as one. Oates stands by the fireplace; seeing me he frowns and looks away to Mrs Gunn. Almost a month has passed since the discovery of the woman's body, but the incident is not forgotten, least of all by Mrs Gunn. What she was told I do not know, all I see is that she treats me now not as she did, but as one might an uninvited guest.

'What is this?' I ask, looking from one of them to the other. 'Has something happened?'

Mrs Gunn purses her lips, but Oates answers for her, so

full of the power of this thing he knows he seems to swell with it.

'News,' he says.

'Of what variety?'

Oates raises his eyebrows, as if to say he will not tell, although from experience I know he will.

'A happy kind,' he replies, but before he can continue we are interrupted by the sound of the door overhead. Grasping her apron in her hands Mrs Gunn hurries up the stairs, Oates behind her. Charles is in the hall, his hat still in his hand; seeing Mrs Gunn he smiles.

'I see my announcement has preceded me,' he says. Rushing forward Mrs Gunn reaches for his hands and presses them in hers. Charles laughs, no doubt as much at the impropriety of this as anything, for Mrs Gunn loves him as she might a favoured son, and he holds her in what seems a special affection.

'Let me be the first to congratulate you, sir,' says Oates, bobbing up and down in what is no doubt meant to be a bow.

'My thanks,' says Charles, giving Mrs Gunn's hands another squeeze. Then he lifts his eyes to me.

'What say you, Gabriel? Will you not give me your congratulations?'

'Tell me first what has happened and then I shall,' I say, although I already know what it must be.

'I am to wed Miss Poll,' he says. 'A date is set.'

Although his words are light I fancy his meaning is not as simple as it might seem. For a fraction of a second I hesitate. Then I step forward, thrusting out my hand in congratulation.

———

Although there are no more celebrations that day, come Saturday we take Charles into Covent Garden. In a room above a tavern there is meat and gravy, wine and dancing. The evening is mild, and the streets outside are thronged with people, all boisterous with drink. There are a dozen of us, including Robert, some I know, some I do not, and together we make a merry party.

By midnight we are drunk, the dozen we arrived with swollen to twenty or more. Two men I do not know, a pair of Irishmen with fiddles and a drum, several women and a pox-scarred man I take to be their bawd. Though the party is for Charles, as ever it is Chifley who is its master. Seated on a chair at the room's centre he conducts the scene, one arm about a girl, the other clasped hard upon a glass, feeding on the scene's disorder like some malefic thing. To me he does not speak, except to call once for me to sing, his face glinting with the challenge he knows I will not meet. Of us all, am I the only one who sees the way he watches Charles, and Charles watches him? – as if between them lay some secret hate, and Chifley sought to do him harm by the very fact of our delight. Charles, though, seems to have no heart for our games, even as he laughs and sings as one of us.

For them to be like this is nothing new. But at one o'clock a girl appears amongst us. Approaching Charles she seats herself up on his lap, an act which provokes great delight among the rest of us, for she is very fat, and he winces beneath her weight. With her toothless mouth she kisses him, and good-humouredly Charles responds, a dreadful sight, then leaning back she pulls down upon her bodice so her breasts spill forth. They are huge and pale, the skin upon them almost transparent, and on one a blue vein is visible, snaking towards the nipple, thick and pulsing like a worm. Leaning forward she presses them into Charles's face, shaking her shoulders so they bounce and ripple against him. Trapped by her weight upon the chair Charles has little choice but to submit. On every side our companions whoop and holler, urging her to continue, and so she does, grasping Charles behind the head and pressing his face into her chest as if to give him suck. As the others cheer, flushed with drink and excitement, I find myself growing tense, afraid of what Charles might do.

After what seems an eternity Charles pushes her away into Chifley's embrace, Chifley grasping her wrists and jigging her about so her naked breasts dance wildly for all to see, this obscenity provoking yet more applause, the woman shrieking like a banshee in his grip.

Forgotten, Charles stands, makes his way towards the open window. While the woman shrieks and spins the fiddlers play a reel, but by the window Charles does not turn, just stays, staring out. I cross to him and see that in the street below, too, people push and cry, sing and dance, full of drink and a wild release. Through our haze of wine this is a scene of great colour, its players moving too quickly and its clamour rising to the window. Our bodies are close.

'I have no taste for tonight,' he says.

'It was a vulgar trick,' I say.

Beneath us a couple embrace, their bodies pressed against each other, lost in a kiss. When at last he speaks again his voice is quieter, less certain.

'I sometimes wish I might live as they do, heedless of the world and its demands.'

I shake my head, uncomfortable. It seems awful to me, that one such as he should wish to unmake his life.

'I do not understand,' I say, although I fear I do.

'No?' he asks, turning to face me at last. I can smell his distinctive scent of fresh laundry and cologne. His eyes meet mine, searching, as if he thinks he shall find something there, the moment seeming to open with possibility. Then he gives a nod.

'Then you are fortunate.' He steps back and stares across at Chifley and the girl, and all at once his mood seems

113

forgotten. Clasping my arm he turns me back towards the room.

'Come now,' he says. 'I would have a song of Caswell.' But though he wears a smile, in his eyes there is no joy.

———

It is late before I find my way home again, my path winding through the darkened streets. Although I have had much to drink I am not drunk, rather lost in some leaden sobriety no amount of liquor will ever shift. On the step I pause. The darkness of the rooms within seems to open up, unfillable, and for a time I stand unmoving, unable to press on.

Inside, the house is asleep, or so it seems until I pass by Robert's open door. I do not know quite when he left the celebration, for he did not speak to me or say farewell. Now he sits before his desk, his body leaned into the candle's light, forehead cradled on his hand. The window is open to the night, admitting the warm spring air, the sound of his pen's scratch upon the paper audible above the distant sounds of the dark city. Although he must have heard my feet upon the stairs he does not turn, so absorbed is he in whatever it is he has before him. I stop, arrested by the still-ness of the scene, its memory of an ease we shared which now seems gone.

After a time he looks up, and regards me with an expression that is not unkind but which saddens me for the distance it contains.

'Have you need of me?' he asks.

I shake my head. 'I am only just returned.' Then I stop, not knowing what next to say. Although a month has passed since my encounter with Mr Tyne in the cellar and all that came after it, things are still not right between us. Nothing has been said, yet both of us know a trust not easily mended

114

has been broken, and lingering in his doorway I wish only to find a way to make it whole again.

Perhaps he sees this, for he lays down his pen.

'Are you unwell?' he asks.

'No.' This is not entirely true. My moods are out of sorts, and I have not slept well these many nights.

'It will be summer soon,' he says. 'My apprenticeship will be at its end.'

'I know,' I say, but in truth it is hard to imagine life here without his presence. 'Have you decided what you will do?'

'I am told there is business in the Indies for medical men.'

I nod, although it had not occurred to me that Robert might consider such a course.

'It seems very far to go,' I say brokenly. What I wish to say is that he must not go, or that if he does he should take me. I wish fervently, for a moment, that I might go with him to somewhere warm.

'I am tired of London,' he says, 'and of the company of the dead.'

There is so much unsaid between us, and I do not see how we can find our way through it.

ROBERT HAS GOOD REASON to be distant with me, for in the month that has passed since the day of Craven's visit and my encounter with Mr Tyne, much has changed. The next morning I woke early, the knowledge of Mr Tyne's act heavy in me. It would not be long, I knew, and indeed it was barely nine when Robert came to me in the dispensary.

'Have you seen the body?' he asked.

I hesitated, tempted to lie. But something in his face made it easier for me to speak the truth.

'I have,' I said.

'What do you know of it?'

A moment slipped by, a heartbeat, nothing more.

'Nothing,' I said.

'It was intact when we washed her two nights ago.'

'I saw what had been done this morning.'

'Why did you not come and tell me of it then?' Robert was searching for a way he might believe me.

'I was afraid you would think me responsible.'

'If you had come to me then I should have thought no such thing.'

Something clenched in my stomach, knotting it tight.

'And now?'

'I will have to report this to Mr Poll. But it would be better if this thing were clear between us before he learns of it.'

Briefly I hesitated, wanting to tell him all. But when I lifted my eyes I knew I would not.

'I can tell you nothing more,' I said.

———

Once Robert was gone I sat blindly in the dispensary. I was sick with this thing, not just for fear of what Mr Poll might say, but for having lied to Robert. Some minutes passed, and in the hall outside then there were feet upon the stairs, the murmur of voices. A door opened, and closed; Robert was back.

'Mr Poll has need of you,' he said.

———

Mr Poll stood by the high window in his study, papers spread on the table as if he had been interrupted in his work. Charles was beside him, and as I entered his eyes met mine. In shame I looked away. Robert closed the door behind us. At last Mr Poll turned to me.

'You have seen the corpse?' His voice was soft, but tight.

'I have,' I said.

'And you say you know nothing of it?'

'Only that I saw it this morning and did not report it.'

'Because you were afraid of becoming the object of suspicion?'

I nodded.

'Yet you see the difficulty here. To be done the act must have an author.'

Opposite me Charles's face had closed. All at once I understood – he had guessed the shape of what had occurred, if not its detail. Yet he would not intervene.

'And you tell me this author was not you?'

I shook my head. 'I know no more of it than you.'

Mr Poll paused, one finger tapping a slow beat upon the other arm.

'It is hard to credit, you understand?'

'I do,' I said, my words clear in the quiet of the room.

There was something I had not seen before mingled with Mr Poll's anger, something that stilled the anger I had in me. For a long time he examined my face.

'I have your word?' he asked at last. 'That it was not you who did this thing?'

'You have.'

With what seemed very like disgust he said, 'Then go. I have nothing more to say to you.'

Each Sunday, when my work is done, I take paper and pen and write to my guardian. That I should do so was never agreed, but I do it anyway, giving him a catalogue of patients seen and places visited, omitting those details I think it best he not know. My letters are careful, dutiful, all that the letters of one such as I to his guardian should be. And yet they are poor things, their words lying dead upon the page, made stale by repetition, and I am sure they must bring as little joy to read as they do to write.

That this should be is doubly painful to me. For seven years my guardian has treated me as he might his own son. I should be grateful, and so I am, but where I should feel more, I do not; rather I feel only clumsiness, a tangled wound inside that I cannot unpick.

In my letters there is little of any consequence – simply the friends I have made, my affection for Charles and Robert, my admiration for my master's skill. Of the world to be found here in Charles's company I say nothing.

Perhaps it would be better to give these evenings to my

books, but I have little taste for them. As the weeks have passed I have found no joy in my studies, no concentration or ease, the things I learn of little use. Something is lost to me, some aptitude.

Those hours I would once have spent with Charles are now spent on my own, walking here and there through the city, searching for diversion, and for something else I cannot find.

———

By Seven Dials I hear my name and, turning, find May standing there. He looks thinner than when I saw him last, his frame in the black suit more spiderlike.

'May,' I begin, taking a step back as he approaches, 'what are you doing here?'

He smiles, and though the expression is genuine it is shot through with shame.

'I have business,' he says, gesturing carelessly. I follow the gesture with my eyes, uncomprehending, until suddenly May laughs his old laugh.

'The Jews,' he says, as if admitting to some foible for which he seeks sympathy, 'I come to see the Jews.'

Understanding now, I nod.

'I have not seen you of late,' he says.

I shake my head. 'I have been busy with my duties . . .' and May grins, nodding, though surely he must know the lie for what it is.

'And Charles? How is he?'

Realising he has not heard, I hesitate. 'He is to be married.'

'Married?' says May. 'That is happy news.' But then he falls quiet.

'And you?' I ask. 'You keep well?'

He nods, but then a low door opens behind him, a young Jew framed in it. May lifts a hand as if to stay him.

'I must go – but visit me, I have missed your company,' he says, smiling.

For a long time I remain there, staring after him. There is no wrong May has done to me, no unkindness I could name. But I cannot bear his company, cannot bear all that it asks of me.

———

I know his face at once, though I have not seen him since that day in the park.

Without thinking I look down, but Chifley lifts his arm.

'Ash,' he calls, rising from his seat. Opposite me Caswell stares at the table in front of him, and I know at once Chifley has some game planned here.

'You two have met, I think?' Chifley asks, drawing a chair towards our table. Looking no better pleased to see me than the last time we met Ash nods agreement.

'Swift,' he says.

I rise, thinking to excuse myself, but Chifley puts his hand upon my arm, calling for another glass. And so I sit again, and wait.

It transpires Ash and Chifley have some business about a horse. As it was that day with Arabella and Amy, Ash's manner is stiff and superior, as if he found himself burdened by our company. Once it is done he stands almost immediately, glancing at his watch.

'I have business elsewhere,' he says, barely looking at us as he speaks. Leaning back in his chair Chifley takes a swig from his glass and smiles.

'I am told her name is Louisa,' he says.

Ash looks at Chifley.

'You talk too much, man,' he says. I think at first he will say more but then he casts a few coins upon the table and turns away. Chifley reaches for his snuffbox.

'What? You did not know?'

'Know what?'

'That silly whore you met is ruined. Ash would have nothing of it.' I have drunk too much, and my face burns, Chifley looks at me mockingly as I rise to my feet.

'Why, Sparrow,' he asks, 'you do not take our jests amiss?'

I push past them for the door, a cold fury seething in my gut.

The night is warm, the streets are thronged with the Saturday crowds, fiddlers and sailors and soldiers and whores, all jostling and shouting. Not caring where I go I walk along the Strand to Ludgate Hill, then south, towards the river. I think at first to find Ash and teach him a lesson with my fists, for I am filled with a blinding loathing for these men and their ways, yet in the streets beneath St Paul's, where the watermen and their many brethren dwell, it begins to fade, replaced instead by a sort of shame, not just for my part in this thing but for my cowardice.

THE KITCHEN IS DARK, and so at first I do not see him in the shadows.

'It is late for you to be about.'

Startled, I jump. He chuckles, leaning forward so I can see the outline of his face. 'Had you thought yourself alone?'

'How come you here?' I hiss.

Lucan makes a noise of derision. 'You would remove me?' With a lazy motion he leans back against the wall.

Slowly I edge away from him. Though he comes to the house often now I am not comfortable in his presence, nor do I trust his motives for coming unannounced.

'I am alone, you need not fear.'

'What of Mrs Gunn?' I look towards the door to her little room.

'She will not wake, I think.' As he speaks I realise that he is drunk. Then, as if anticipating me, he adds, 'Nor Tyne either.'

I do not reply.

'He has wronged you, has he not?'

'He has.' Although the room's full width separates him from me, his presence is like a physical thing.

'You are afraid of him?'

I do not answer, and he nods.

'There is no shame in it. He is a man to keep always in one's sight. I fear it is on my account you have been wronged.'

'Perhaps,' I say.

'Would you have me teach Tyne a lesson on your behalf?'

I hesitate, for the idea is an attractive one, but then I shake my head. Lucan laughs.

'Good. I admire a man who does not incur debts easily.' He pauses thoughtfully.

'They say de Mandeville is to marry your master's daughter.'

'He is,' I say.

For a long moment he lets the statement hang between us.

'You know more of him, I think, than when last we spoke.'

'Perhaps,' I say.

'Her father but a miller's son. And he so great a gentleman.' He comes closer.

'I do not understand.'

'No?' he asks, his voice amused. 'They say she brings a fortune a better man than he might still desire.'

'I do not take your meaning,' I reply, but I feel a chill, for in truth I think I understand.

'You met an actress once, a child which died.'

I shake my head. 'I gave my word I would not speak of it.'

'Nor have you broken it.'

'He has debts? I ask. Then, with a startling suddenness, Lucan lifts his hand and grasps my face. His grip is almost tender, yet I feel the strength of him, the power which tenses in his hand.

'Surely you have seen enough of death by now to know something of life?' he asks, his face so close I feel the heat of his breath. My own comes raggedly, the blood hot in my throat, our bodies caught in this strange embrace.

'Do not be a fool for them,' he says at last, then all at once releases me.

DRIPPING MAY. Rain everywhere, a week of it. Inside the house everything feels damp, and in the cellar there is water. Then one morning a knock – a boy on our doorstep with an unmarked letter he says is for me, though he will say no more. I open it, afraid. Inside, a note bearing news Amy is taken ill and begging me to bring Charles at once. The ink is spilled upon the paper by the rain. Looking down I see the boy's frightened face.

'Wait here,' I say.

In the dissection room Charles is bent over a body with Mr Poll. Robinson, a seller of hats, dead two days of a strangulation of the bowel. Charles is drawing forth the spilling mess of his guts, a slippery mass which bulges evilly here and there as he scoops it into a pail. The stink clotting the air so I must lift a hand to my face.

'What is it?' he asks, and coming closer I hold the note out so he might read it. Barely pausing in his work he scans it quickly, then glances down into the opened cavity of Robinson's belly. Across the table Mr Poll is waiting. Charles twists his hand, chivvying the liver free. Then at last he sets his scalpel down and looks at Mr Poll.

'I am needed,' he says. Mr Poll regards Charles for a second, perhaps expecting some further explanation. But Charles offers none. Something silent passes between the two of them, then Charles takes a rag and begins to wipe the fat from his hands.

'Is the messenger still here?' he asks, and I nod.

'Say I will be there presently.'

———

The day is wet, rain falling steadily from heavy skies, and though we walk quickly we are wet before we have gone a hundred feet. Charles's handsome face is closed.

As soon as we arrive Mary opens the door. She looks less fierce today, I think, her face pale, and scared.

The house is hot, as close and over-warm as the first day I visited. Along a little corridor Mary stops before a door and half-turns to Charles. Her sallow face is tight and grey with worry, yet there is still that mixture of defiance and need I saw in her the first time we met. It seems she means to speak, but cannot find the words. Charles reaches out a hand and places it on her arm, his touch seeming to dissolve whatever it was that burned inside her.

'Do not fear,' he says, and Mary nods, letting her hand press upon the door so it swings open.

The room is dark, the curtains drawn against the day. Upon the floor mounds of bedding are tumbled here and there, crumpled and stained with blood. On the bed in the room's centre Amy lies, her face ashen, her head cradled in Arabella's lap. Arabella looks up as we enter.

'Please,' she says, one hand stroking the tangled mess of

Amy's hair, 'help her.' I am not sure what is worse, the sight of Amy's blood or the way Arabella's voice breaks with fear.

'How long has she been like this?' Charles asks, setting down his bag and seating himself behind her. Arabella shakes her head.

'I had a performance last night, and she was in bed by the time I came in. When she did not rise this morning, I came in, and found her.' Her voice trails off.

Charles nods, placing a hand upon Amy's brow.

'It was a woman in Ludgate Hill,' Arabella says. As she speaks Amy opens her eyes.

'Charles,' she says, smiling, and Charles takes her hand.

'Amy,' he says, 'what have you done?'

She shrugs, then seeing me, 'Mr Swift,' she says, 'you did not come to visit.'

I shake my head. 'No,' I say, and she smiles.

'You will not want to, now, I think.'

'Yes,' I say, 'I will come again.'

She laughs raggedly. 'And your carriage, you will bring your carriage?'

I swallow hard. And then she winces, her body doubling up in pain, and turning aside she closes her eyes and seems to slip away.

'Tell me you will help her,' Arabella pleads, but Charles only shakes his head.

'I will do what I can,' he says. 'After that it is in God's hands.'

From his bag Charles takes a draught to thicken her blood, mixing it with opium and spooning it carefully into her mouth. With the opium her breathing grows slower, more regular. Mary glances at Arabella; this change calms them a bit. But the bleeding does not stop. It is not the first time I have seen a patient haemorrhage, but it is still hard to credit the sheer volume of the blood. Again and again Mary sops it up with sheets and towels, carrying them away, yet always there seems to be more of it, leaking forth like a tide. At last Arabella bids her stop, her face hopeless. She extends a hand and takes the girl's in it, the gesture so tender I feel my throat tighten. By the window Charles stands, his face half-turned away; as if he wished only for the end to come.

All afternoon we wait, barely speaking. At some point I seat myself beside Amy, and take her hand. It is cold, and limp, the pulse in it shallow. Then Arabella slips Amy's head free of her lap and stands, crossing to the door, as if she cannot bear any more to be close to her.

The life in Amy ebbs slowly, her breathing growing softer, less regular, until with a little start it gives out altogether. For a time we remain still, then at last Arabella's voice breaks the silence.

'It is over, then?'

Charles kneels, pressing one finger into Amy's throat, then nods and steps away. Slowly Arabella approaches, and still holding one arm to herself extends the other to touch Amy's face, arranging the hair upon her brow carefully, as if she were a child. By the door Mary has begun to weep.

Quietly Charles takes up his bag, and head bowed begins to move to the door. I cannot move though. Silently Arabella turns to look at me.

'Arabella –' I begin, reaching out for her hand, but she shakes her head, pulling her hand away.

'No,' she says, 'do not say it. I could not bear it.'

OUTSIDE THE RAIN HAS STOPPED, the water on the cobbles lying dark in the dusk's soft light, deep as mirrors. After the heat of the house, the air in the street is cool, yet it feels remote, the motion of the passing traffic unreal.

Though I wish from Charles some word, some sign that would make sense of this, perhaps it is better without. Only when we reach our door does he turn to me.

'This should never have been,' he says. 'These women are no concern of mine.'

Suddenly the door opens to reveal Mr Poll, Oates at his side. Caught for once without his mask, Charles seems to stand naked before the older man, exposed in all his frailty. Yet Mr Poll does not flinch, nor reprimand him, indeed his expression is more one of regret than of anger. Again that something passes between them, then, touching his hat, Mr Poll bids us goodbye, reminding Charles of his appointment to dine at his home that evening and stepping out into the waiting door of his carriage. For a moment I think Charles will turn to follow him, say some word to hold him there, try to erase what has just passed between the two of them. But he does not, the wheels of the carriage loud upon the cobblestones as it departs.

It is only when Mr Poll's carriage is out of sight around the Square that I see the way he trembles, though whether with rage or shame I do not know.

I follow Charles up the stairs, watch him gather his things. I know I should leave him, let him be, but I feel the need of some word with him, some way to undo what I have just seen. In agitation he turns about the room, search-ing for something, and thinking it is a draught he had me mix for a patient of his this morning I take it down from the shelf. But as I offer it to him I realise he had not understood that I was there, for he starts, something flashing behind his gaze. I think at first he means to speak angrily to me, so great is his agitation, but instead he takes the medicine from my hand.

'Oh Gabriel,' he says, 'she is a pretty thing, but do not be a fool.'

Something in me hardens. Charles, though, only smiles coldly.

'I see you have no stomach for my words, but trust me, it does not pay to become too attached to these sorts of people.'

'No doubt you speak from experience,' I say, my words coming too fast, too easily. Charles's expression stiffens.

'Very well,' he says. 'Only remember: she can be yours for the price of a few ribbons. I can even arrange it for you if you wish.'

I am struck motionless. In his face something shifts – regret dawning perhaps – and it seems he will apologise. But then he brushes past, out the door and down. When I hear the sound of the door to the street close, I turn – and see Mr Tyne. It is clear at once he has heard all that passed between the two of us, for he watches me with a look of delight. He takes a step, and I back away, then another. Suddenly afraid, I lunge past him and out.

———

In the street I walk blindly, pushing through the moving crowds. Already the windows are ablaze, the city filled with light and sound. From Compton Street I cut east, towards Covent Garden where the crowds are thicker, the sound of fiddlers and Scots pipers pressing hard upon the air, though I barely hear them. From the windows women lean, their breasts hanging free in loosened stays, and they call lewdly after me. Without thinking I call back, my words angry, and they respond in kind; by the market a pair of gentlemen, students down from Cambridge perhaps, collide with me, and I push at them and shout. They are drunk, and though there are two of them they do not raise their fists, simply back away, leaving me to call angrily after them. And then, upon the Strand, there is Chifley, Caswell beside him. For a moment I might strike at him but Chifley grabs my wrist, staying me.

'Sparrow,' he laughs, 'where do you go?'

I shake my head, twisting free. Though he is almost a head shorter than me Chifley's pouter-pigeon frame is powerful. He smiles.

'You will come with us, I think.'

At first I resist, for Chifley's mood is dangerous. But then I realise I do not care, and taking the bottle he holds out, I lift it to my lips and drink.

They have won at billiards, and are already full of their success. Chifley holds it well, the only sign that he is drunk the purpose in his stride, but Caswell's face is flushed and his step uncertain. They lead me through the lanes, first to a shop which sells eel pies, then on to a ginshop Chifley knows near Monmouth Street. From the way the serving girls make merry with Chifley it is plain they know him well enough. It is a dreadful place, low-ceilinged and close, yet the gin is cheap, and the music loud. On the counter sits a woman, no taller than a girl of five. She wears a child's dress, a filthy thing stained all about, her face garishly painted. Although two men stand talking with her, Chifley demands that she be brought over, for he says he wants to dandle her on his lap. Her companions glower at us, but Chifley pays them no heed.

Her name is Rosa, and she moves with the swaying gait of her kind, her shrunken limbs no longer than my forearm yet she slips up onto Chifley's lap as might a dog, writhing against his grabbing hands and laughing with a deep mannish sound.

With the sharp sweetness of the gin in my throat and my first cup gone, I call at once for another. Beneath the paint which cakes her cheeks and brows her face is grotesque, its features heavy and misshapen as an ape's. Giving me a sly smile, she slips her hand into Chifley's jacket. I do not like this look, its taunting challenge, but I do not speak, not even as she draws his wallet out and deftly slips it into her bodice. Quite suddenly I have the desire to be out of myself, forgetful with drink, and so with ferocity I lift my glass and pull back once more upon the gin, closing my eyes at the heat which floods my brain and belly.

The next hours pass in a blur. Somewhere we lose Rosa although before that I remember stumbling into a room to see Chifley standing against the wall, fly buttons undone and her before him, her head moving quickly back and forth. Afterwards we eat again, and then Chifley discovers his wallet is gone, which blackens his mood. And after that, or later perhaps, I say that I must go, but Chifley and Caswell demand that I stay, and when I insist, they declare their intention to come with me as an escort, so I might be protected from brigands. And so the three of us stumble back together, arms hung about each other and very drunk, through the lanes to Greek Street. On the doorstep I take my leave, turning the key in the lock as quietly as I can. But then Chifley leans in and grabs my arm.

'Hey, Sparrow,' he says in a slurred whisper, 'what of those ladies you promised us?'

'I promised you no ladies,' I reply, but he only laughs.

'I think we'll look for ourselves.' He glances at Caswell, who wears a drunken smile, half-eager for this new delight, half-frightened at what might come.

'No,' I say, moving to keep him out, but I am too slow, for he is already past me and inside.

'They are asleep.' I gesture upwards, but Chifley is not to be dissuaded. Grasping the handle of the door to the front room, he swings it open, lurching inwards to see what is there. In the hall Caswell collides heavily with the table, and Chifley turns, looking about.

'The cellar, I think,' he says, fumbling in his pocket for a match.

In vain I try to slow him down, grabbing at his coat, but Chifley is not to be deterred. Caswell follows us, tittering delightedly at this new scene of chaos. As chance would have it the cellar door is unlocked, and Chifley slips through. Trying to stop him is futile. I follow him down into the darkness. The light from the match dances wildly on the walls, but then the match burns down to his fingers, and with a curse he casts it to the floor, where it gutters and dies.

'Find me a candle,' he hisses, taking the last few steps with a thud, and a second later the light flares again at his fingertips. From somewhere Caswell passes him a candle, and Chifley lights it, before swinging out into the room's centre.

On the tables lie three corpses, two women and a man, and here and there the other remnants of our trade: a pair of arms, a leg still bound in muslin, three torsos hollowed out and a head, this last laid upon its face by Robert earlier today, for it would not sit still in any other way, persisting instead in rolling here and there. The smell is foul, and Chifley makes a face.

'It's a rare stink you have in here,' he says, raising a finger to his nose. Caswell snorts.

'Winter work,' Chifley says inscrutably, and slowly moves his hips back and forth. Beside me Caswell giggles again, but already Chifley has forgotten. Creeping towards the man, he leans close beside his ear and says hello, lingering upon the word so it is made ridiculous. When no answer comes, he tries it again and, unable to bear this latest hilarity, Caswell's nervous giggles explode into laughter. Wildly I try to silence him, but this only provokes him further. He clasps his hand over his mouth, unsuccessfully attempting to stifle himself. Glancing round at us Chifley lifts a finger and with a sudden motion jabs at the man's arm. This done he rises and moves to one of the women, making a show of tiptoeing towards her, only to lean down at the last moment and cry 'Boo!'. Despite myself I grin at this, while Caswell laughs so much that he must lean against the stairs. With a finger Chifley presses down upon her nose, squishing it first this way and then the other. Then, bored with this, he turns to the second woman. She is younger than the first, and although her expression is gaunt and blotchy and her stubbled scalp bare, there is a quality to her face which suggests she might once have been fair enough.

'Good day,' Chifley says, with another glance at us to see that we are watching. He pauses then, as if waiting for an answer.

'What's that?' he asks. 'You have something you wish to tell me?' Leaning closer he places his ear at her lips.

'You want me to do what?' Once more he pauses, as if he were listening, then he giggles prissily, as might a girl, batting his eyelids and covering his mouth.

'Oh no,' he titters, 'I could not.' But then, as if answering, he wriggles his shoulders. 'Oh, alright,' he says, 'but only once,' and with a mincing motion he lifts his hands and cups the sunken remnants of her breasts. Lovingly he massages them, then slowly he puts his lips to hers, mumbling and murmuring, *mm-mm-mm*, a sound as if he were eating. Then all at once he slips an arm beneath her, pulling her towards him in an embrace. It is monstrous yet I am laughing. Perhaps it is the gin, perhaps it is the lunacy of the moment, but I cannot help myself. Wildly Chifley looks about, and for an instant our eyes meet, then he pulls her from the table, one arm about her waist, the other pressed beneath her arm so he may hold her upright, and marking out a wild tune he begins to dance, swinging past Caswell and me. Caswell is laughing his idiot laugh, and Chifley is making the sound of a trumpet, *ta-ran-ta-ran-ta-ran-ta-ra*, as Caswell chases after him, clapping his hands. Around and around he goes, Caswell swirling after him, myself too, for I am laughing and laughing, and then suddenly I am crying, although I do not know it at once. I fall still, letting them swirl on, shaking my head. Away they go, then back again, Caswell now dancing with his hands upon the girl's shoulder. They pass close by, Chifley's eyes meeting mine, filled with a sort of exaltation. I step after him, but I do not have to, for he trips upon a bag and stumbles, sent sprawling to the ground with the girl's body on top of him. Caswell lands heavily upon his backside. Still laughing Chifley begins to clamber to his feet, but I am upon him, and grabbing him by the coat I haul him upright, pushing him towards the door.

'Get out,' I say.

I push him up the stairs, into the hall. Behind me I hear

Caswell coming up too, and with a shove I send Chifley sprawling into the street outside. His collar crooked and jacket torn he stares up at me, neither angry nor ashamed but rather pleased, and though I know that I should strike at him, drive him away, suddenly I do not care, and, shaking my head I step back and away.

'Go,' I hiss, 'go!' And going out the door Caswell is laughing still, but I cannot look at him, and so I close them out and stumble down the stairs to try to right the wrong there.

I WAKE ILL and miserable. The room is hot, the air close: somewhere in the night I remember waking, my stomach heaving its contents into my chamber pot, and the smell lingers foully. My eyes ache and my throat and nose are sour with bile, and for a time I just lie, face pressed against the sheet, wishing only to slip back into the cool refuge of sleep. Somewhere just out of reach something nags at me, some sense that there is something I have forgotten, and dully I struggle to remember, until all at once the recollection returns, descending like a weight.

By the time I muster the strength, the day outside is bright, the air in the yard fresh with the smell of leaves. Crouching low before the butt I close my eyes, let the water course across my head and back. Though it is cold I do not pull away, glad for its icy trickle on my swollen face, the sound of the falling water flat upon the stones. When I am done I rise, blinking, to find Robert there, a towel held out to me.

'Your shirt is soiled,' he says.

'It will do,' I retort, more sharply than I intended. Lifting my hand I think at first to apologise, but then do not.

'Gabriel . . .' Robert begins.

'What?'

'I do not pretend to understand all of what occurred last night, but you harm only yourself this way.'

I nod. Although my memory is confused I recall now being found by Robert, hopelessly trying to tidy the mess left by Chifley and Caswell.

'Was there any damage?'

'Nothing that was not easily repaired, although I need not tell you it could have been worse.'

'And Mr Poll?'

Robert pauses, watching me.

'I see no reason for him to be informed,' he says.

'Thank you,' I say stiffly.

'Give me the shirt,' he says. 'I will have Mrs Gunn clean it for you.'

———

The day creeps past interminably, a long sullen march towards evening. By midday the nausea has passed, replaced by a headache which presses hard against my eyeballs. I am clumsy with it, and twice Mr Poll reprimands me for dropping instruments. Our first task is to open the girl, and as I help bear her up the stairs with Robert I am consumed with shame for the events of the evening before. Unfeeling I watch as her body is unpicked, piece by piece. Although I have seen this done many times, today I stare almost unblinking as her throat is opened, the gristled column of the windpipe removed, thick as a child's arm. Atop it the swollen mass of her tongue still attached, ridged and coated like that of some beast in the market place.

When we are done I gather the pieces and the pails and bear her back to the cellar, depositing what is left upon the table with a twinge of uncustomary disgust.

During the afternoon I slip away and conceal myself in a corner of the dispensary. Resting my head upon the bench I fall into a shallow doze, a fitful half-waking thing, disturbed by phantoms which flit just out of reach. How long I sleep I do not know; a few minutes perhaps, but all of a sudden I wake with a start. Charles stands in the door, one hand upon the knob. That he had not thought to find me here is clear, for he stands poised to turn, as if about to slip away once more. We look uncomfortably at one another: all day Charles has been out of sorts, his mood brittle, and now we are alone together I see he wishes we were not.

'I am sorry,' I say, rising. 'I thought only to rest awhile.' Although my words are apologetic my manner is not.

'No matter,' he says stiffly, and we are so close we might touch. Even now, when I know so much more of him than I did, Charles possesses a sort of grace, a beauty few can resist, and I find myself wishing to forgive him, and so, I think, does he. But it is not to be.

'I have work to do,' I say, stepping past him and away.

————

That night I cannot sleep, floating in the darkness of my room. From the street below come the cries of the night – drunkards singing and the clatter of the wheels upon the stones. At three I hear the bells of St Giles, and slipping from my bed I make my way downstairs. Through the window moonlight falls, soft rectangles of light upon the stairs, the wood cool against my naked soles. In the dispensary I draw opium, and drink. It brings sleep, a drifting restless thing of sound and fire, a restless motion in which I move, as a swimmer might, just beneath waking's surface. That I dream I know, yet still I dream and cannot break away, even as I feel myself pursued. What follows me I do not know and yet can only fear, something both horrible and familiar, and whose touch upon my shoulder stills me so I turn to face it, my body sick with terror, turning once and then again and then again and then again until suddenly I see it and in that instant wake.

THE DAYS THAT FOLLOW pass in sullen silence. Though we have work enough I am left much to myself. Twice I bear messages to Whitechapel and Kentish Town, winding my way gratefully through the city streets, and in between I bend to my books or idle in the yard. What it is that ails me I do not know: though I grieve for Amy it is more than that, my anger mingling with a shame which will neither shift nor dissolve, and with it too the remembering of my desire for Arabella.

It is Charles who tells me of Amy's funeral, drawing me aside in the morning of the Saturday. For three days we have barely spoken, and now he is awkward with me.

'They bury her this afternoon,' he says. I look at him coldly.

'If you wish to go I will tell Mr Poll you are on business on my behalf,' he says. I nod uneasily, for I have no wish to be beholden to him. Perhaps he sees this, for he does not press the point, and so it is me who must accede.

'Thank you,' I say, though stiffly.

And so, an hour after noon I am at the front door. But then comes Mr Tyne's voice from the stairs.

'You're wanted,' he says.

At first I think to keep walking, to close the door behind me and leave him there. But I hesitate, Mr Tyne watching with a mocking smile.

'What?' he asks – 'there is somewhere else you must be?'

————

In the theatre Mr Poll has a body, brought last night by Lucan, laid out for examination. Banister, owner of a counting-house in the city, struck down by a spasm of the brain three nights past. As I enter, Mr Poll glances up at me, telling me to gather his instruments.

I do not protest. Removing my jacket I roll up my sleeves and tie on my apron. Barely looking at me Mr Poll motions to me to pass him the scalpel, and with a practised motion he slices from ear to ear across the dome of the skull, bisecting the scalp, then, putting aside the scalpel, he slips his fingers into the cut and pulls the face down, exposing the yellow bone of the skull. There is always something unsettling in the way the face slips so cleanly from the bone, as if it were merely a mask, worn and discarded. Repeating the process at the back of the scalp he takes the saw and begins to cut away the dome of the skull. The bone is dry, the saw's motion bringing first fine yellow dust, then a smell of burning. It is not quick work, but to appear impatient will only earn me some reprimand, so I will myself not to look up at the clock which stands above the fireplace. The minutes tick by, the saw moving in the quiet of the room, until with a last slide the skull splits. Handing me the saw Mr Poll draws forth the brain, severing the column which holds it in its shell; then, placing it on the slab, he regards it thoughtfully.

'I have measured the brains of halfwits and simpletons,' he says. 'They do not differ from ours in weight.'

Since his words seem not directed to me in particular I do

not reply, and a moment later he takes up his knife, bisecting the brain once and again until the dark and white of the haemorrhage comes into view. Pleased, he grunts, scooping up the brain and squeezing it so the jellied blood drips forth. Not for the first time I wonder at the way these lumps of meat contain us, at the wonder of the motion of our selves through this brute matter. What must he have felt, this Banister, as the blood spilled forth into his mind? A sound like water, or wind? The falling away of himself?

———

The hour of the funeral is already past when we are done, and I leave the house at a run, dodging through the carriages and passing traffic. The church lies not far from Percy Street, in a little close behind Charlotte Street, and at its rear the graveyard is a quiet place shaded by a beech, walled in on each side by houses to which ivy clings. As I come about the church's side I see the funeral party in the far corner, silent while the priest intones the words of the service.

Quite suddenly I am uncomfortable, hot and awkward, as if my presence here will be unwelcome.

Arabella stands alone in the centre of the group, staring downwards at the coffin. She stands so still, so stiff it seems her very body refuses all sympathy. Mary is behind her, dressed all in black, face set.

The service is not long in finishing, the party breaking up as the gravediggers lower the coffin into the earth. Beside Arabella a ginger-whiskered man says something I cannot hear, bowing close to her as he speaks. She nods curtly, and her eyes catch mine across the yard, but she gives no sign. As she passes through the group the others touch her arm and hand, murmuring words of sympathy; only when this is done does she approach the place where I stand.

'You came,' she says, extending her hand. I press it tight, not wanting to let it go. Many times I have heard Robert and Charles offer consolation to the grieving, but it is not an art I have ever shared. There seems so little to be said, and yet everything, as if words cannot encompass it. But as I see she does not want my pity, nor my grief, only quiet, only for this thing to be done and her to be away.

'I did not know . . .' I falter.

'Know what?'

'If I would be welcome.'

'She was your friend,' she says softly.

'Had she family?' I ask, but she shakes her head.

'None that would have seen her were she alive.'

'Then they do not know?'

'I wrote to her brother, and to an aunt she spoke of, yet neither have replied.' Shaking her head she looks away, then back.

'Then those here?'

'Friends,' she says. 'And few enough of them. No mind, it will be over soon.'

I shake my head. 'It should not be like this.'

'No,' she says angrily, 'it should not.' Then catches herself, as if she will not show this thing, nor give it voice.

The man with the muttonchops appears at her elbow.

'Gabriel, this is Mr Gardiner. It is his theatre in which you have seen me play.'

Gardiner looks at me. Though his face is ruddy and his shining features coarse there is a shrewdness to his gaze I cannot help but like.

Begging my pardon, in a booming Scots accent, he turns to Arabella. 'The carriage,' he says, and she nods.

———

145

Back at the house the few who came to the funeral stand in the drawing room and speak quietly. The occasion is not an easy one; those who have gathered seeming uncomfortable and anxious to be away. Only Mr Gardiner seems in his element, speaking casually and cheerfully. Sitting sullenly in their midst I feel awkward, out of place, yet it is not them I watch, but Arabella. As she moves and speaks I see the way she hides herself, the way she laughs and smiles, and anger rises in me at her pretence. Finally I stand and absent myself, descending to the kitchen. From upstairs comes the sound of voices, the opening door, but still I do not move, willing her to come to me, to find me here. An hour passes, then another, and only then is there a foot upon the stair.

Her hair is awry somehow, her face composed.

'You are here,' she says. 'I thought that you had gone.'

I rise so I may face her.

'I am glad that you have not,' she says. All at once I know why I have stayed, that I am angry with her now, angry for the way she will not let this thing affect her, and suddenly I want to strike at her, to make her weep, to jar her somehow into some sign of grief. Perhaps she sees this in my face, for she shakes her head, and comes close.

'Why did you come today?' she asks.

I pull back. 'How could I not?'

She hesitates. 'You are angry at me.'

'No,' I say, but she takes my hand, holding it firm as I try to twist myself away.

'I am glad of it,' she says. The two of us stand so close I can smell the scent she wears upon her throat, see the way her powder is clotted here and there upon her face. I feel it all within me then, the anger and the grief, and I do not know whether I should strike at her or take her in my arms. And then she lifts her face to mine, and with a hungry, urgent mouth kisses me, once and then again, her body pressing close against my own, as if she sought to lose herself in this, to be unmade in the dissolving need that rises in our chests and mouths and hands.

So this is what it means to know a woman. This ragged wanting. My hands mute implements, raw and clotting, my desire more like a pain that cannot be salved. Outside the summer days are long, the city quarrelsome and bright.

Perhaps it would be better were we busier, but with the heat there is little for us to do. The bodies will not keep, and we may not teach, our days lost in idleness. I am sure Robert guesses much, of the cause of my distraction and my absences, of my estrangement from Charles. On those evenings when I may not be with her, he walks with me through the dusty streets.

———

As the weeks slip by I go to her as often as I may. She has her life, and I have mine, but since the night of Amy's death something has changed in me. Though I go about my work I no longer care for this, for any of it. When we are apart I wish myself in her company, when we are together I cannot concentrate. And always I wish only to leave all this behind, to be away from it. Always this desire for her being, opening unanswered inside of me: no matter how I try I cannot cross whatever gulf it is that lies between the two of us, cannot translate myself into that heat.

———

Beneath my pillow I can feel the flat of the bottle that I filled in the dispensary this afternoon, its shape pressing hard against me. I will not drink tonight, I tell myself, though this is a lie, and turning over in the bed I reach for it, the glass cool against my hungry hand.

A T THE DOOR Mary shakes her head.
'No,' she says. 'Not now.' From the window overhead there comes a man's voice, low and teasing, then Arabella's, raised in laughter, the sound spilling into the evening air. Mary does not move, her body blocking my way.

'Later,' she says, 'come later.'

————

The house is quiet when I return, the windows open to the summer air. Mr Poll and Charles are gone for the day. But as I enter the kitchen I hear the voice of Mr Tyne.

'Back from your whore already?'

Startled, I see him standing in the door to Mrs Gunn's room.

'What?' he asks, coming closer. 'You did not know that is what she is?'

'Do not use that word,' I say, but he only laughs. Behind him I see Mrs Gunn appear.

'Whore,' he says, 'whore,' and perhaps he might say it again, but before he can I hurl myself towards him, grasping his collar so we crash into the wall and door. We land heavily but if he is hurt he does not show it. Instead he laughs, his pockmarked face grinning – and so I swing him round and away, sending him stumbling through the chairs onto the floor. On the table the lamp spills sideways, falling to the ground with a crash of breaking glass. Without thinking I lunge at him again, meaning to strike him once more, but I lose my footing and in a moment I am on my back and he is up, one hand about my neck, the other thrust inside his coat. Seeing he means to draw his knife I kick out, trying to throw him off. His head is bleeding, dripping down from a cut above his eye.

'I said once I would kill you,' he says. 'It is a promise I mean to keep.'

The knife is out, held close to his body and low so it might strike upwards, and hard. Desperately I grab at his arm, staying it just above my belly, yet the angle is awkward, and he has the advantage. His face is close to mine, his hard little eyes boring into me, their whites all but invisible. Then suddenly Robert is behind him, yanking him away from me.

'What is the meaning of this?' he demands. Mr Tyne leans back against the wall, one hand raised to his head, the knife still clasped in the other. He is panting, his breath coming in ragged gasps. Rubbing my neck I begin to lift myself to my feet, watching Mr Tyne. I cannot believe he will let it end here, but he does not move.

'Well?' Robert demands.

I shake my head. 'Nothing,' I say. 'It was nothing.'

Behind me Mrs Gunn steps forward. 'It was him,' she says, pointing at me. 'He struck first.'

Robert closes his eyes, his breath seeming to catch. Then, with an expression of resignation, he turns to me.

'Is this true, Gabriel?' he asks. 'Did you start this?'

For a moment I think to shake my head, but I cannot, and so I simply say, 'I did.'

Robert nods, his thin face seeming stricken by some awful certainty.

'You know I must report this.'

'I do,' I reply.

For a long moment he stands, staring at me, then at last he turns away.

'Clean this up,' he says, moving away to the stairs. Mr Tyne straightens, a triumphant grin upon his face.

'Where are your airs now, boy?' In my chest I feel my breath move hotly – but before I can speak Robert turns on him.

'Silence!' As he speaks he descends once more, his eyes fixed on Mr Tyne and Mrs Gunn.

'Gabriel is the apprentice of your master, man, and whatever tomorrow brings, in the meantime you shall treat him with the respect that he deserves.'

Mr Tyne begins to reply, but Robert cuts him off. 'Do not think I am ignorant of your part in this,' he says, advancing on him until they stand face to face. For a long moment Mr Tyne does not move, then, quite suddenly, he turns, and with a backward glance that drips with hatred vanishes up the stairs and away.

Once he has gone Robert turns to Mrs Gunn.

'You would do well to remember what you heard me say,' he says firmly, but without anger. 'Mr Tyne is not master of this house, whatever he believes.'

Mrs Gunn hesitates, then she nods. 'Yes, sir,' she says quietly. At this Robert softens.

'You have been a good friend to me these last six years, Mrs Gunn,' he says. 'I shall miss you when I go.'

Mrs Gunn looks down, a blush colouring her scrubbed cheeks.

'I hope you will be the same to Mr Swift once I am gone.'

Looking up she glances first at Robert, then at me, then back to Robert. She is a kind woman, if a foolish one, but she is caught, and we both see that.

'Yes, sir,' she says.

———

I do not follow Robert up the stairs at once. Instead I linger in the kitchen, intending to help Mrs Gunn repair the damage. Yet as I lift a chair she takes it from me and shakes her head. Understanding, I relinquish my grasp.

Upstairs Robert's door is open, and he sits upon the sill by the window. Outside the city is alive with light.

'Thank you,' I say.

Robert shakes his head. 'No,' he says. 'My temper will only have made things worse. Tyne is the worst sort of man.'

Robert looks out at the lights once more.

'This was his purpose, you know. Ever since that night with the child.'

'Yes,' I say. 'I do.' Briefly, I consider. 'I will be dismissed, will I not?'

'Most probably.'

'I am sorry,' I say.

'So am I.'

'You are to go away?' I ask. Turning back to his desk he takes up a folded sheet.

'It is confirmed today,' he says. 'I leave in a month for St Lucia, a practice in Castries.'

Though the news is not a surprise, it strikes me hard, for it is only now that I realise how keenly I shall feel his loss.

'Perhaps you could come with me,' Robert says, holding his hand out. 'Some accommodation might be made

153

between your guardian and Mr Poll and me. You could train with me, or take some work.'

Robert's thin face is set in a look of such affection I am ashamed he should see so much in me. But then I shake my head.

'No,' I say, 'that life is not for me.'

———

In my room I lean back against the wall and stare up at the cracked ceiling I have gazed at so many times before. The narrow bed is hard, its familiar smell of dust and sleep rising faintly. If I close my eyes I can imagine her face, feel her touch. I feel weak. Were I to lift my hand and hold it still, it would tremble: his purpose was to wound and indeed Mr Tyne has touched something I must fight to deny – the way she gives herself to other men, and what that means. Through the wall I hear Robert in his room: with him gone there will be nothing left to keep me here. And all at once I want it to be done, to be away from here, from all of this.

IT IS LATE the next day before Mr Poll arrives, the after-noon already done. Seated in the kitchen, I hear his carriage outside, muffled voices in the hall above. Soon enough Robert is on the kitchen stairs.

Mr Poll is in his study, Mr Tyne standing to one side. Where he has been since last night I do not know, but seeing now the swelling of his cut and blackened eye, the bruises on his cheek and neck, I realise I am no longer afraid of him, of any of this. Mr Poll stands watching as I take in those injuries, my gaze clear and cold, then with a glance he directs Robert to close the door.

'What is the meaning of this?'

Before Mr Tyne can answer I speak, my voice coming almost proudly. 'It was my doing.'

'You struck him? To what purpose?'

'Because he is a villain.'

'What kind of an answer is that?' snaps Mr Poll. Then, recovering himself, he turns to Robert.

'What do you know of this? Who struck the first blow?'

'I was not present, sir,' Robert says.

'It was I,' I say, before Robert may say any more.

Mr Poll looks at me, then back at Robert.

'Well?'

Robert looks down. 'I have the word of Mrs Gunn that the first blow was Gabriel's.'

Mr Poll nods. Then he turns to Mr Tyne.

'And you? What have you to say to this?'

'The boy speaks the truth,' Mr Tyne replies. 'He attacked me.'

'And you did nothing to provoke it?'

Mr Tyne only smiles, his eyes meeting mine for a moment.

'Fetch Charles,' says Mr Poll. 'This matter is his concern as well.'

It is almost an hour before Charles arrives, summoned by Robert from somewhere or other. Directed to wait in the library I hear him come in and speak with Mr Poll for a time. Then Robert appears at the door and summons me to join them. This time Mr Tyne is not present, but in truth it would not matter if he was, for the sight of Charles standing with my master revives in me my desire for this thing to be done. What Charles thinks I do not know, for he does not speak, and so it is Mr Poll who begins.

'I will ask you again,' he says, 'is there some cause for this behaviour, some reason you can give for it?'

I shake my head, looking not at Mr Poll but at Charles.

'Think carefully,' says Mr Poll. 'I know there has been ill feeling between you and Tyne for some time, and I do not doubt that you were provoked.'

'Please, Gabriel,' Robert says, but I only shake my head.

'The first blow was mine,' I say, 'that is all there is to be said of it.'

'Then you give me no choice, you understand that?' asks Mr Poll.

'I do,' I say. There is quiet then, Mr Poll standing silently.

'Then go,' he says at last, 'you are dismissed.' As he speaks he shakes his head, the expression on his face is one of sadness, not of anger, and all at once I feel the blood hot in my face, and so I turn away, unable to remain.

———

In my room I pack my things, a process quickly done, and gladly, for my hands tremble as I work, though whether from rage or shame I do not know. As I work Robert watches me from the door, unspeaking.

'Where will you go?' he asks when I am done, and I shrug.

'I will find a room,' I say.

'Have you money?'

'A little,' I reply. He nods, his eyes regarding me steadily, then extending his arms he draws me to himself.

'God keep you, Gabriel,' he says, 'God keep you.'

———

Outside in the street the air is warm, the day not quite yet done, and to the west the sky burns red. In the air above, the swallows shoot and wheel, their small bodies describing arcs against the fading sky as they chase their prey. Before his shop, Clark's boy sweeps the pavement, next door the maid chatters to the waterman; all about the life of the street continues as it ever does, it is only me that has changed. For these moments I hesitate, not knowing which way to turn. In the hall behind me Mrs Gunn stands with Robert, Charles beside them and so, not wanting to linger, I turn left, my feet following themselves into the city's roil.

I WAKE TO EVENING'S fading light, the air about me close and foul. Through the thin partition of the wall beside me comes the sound of coughing, a noise both wet and horrible that continues on and on. At first I am unsure of where I am, or when, and for a brief moment I fancy I may have slept only a heartbeat or two, slipping in the shallow, skittering sleep of the opium, that the light outside might be that of the dawn, but even as I do I know that it is not, and that the day is gone, and it is dusk.

Sitting up I rub my hands against my face. My head is thick, and some sense of loss weighs down on me, a regret for which there seems no cause. With one hand I find a match upon the table by the bed, and striking it I light a candle stub, the room flickering into light as it flares and takes.

Rising I fumble with my flies, watching the stream of my urine drum into the pot. It is dark and pungent, its stink rising hotly. Then I reach for my coat upon the chair, only to remember my watch is gone, pawned yesterday. From downstairs comes my landlord Scarpi's voice raised in anger at his wife. Outside, people will be gathering, talking and laughing as they go about the business of the last hours of the day. Lifting my eyes to the window I picture them, feeling their motion somewhere inside of me. I would be out there, I think, amongst their busy movement, and I reach again for my coat and hurry out the door and down the stairs into the street.

———

Six weeks have passed since I left my master's house. That night I walked without direction, feeling a lightness at being free again. On every side the streets teemed with life and noise, the ceaseless press of the city's motion, and yet I barely noticed. Only when I came to Ludgate Hill, the great bulk of St Paul's afire against the fading sky, did I falter, realising I did not know where it was I went, the implications of what I had done suddenly pressing down on me.

Not knowing what else to do I turned aside, seeking out a tavern or eating place where I might sit awhile; finding one, I took a place before the window, staring out through the smoky glass into the street. I ordered wine, and at the owner's insistence bread and soup, though I had little appetite.

The food was quickly brought. In my mouth the bread was dry and stale, though in truth I barely tasted it. Once and then again I drew out my purse and counted the coins within. It was not much, enough for a week or two, no more. Perhaps I might find work, I thought, though I recoiled, so horrible was the idea of losing my days as some schoolteacher or counting clerk. And so I sat, staring at the street, my mind lost in the implications of what had been, what was, and what would be, each becoming tangled in the others.

At last I tried to eat the soup, but it was long cold, the greying meat repulsive in my mouth. Pushing it aside, I sought out the owner. For a few shillings he led me to a room, and casting off my boots and jacket I stretched myself upon the bed. The mattress was hard, rank with the smell of mildew and the other bodies that had lain upon it; through the window from the street below the sound of the passing revellers rose, seeming to fill the space as if they cried and shouted in the room itself.

———

In time I heard the clocks ring out two o'clock, then three. Somewhere not far away musicians played, men's voices raised in song. Yet within me was only space, huge and unfillable. Finally I rose, and opening my bag brought out the flask of opium I had hidden there. Even then I felt it, that awful mingling of desire and revulsion, as if my hand were guided not by my will but by something stronger. I like to think I hesitated, seated there, that I might have set it aside – but I did not, and so instead I raised the bottle to my lips and drank, feeling myself sink back into its embrace.

IN THE STREET the lamps are lit, setting light upon the faces of the passing crowd. Though the night is cool the air is clear, and in the windows and doorways the people of the district can be seen. Here a bookbinder bent at his work, there a shopkeeper in conference, in other houses families and children. My pace quickens as I pass them by, grateful to be moving free. Amongst the crowd I am anonymous, another face to be glanced at and easily forgot, and though there is something exhilarating in this, so too it frightens me, the restlessness it provokes. All about me so many people, passing close and past and past again, and me untethered in their midst.

On the Strand I hurry past the doorways one by one, watching for somewhere that I might stop. Reaching into my coat I count my coins between my fingers. Not much perhaps, but enough. I have discovered that the city offers many pleasures for those who would sample them, easy companionships of dice and drink.

Finally I stop outside a place I am familiar with. Inside the fire is lit, the room already thick with tobacco smoke. Taking a seat I look about, seeing faces that I know and others I do not. At a lift of my hand, the serving girl brings brandy. She smiles as she places it in front of me, and I smile back: she is a pretty thing, and popular, and she has a weakness for me which is flattering. Lifting the brandy to my lips I take a sip, feeling its warmth down my throat and neck. Another sip and then another one, and finally my restlessness begins to ease. I scratch my neck; I have a rash there these last two weeks, an angry thing which comes and goes, and against the collar of my shirt it bothers me.

In Covent Garden, Arabella will be on the stage. Shakespeare perhaps, or Sheridan, the words somehow irrelevant. In the stalls and boxes they will be listening, their eyes transfixed, lost to whatever illusion is woven on the stage. Every night she is thus, her body bound into its costumes by the dressing girls, her face painted for the stage.

There was a time when it seemed marvellous, when I would go and watch her there and find happiness, but in these last weeks I can hardly bear to see the way she surrenders herself to the part. Last night I waited for her, seated in her dressing room. My watch just pawned, I had money in my pocket, money I was determined would be kept. She came from the stage, hard with it, and somehow not herself. All I wanted was to touch her face, to feel her close against me once again. But as she entered I saw she was still half in her part, her gestures somehow false, and so I contrived an argument, wanting to see her weep, to know the power over her that this would give. But that power when it came was hollow, and cheap.

————

Much later, and I am unsteady on my feet. My purse is light, my money gone, and myself no better for its loss. Arabella plays late tonight, and I would go to her, though I am in no state for it. Tonight I heard my voice as I spoke to the other men, too loud and artificial in its tones, as if it were I who played a part, and one which did not fit.

I GET TWO CROWNS for my books, a shilling each for my spare boots and shirts. Only when he reaches my Bible does the pawnbroker pause.

'I have too many of these already,' he says, sliding it across the table towards me. I push it back.

'Surely you can take another?' I ask. He looks at me impassively, then slides a ha'penny across the counter.

I take the money quickly, slipping out the door again. Not much, perhaps, but enough to buy food for a week, and opium. Out in the streets I feel my spirits rise, free of the captivity of that little room with its rows of parcelled goods. I know this feeling, know the way it pulls. I move too fast, too carelessly, afraid somehow to be still, or at rest.

————

Two nights past she pressed a guinea in my hand, bidding me take it. Opening my hand I looked at it sitting heavy in my palm.

164

'What is this?'

'A gift,' she said, but I shook my head.

'I have money.' Standing there I felt a fool in front of her, a sullen child.

'Your watch,' she said, 'your books.'

Angry, I pushed the coin back at her so it slipped and fell onto the floor.

'And how was this money made?' I demanded.

Behind her Mary watching me, her sallow face expressionless.

B Y St Martin's he lunges out to catch my arm.
'Which ones have the pox?' he demands. A gentleman,
at least in name. I shake my head and pull away. Letting go
he takes a step back.

'What, you mean you cannot vouch for them?' His arms
are held wide to indicate the women who line the streets
hereabouts. Behind him his friends hoot with laughter.

Shaking my head again I make to push past these five
revellers.

'I think he is a Methodist, gentlemen!' he shouts, but I do
not turn around.

Cheeks flushed I take the corner at a rush – and then
come face to face with a pair of women. They stand close,
locked in argument, the fist of one raised threateningly. Per–
haps I startle them, for they turn, faces already taut with
rage.

'Molly?' I ask.

At first I am not sure she knows me, but then she laughs.
'A fine place for you to be,' she says.

With a last burst she shoves the other woman back down the street.

'What are you doing here?' I ask. 'Where is May?'

'Who knows?' Though she is still beautiful she looks older, and thinner too, the skin about her eyes and mouth bruised and drawn.

'You have left him?'

She laughs, the calculation visible in her face. 'You think I did not come here anyway?'

'You do him an injustice,' I say. 'He loved you, no doubt he loves you still.'

'Here men give me sovereigns for that same love,' she says, coming closer. I back away, and she curls her lip. 'What? You do not care to know these things? Come, perhaps you would try what he found in me.' Though she does not touch me, her closeness is unsettling. Her breath is foul, sweet with the scent of gin and opium.

'No,' she says then, stepping back and away from me. 'You are no more a man than he.' Some of the other girls have gathered to watch, and now they laugh and jeer amongst themselves. Shaking my head I take two steps back, then turn, and walk away into the night.

That Molly should have deserted May should come as no surprise, yet it unsettles me. I linger on a corner, feeling powerless, repulsive to myself. Then, determined to find him, be the friend I know he would be to me, I set off for Marshall Street. Yet it is not May who answers my knocks but an older man. He stares at me as if I have offended him somehow.

'The room is let,' he says gruffly.

Confused, I look past him. 'Let?' I ask. 'To whom?'

'Try Pizzey's,' he says, gesturing across the street, then starting to close the door.

'No,' I say, stepping forward, 'wait. What of the former tenant?'

'The painter?' he asks, incredulous. 'Gone, gone these last six weeks.'

'Gone where?' I persist.

His face softens, but then he shakes his head.

'You find him, you tell him he owes me two pounds six,' he says, shoving the door closed.

A ND THEN MY OWN LANDLORD, Scarpi, at my door. Against his blows the door shaking in its frame, bowing at the bottom at his kicks and shouts.

Standing up, I pull on my boots and shirt, rubbing my eyes to give some impression of industry. When I took the room five weeks ago I told the Scarpis I meant to find employment for myself, and it was on this basis that they gave the tenancy to me. Glancing in the dirty mirror by the door I press down my errant hair, and leaning on the door turn the key quietly within the lock. Even through his angry shouts Scarpi notices, and his voice subsides. Still with my weight on it I open the door to look at him.

'Do you mean to sleep the entire day?' he demands as he sees me there.

'My hours are no concern of yours,' I reply, but he is not listening.

'Your rent,' he says, peering past me into the room. 'You said two days ago you would have it soon.' There is something calculating in the way he speaks which makes me realise he has some need himself.

'I have money due,' I say, 'very soon.'

Scarpi looks at me, then gives a laugh.

'An uncle perhaps?' he says mockingly. 'You Englishmen always have an uncle.'

When I do not reply he shakes his head.

'I am told there are others you owe money to.'

In my gut there is a twist of anger, but carefully I hold my tongue.

'Tomorrow,' he says, 'or you will be out of here.' He walks away; at the head of the stairs he turns around.

'An uncle,' he says, then pleased with his witticism he laughs again.

———

As I listen to him clatter down the stairs I seat myself upon the bed, rubbing at my face. Panic scratches in my chest. There is little left to pawn, no way of earning I can see. I need a plan, a way of finding my way out of this. Taking up my purse I look at the few coins there, trying to see some way to make them multiply. A few shillings, nothing more, the rest already spent. This time will be different, I tell myself, these coins will not be frittered away.

Outside it is cold, the evening already drawing in. Before I go to her I need a drink, and so I find a little shop where wine is served and cards are played. The room is warm, and there is talk, and song, and though these men are strangers, I find some measure of calm in their company. Even with this money in my hand I feel a sort of wretchedness, as if I have erred somehow, and so I drink a glass of brandy, and then another. Meanwhile I watch a game, and thinking I have the measure of the dice I place a little bet and win. This provokes much cheer and so I have another bet, and win again. Three times, or four, the dice fall my way, and soon I have three times as much as I started with. But then I miss, and then again. Though I should stop, leave the game and save what of my money remains to me, I cannot. Instead I bet angrily, as if to force the dice to fall my way, but soon enough I have nothing but a shilling left to me.

Angry at myself for my foolishness I place a wager on the dice at ten to one, thinking to win back all I have lost and more. Shaking them in my hand I feel my heart begin to skip, my stomach light and queasy with the thrill. They fly fast from my hand and skitter on the bench, and for the time it takes them to fall I am exultant, abandoned to their flight and its possibilities. Then, with one last turn, it is gone, and my excitement replaced by the numb certainty that I have erred again, and, like Icarus, must fall.

In the street outside I feel sick with what I have done. My money spent, lost again to dice and drink. Looking back towards the door I wish to undo these last hours, unpick the fabric of my act, but it is done and cannot be reversed. From a window voices come, a woman's high and shrill, then a man's brittle with rage. Thinking of my room I cannot bear to be alone. I want nothing more than to go to Arabella, to lose myself once more in her body. But I feel soiled by my foolishness.

———

Alone in my room, I draw the locket from my bag and open it. Inside the painted image of my mother's face behind its speckled glass, the awkward lines of her neck and throat rendered by some clumsy hand. How many times have I gazed on it, how many times tried to imagine her voice, her touch? Only seventeen, dead in some rented bed, and me the bawling cause of it. With my finger I stroke the glass, imagining it is her face. I feel a tightness in my throat. Our parents live in us, I sometimes think, like ghosts, or prophecy.

THE HOUSE IS STILL, its grimy windows shuttered close, as if it were home only to ghosts and memories. At the door I knock, aware of the eyes of those passing by upon me here. For half a minute, maybe more, I wait, then I lift my hand again, but as I do the door opens a crack, a girl's face appearing in the space.

'I would see your master,' I say. She is not pretty, or not quite, but in her face there is some quality I cannot define, some loneliness perhaps, which makes her silence give me pause.

'I am known to him,' I add, hearing the way my words sound somehow too loud or pressing, as if I need this thing more than I should. Yet even now she does not reply, just gives a nod, and steps aside so I may pass.

Inside the house is deserted, rooms closed up, furniture covered with sheets. In the hall a pair of paintings stand facing the wall; on the wall above pale squares show where they once hung. Opposite is a clock stopped on a quarter after three who knows how long ago. And everywhere the sense of many years' abandonment, the dust thick upon the floor.

Without a word she leads me down a hall into a drawing room. Inside it is dim, the curtains drawn; opened, they would reveal the yard of St Ann's across the street. Taking a few steps in I see candles burning in a great candelabrum on the mantel. Thinking to ask the girl where her master is I turn, but she has gone, as quietly as she came. All at once I wonder if she is mute, or simple, and if she is, what place she has here, with him. Alone I feel unmanned, unsure of whether I should wait or go, the echoing space of the house seeming to stretch hugely now on every side. And then from behind me a voice, low, and deep, so I jump, as a child might.

'I had not thought to see you again,' he says. He stands beside the fireplace, though it is cold and dark. To hide my nervousness I clear my throat and take a step closer to where he stands.

'No,' I say, 'no doubt you had not.'

'It is said you fought with Tyne.'

Looking round I see no door where he may have entered; he must have been here when I came, invisible, or hidden somehow.

'I did,' I say.

'You were lucky he did not kill you.'

'It was not for want of trying on his part.'

He nods. 'I had thought you would return to the home of your guardian.'

I shake my head. 'You said once you might be a friend to me.'

For a long moment there is silence. 'And you said you had friends enough, as I recall.'

I do not reply.

'What is it you seek?'

'Money,' I say. 'A bed I might call my own.'

He laughs. 'And what shall I have in return?'

I shake my head. 'I do not understand.'

'No?' he asks, watching me. 'You see this house? It once belonged to a man who placed himself in my debt.'

As he speaks he comes closer to me, his heavy eyes on mine.

I do not answer and so it falls to him to speak.

'We understand each other then, I think.'

THOUGH HE GIVES NO COMMAND I follow him, uncertainly at first, and then with more clarity. In the street his carriage waits. The day is drawing in, and about us people hurry and shove. As he moves ahead of me he draws a flask from his coat and lifts it to his lips. Raising an arm he beckons a man he calls Bridie closer, striking the carriage roof as he opens the door then passes the flask to me, his hand callused and rough where it touches mine.

As he clambers up into the driver's seat Bridie glances down at me, something in his manner enough to make me lift the bottle to my lips. The neck is wet and warm from Lucan's mouth, and the brandy burns as I draw back on it.

We ride eastwards into the gathering dusk, the carriage winding through High Holborn and up Snow Hill into less familiar streets. In the cabin Lucan and I are bucked and thrown as the carriage bounces on the stones, and yet I do not care, drinking the brandy that he passes me. Outside, fires burn in grates beside the roads, sellers of rags and other ruined things piling their merchandise upon the cobblestones alongside.

In time the buildings give way to muddy fields and houses half-made, the rutted roads and unplanted gardens somehow suggesting not industry, but rather a place already in decline. Finally we come to a halt before a warehouse and clamber out, my face already flushed and foolish with the drink. About us men are gathering, women too.

Inside there is a low-beamed space, the air in it thick with smoke, and everywhere men press and jostle, their faces alight with an edgy excitement, something heady, and quick. Some hold bottles which they pass from one to another, others laugh. In the room's centre a chalk line marked out on the floor, a figure seated on a chair, arms folded and naked to the waist, square head shaved close.

'What is this place?' I ask, but Lucan merely presses a bottle in my hand and bids me drink. The noise and the heat and the mass of the bodies is overwhelming, exhilarating. Men are shouting, calling for it to begin. Bridie has a smile on his freckled face. He is a man who finds humour in everything, I think, and value in none.

Then a shout goes up, the crowd surging forward, the spruiker for the man in the chalk ring circling, baiting the crowd. The man is Byrne, and as his spruiker bawls out his achievements he rises to his feet, bellowing an Irish song. On every side the crowd is shouting, screaming insults, waving betting chits and bottles and fists up in the air. For a minute, maybe two, this is all there is, and then a door at the back opens and through an opening in the crowd a second man enters the ring.

His name is Levi, and where Byrne made his way about the ring, arms raised and bellowing his song, this one seems oblivious to the crowd. Even as Byrne shouts at him, and beats his chest, Levi barely seems to notice him, standing instead by the edge of the ring and quietly removing the shirt he wears, unbuttoning it and folding it as carefully as he might were he undressing for his bed. Though he is a man of no great size, there is a delicacy in the way he holds himself, something sharp and dangerous. Placing his shirt in the hand of one of the men who followed him out he binds his hands, pausing every now and then to pull at the cloths and straighten them. On the other side Byrne is still bellowing and pacing up and down, but Levi will not look at him, and it is clear even as Byrne raises his fists once more so the crowd will cheer for him, that he seeks from Levi something he might fix upon. The bindings done, Levi extends his arms to his second so they may be knotted off, and only then, when that is done, does he turn and face Byrne across the ring.

Like some conjuror the spruiker lifts his hands into the air and sweeps himself down and away, the gesture huge and theatrical, drawing a great cry from the crowd gathered about the ring. Overhead the lamps flicker and burn, casting smoky light on everything. Not bright, but bright enough to see Byrne wears a grin. Opening his mouth he calls to Levi, taunting him, calling him Christkiller and usurer. Between each insult he twists his tongue into his teeth as a child might. But Levi does not reply, simply tilts his head from side to side, and shakes his arms as if to loosen them, moving out and round the circle's edge, so Byrne must follow him. Byrne has a head and a half on him, but Levi does not look afraid or uncertain, just businesslike. Facing each other thus they turn once around the ring, and then back again, neither coming closer, neither backing off. On every side the crowd are crying out, urging them to strike now and strike hard, to win for them – but they take their time and watch each other, seeming to seek out a moment, a sliver in the other's guard through which they might enter a blow. Byrne has the advantage, for his reach is longer, and Levi may not come close to him without being struck. And so it is no surprise when he steps in and jabs a fist at Levi. But Levi dodges down and around, rolling under the blow, catching Byrne in the side with his elbow while the bigger man's flank is exposed. The blow is hard, and even the audience feels it, and Byrne grunts as if it has hurt. Turning then he jabs again, and once more Levi slips under him and strikes him in the side, so this time Byrne stumbles a bit, and then again. This third time Byrne is ready for him, and as Levi slips under his guard he catches him a glancing blow across the head, the strength of it taking Levi off-balance so Byrne follows him with another, landing this with the full weight of his strength, and sending Levi stumbling back. Lucan stiffens, his hand closing tighter as he follows the smaller man's every move about the ring.

Now Byrne's greater strength denies Levi any respite. Though he is quick, weaving and dodging and avoiding most of Byrne's blows as he did the first two, countering each time with his short, hard jabs to rib and kidney, with each successive punch that Byrne lands he grunts and falters, until his nose and lips are bleeding, and the skin upon his forehead contused and split. A change grows in the crowd's mood, excitement turning into something closer, more attentive, as if the spectacle of Levi's besting swells within their chests. Blow by blow Byrne wears away at him, countering each of Levi's blows with two of his own, until the moment comes when Levi stumbles. At this signal the crowd begins to growl in its throat, their voices rising one by one, calling to Byrne to finish him. But Lucan does not speak, just stands watching as Levi reels and falters, his efforts directed more and more at simply avoiding the fists of the larger man. Byrne wears a look of concentration as he follows him, striking and jabbing and forcing him back against the circle's edge. Faces press close everywhere, their features contorted in the reddish light, the air heavy with the smell of sweat and smoke and beer and blood. And then quite suddenly Byrne swings again, and Levi rolls past the blow and under it, coming up to strike Byrne in the kidney from behind. Byrne arcs his back, his balance lost, and Levi strikes again, hard in the side, the blow throwing Byrne off-balance and letting Levi land a fist against Byrne's unprotected cheek, the force of it sending Byrne's head flicking back. Levi himself is unsteady on his feet, and yet he follows Byrne as he stumbles back, striking him again and then again, hard cuts into his face and side and back and gut. The crowd are angry now, and confused, and where before they watched with horrid satisfaction, now they shift and strain. Byrne no longer swings at Levi, it is Byrne now whose arms are raised in defence, as he swings here and there like a bull worried at by a gnat. Once and again Levi strikes at him, the larger man reeling back, fighting to recover himself, until at last with one more blow Levi sends him crashing to the ground. Standing over him Levi sways, twitching and trembling, as if he thinks Byrne may rise again, but Byrne only turns upon his side.

I give a cry, exalting in Levi's triumph, and so too Bridie, and even Lucan nods. But the crowd is restless, stirring and calling, as if seeking a focus for their anger. I do not care, I have made three guineas on my wager, and won besides, and it thrills in me. Lucan passes the flask and I take it, feeling the brandy choke and burn. In the ring's centre the man who took Levi's shirt, a black-coated Hebrew with earlocks, holds Levi's arm in the air, but the crowd do not cheer, rather they cry insults, and hurl bottles and food, and yet Levi looks not frightened but as if he takes pleasure in their hatred, as if it meets something in him.

'Come.' Lucan pushes me out of the crowd. 'There will be violence done tonight,' he says, as we pass the Irishmen on the door, 'mark my words on that.'

———

Outside in the air, by the carriage, Craven is waiting.

'Who's this?' he says, looking at me, and Lucan shakes his head.

'Poll's prentice, as you know well enough.' Opening the door he ushers me in, pausing to draw a cigar out from his case and light it with a Lucifer. But Craven is not to be put off so easily.

'Why bring him here?' He comes nearer to the door. Though he is thin I do not care to have him so close.

'There is something I would have him do for me,' Lucan replies, casually enough. I think Craven will object again, but he does not, just steps back and follows Bridie up onto the driver's seat.

'What is it you would have me do?' I ask Lucan as he pulls the door closed. In the darkness his cigar flares, catching the lines of his face.

'A simple thing,' he replies, 'easily done.'

———

We make for Camden, passing through the open spaces of the fields. Overhead the moon is bright and the buildings seem to glow, light chasing in front of us upon the road. I am a little drunk, the thrill of the fight still there in my veins and limbs. And yet I grow uneasy as the road spools away beneath us, imagining what this thing we go towards might be.

At last we stop beside a little church. Pulling down the window Lucan looks out across the fence.

'Within there is a girl called Jenny Carpenter,' he says, 'not twelve hours dead. We would have her corpse and you shall fetch it for us.'

'Why not fetch it yourself?' I ask, and Lucan chuckles, leaning back.

'The Rector knows my face, I fear, and Craven's too.'

'Why would he give her to me, if not to you?'

'She has no relatives nor friends, and so it is the parish which must bear the cost of her burial.'

There is a moment then when neither of us speaks. Then Lucan opens the door.

'Go to him now, tell him she is your sister, lost these many years, and you would have her back so you may bury her.'

'Why would he believe such a thing?'

'Because you will make him,' Lucan replies, then with a laugh he gestures out at the house. 'And besides, he will welcome being saved the cost.'

Slowly I climb down onto the road, and Lucan calls after me in a low voice. 'The sexton is a friend to us, be sure you put a crown into his hand.'

————

The Rector is a pale man, with an impatient air, and even as I tell him my business I can see his irritation at being disturbed.

'You call late, sir, especially on such weighty business,' he says. Worried he suspects, I hesitate.

'I came as soon as word was brought to me,' I say then, aware of the sexton's scrutiny. The Rector taps one hand against his arm in a sharp tattoo.

'Did you know her, sir?' I ask then in a rush – 'how was she in life?'

The Rector glances at his sexton.

'She was a courteous child, was she not, Mr Carroll? Well-liked?'

'Indeed, sir,' replies the sexton with a bland smile.

'Yes,' I say, 'well-liked, I am sure.' Sensing the Rector's reluctance I take a step forward. 'I have not seen her these nine years,' I say. 'Pray tell me all you know.' The Rector shifts uncomfortably and as he does I feel a sudden dislike for him, for this pompous little man.

'When we were children she was much-loved by all who knew her,' I lie. 'A beauty too.'

The Rector has stopped the tapping of his hand, and whether it is my words that have convinced him or merely the desire to be rid of me and my confidences, now he means to let me take the girl.

'You have a carriage?' he asks, and I nod, and with an abrupt gesture he directs the sexton to go with me. I thank him, shaking his hand. When we are at the door he speaks again.

'The sheet she is in, it is linen.'

I face him. 'A shilling then?' I ask, and he hesitates, calculating.

'A shilling.'

IN THE CARRIAGE Lucan leans over the girl's body, drawing open the sheet so he may look upon her. She was pretty once, but Lucan seems not to see it.

'Well done,' he says, leaning back in his seat to smile at me, 'well done.'

———

The carriage bears us back towards the town, through the quiet lanes and streets and thence to Blenheim Steps. There we stop before a building I know to be the School of Anatomy maintained by Joshua Brookes. Opening the door Lucan bids me alight. The street is dark, the only noise the broken sound of music through an open door.

'Knock,' Lucan says, and so I do, and a moment later the door opens to reveal a boy of sixteen or so dressed in a leather smock.

'Who do you seek?' he asks.

'Your master,' Lucan says from behind me then, and the boy looks up at him, and smiles.

'Come in.' He steps back so we may follow him. Behind me I hear the carriage door, a thumping sound, and a moment later Craven is past me through the door, Jenny Carpenter across his shoulder.

———

The house is plain, kept neat and clean, though in the air there is a smell like ham, somehow cloying and too sweet. With the boy leading, we make our way out to a space at the back, a room that was once a yard, but now is roofed in glass and iron, in which four tables sit all in a line. In here a dozen candelabra burn, filling the room with their flickering light. Upon the tables lie three bodies in different states of disassembly, buckets are strewn around, and by the third corpse stands a man of immense girth, his shift open at the neck and sleeves rolled up, dressed in a smock so large it must have taken an entire cow's hide to make it. Hearing us he looks up from his work, a syringe of some sort still held in one pudgy hand, and chuckles.

'You brought her!' He wipes his hands upon his smock as he comes waddling towards us, motioning to the boy to clear a space upon the nearest of the table tops. His face is unshaven, specks of food have caught in the stubble of his beard and stained his collar, his skin is scrofulous and filthy, snuff caked beneath his nostrils. As he approaches, the smell grows stronger, as does the reek of his body.

Craven sets the girl's bundled form down upon the table and, snuffling delightedly, Brookes prods and pokes at it.

'Good, good.' He turns to Lucan, but then notices me, and holds out a hand to touch my cheek.

'Who's this pretty one?' he asks, and for a long moment Lucan looks at me.

'Gabriel,' he says at last. Brookes gives a nod.

'Twelve guineas then?' he asks, all business again, and Lucan smiles.

Then I gasp, for behind Brookes I see a line of cabinets, all filled with waxwork renderings of veins and arteries, delicate as filigree, each poised and posed with hands outstretched and heads half-turned, the flesh and bone and organ which once contained them dissolved away.

'Ah. You have seen my beauties.'

––––

Outside in the street Lucan bids me leave him, placing money in my hand as he does.

'Do not let this matter mislead you,' he says. 'Brookes is no man's fool.'

Above us, Bridie shakes his head and whistles soundlessly. With a sudden motion Lucan grabs my arm just below the elbow, his hand closing about it like a vice.

'Craven thinks I am a fool to trust you,' he says, drawing me closer. I can feel Craven looking on behind me. 'You will not make a fool of me, will you, Swift?' he says, his voice measured and low.

Slowly I shake my head, looking deep into his eyes, their pupils dark, whites stained and yellow. He holds me there, close in that embrace. Then with a low laugh he lets go so I stumble back.

'Come,' he says to Craven, turning away as he speaks, 'there is work yet to be done tonight.'

––––

Her house is dark when I arrive, all within long abed. Her body warm and thick with sleep, its skin against my own. Within my arms I feel her breath, its motion in her chest. We

185

are each of us alone in this, I think, contained inside the cages of our selves. And yet as I press my face against her neck I wish that I might lose myself in her, might find some comfort there, the wishing like a pain that keeps me long from sleep.

NOTHING IS DIFFERENT when I awake, yet all has changed. The money made is real enough, as is my memory of how it was earned, the knowledge of that lying on me like a stain. But here, in her bed, it seems somehow far away, the doing not of myself but of some other, a thing remembered as if dreamed long ago.

Were I to close my eyes it might be gone again, left behind, were it not that the violent pleasure of the hours passed with Lucan lingers yet.

Rain has come while we have slept. Outside the day is dark, water moving in waves against the glass behind the drapes, and as I rise to dress, Arabella does not wake. On the doorstep I turn my collar up, but the water runs cold against my skin as I step into it. I am clear, and free, and yet restless, uncertain of where to go. Inside my coat I take the coin Lucan gave me the night before in my hand, pressing it close into my flesh, feeling the way I shiver at its touch. There is some secret here, it seems, I feel it – as if I am divided some-where, the money made by some other self, one I might hide inside as if it were a part I played, and in its playing were made free.

On Poland Street I come to a stop outside the apothecary's. The burnished light within is warm, a yellow glow against the darkness of the day. In my hand the money seems to itch; inside, the bald head of the apothecary's assistant dips up and down as he works, the bottles racked upon the wall behind him. I must not, I know, but even as I tell myself I will not enter, will not spend the money, I know I will, the door already opening, the bell ringing out above my head.

Later, in my room, I watch the grains of the opium turn in the glass, the light of the lamp breaking and shimmering on its curve. Outside the rain still falls, yet the room might be a bubble, and I suspended in its centre. Downstairs the Scarpis' voices are raised in argument but I barely hear them. There is sadness, or close to it, as if something is sundered here, divided where it should not be. But then there is only this, the whispering of the rain and the flare of the lamp dancing in the windowpane.

And when I go to Lucan again he is waiting. I do not need to speak and nor does he. Instead he looks at me as though I have answered some question for him, and then he turns away as if I am not there at all.

WE GO TO CORNHILL, riding fast and hard. The streets outside unfamiliar in the dark, made strange by the fog. At last Lucan strikes at the carriage roof to bid Bridie stop. Climbing out he nods up to Craven, and they set off into the gloom. I follow after them, down a covered passageway and out into an alley. In the fog all is quiet, just the dripping of the water from the trees above, the distant rattle of the traffic. Somewhere nearby a bird cries out, and then a baby coughs and begins to sob. Lucan and Craven turn aside, off into a lane bordered on one side by a high wall, overgrown with ivy. Here Lucan takes my collar in his hand and draws me close.

'Make sure we are alone,' he says, glancing upwards. I consider the wall, then carefully thrust my hand into the ivy's massing leaves, seeking to find some purchase there. It is wet, and slippery, its dusty smell thick, but I manage to claw my fingers into its grabbing stems, and scrabbling upwards begin to climb. Almost at once though my boots slip, my knee and anklebone striking and scraping against the wall as I crash back onto the ground, jarring my leg and spine and falling hard enough to knock the wind out of myself.

Before I can recover Lucan grabs me by the coat.

'Would you have us spend our evening in a cell?' he demands, hauling me to my feet, and pushing me back at the wall.

Wincing at the pain in my ankle I grip the ivy to steady myself, and begin again. This time I do not slip, and soon enough I reach the summit of the wall. Peering through the foliage I see a narrow space, welled in on all sides, and at the end a building, its window dark, the church tower rising like a shadow in the fog behind it.

Beneath me Craven laughs, and I feel anger flare inside me. Turning back I hiss that the coast is clear; with a quick movement Lucan throws the bag he holds to me, and then reaching out he drags himself up to where I perch. He does not look at me, just scans the ground below, then swinging his leg over drops into the yard. Clutching to the ivy to slow my fall I follow him, landing heavily in a boggy puddle, the water soaking into my shoes immediately. A moment later Craven lands, then takes the bag from me and heads through the ragged line of the tumbled stones.

We take two, a man dead not two days and a slack-jawed crone already on the turn. The work is hard, and brutal, and before we are done my body shakes with it, my legs trembling beneath my weight. And yet I get no quarter, Craven taunting me with threats the sexton here is a jealous man, and handy with the shotgun that he keeps.

We sell them to the porter at St Bart's, a leering rogue called Atkinson, who gives us ten guineas each for them. My hands raw and blistered, my suit torn, and muddied beyond repair. Watching Lucan bargain with Atkinson I feel something dull inside of me, as if I grew heavy within, and yet I follow him back to the carriage.

Then by Holborn Hill he bids Bridie stop again. Reaching into his coat he draws forth a five pound note and holds it out. At first I do not move, thinking to shake my head and turn away – but instead I lift my hand and take the proffered note, feeling the paper fold as I close my hand about it.

But that is not quite the end of it. As Craven takes his leave of us I rise to go, but Lucan stays me with his hand.

'No,' he says, 'we are not finished yet.'

Striking his stick upon the roof he sets us travelling once more, through Grevil Street to Leather Lane and Clerkenwell, and thence to Windmill Hill. By Liquorpond we turn into a little close, and winding down go to its end. It is silent here, and though the houses once were fine now they are dilapidated and abandoned, their windows boarded up, and blank. Bridie slows the horses, turning the carriage through an arch, and up a drive into a yard.

It is so still here, so dark, that all at once I am afraid, certain they mean to do me harm. But instead Lucan steps down and makes his way across the yard, to knock upon a door at its side. Again I follow. Within, the sound of voices is stilled, and then a man calls out, demanding our business there, for it is late, and all are asleep. Lucan gives his name, and almost at once a bolt slips in the door, light spilling out, the shape of a man half hidden by the glow of the lamp he holds.

'What?' he asks. 'You coming here?'

'I have a gentleman who would have a room of you,' Lucan replies. In the light of the doorway the fellow seems to hold himself poised, as if at any moment he might spring away. Yet he approaches me, half-sideways like a crab, rubbing his hands together, as if I am some pleasure long-anticipated. This close I see he is not as old as I had thought, thirty perhaps, or thirty-five, nor ill-looking either, save for the way he holds himself, and his eyes, which are crossed in a squint so severe it makes him look a simpleton. Holding his lamp up to my face he snuffles delightedly.

'This is Graves,' says Lucan.

———

The house is poor and dark and seldom cleaned. In the kitchen behind the door a woman sits, half-stupid with drink. Seeing us she lifts her head with sudden interest.

'Who's this?' she asks, looking first at Lucan and then at me.

'A gentleman,' Graves says, 'to have a room.' She looks at me appraisingly, then snorts.

'Gentleman indeed,' she says.

How Lucan is known to Graves I could not say, but known he is, for Graves fawns on him and flatters him, pressing him to stay awhile and talk. But Lucan will not linger, and soon is gone, leaving me alone with them.

Graves shows me to a room on the second floor. It is small, and dusty, large enough for a bed and washstand and little more. As I enter he follows close behind, pushing things and twittering as if he means to help me settle there. Only when I turn does he shuffle back, raising his hands to mollify me and giggling foolishly. At first I think to swear at him, but something in his manner unsettles me.

'Please,' I say. 'I would be alone, if I may.' As if he does not quite believe me he lingers even then, but when I turn to him again he backs away into the hall outside.

Once he has gone I seat myself upon the bed, touching it with an open hand. The sheets are thick with dust and the windows dark with soot and grime. Under the bed there is a chamber pot; with my foot I draw it forth, grating on the floorboards as it slides into view. Inside there lies a human turd, coiled and long and dried to a sickly yellow brown, surrounded by a scurfy tide. For a long time I sit and stare at it, and then I place my boot upon its rim and push it back beneath the bed and out of sight.

Later I will learn that Graves is ever thus, his time spent seated in the kitchen of the house, seeking to corner those of his tenants who would speak to him. There is something needful in him, placatory and insistent, as if he is afraid of his own company. Always he would have more of one, and more than once he follows me out into the close, cajoling me to stay with him, to talk with him.

At first this might seem innocent, the neediness of a foolish man, yet three days after I arrive I wake to the sound of voices raised in anger down below, and descending to the kitchen find one of the tenants there, an Irishman called Murphy, drunk and in a rage. In his hand he holds a belt, and he strikes his wife with it about the head and back, bringing it down again and again until her face is cut and her skin is livid. It is not this scene though which brings me to a stop, but the sight of Graves, who sits watching, hands pressed together in delight, his body on the chair seeming to quiver with some scarce contained excitement.

A ND SO I BEGIN to learn the work. The digging and the drawing forth. With rope and hook and shovel, piece by piece I gain the craft. How to dig the shaft to the coffin's head, how to use the earth's own weight to snap the lid, how to break a body for the sack.

It is well that I am tall, and strong, for the work is back-breaking hard. To dig a hole in as little time as possible, to draw a body forth, to bear it across walls – never have I known labour such as this. Where once my hands were soft, they grow hard and rough, my nails broken and blackened with the dirt.

And though the work is hateful to me, in time I give myself to it. To be Lucan's creature as he would have me be, to lend my will always to his cause. There is no love in this, nor any lost between those of us who work for him, but there is money to be made, and money to be spent.

I learn that the house on Prince's Street is not the only one that Lucan keeps. There is one on Water Lane, near Bridewell Prison and its cemetery. He keeps it always locked, its windows and door all boarded up, but at the rear, in a little lane, there is another door by which he enters. Inside, this house is mostly bare, save for two rooms in which are a bed and a table, and another by the street in which lie jumbled a great many pieces of furniture, all broken and chipped and ruined. In Southwark too another, overlooking the cemetery of Guy's. And there are more, I am sure, places I have not seen but only heard the rumour of. The bodies we take from the graves stay briefly in these places, stored in their cellars and empty rooms, our tools wrapped and hidden beside them.

Nor am I alone in being bound to him. There seem few he does not know, few places he has not ears and eyes. Women who watch the cemeteries, sextons, and pall-bearers. Beadles from the parish houses, nurses in the hospitals and porters on the riverbanks, bailiffs and crossing-sweepers; from everywhere he gathers close the rumours of the dead and where they lie so we may fetch them back. And though there are those who would keep us from what we seek, those who guard the dead with gun and trap and even sword, more often our search corrupts their will, and we may buy complicity if not love.

And perhaps this is all he ever sought from me as well, that I give myself to him. To know I am made subject to his will, that my nature is obedient to his own. To know that I am his, even though I wish only to be free.

A COLD NIGHT, ice seizing on the branches and the windowpanes. By Brookes's house we part, Lucan's money in my hand. I would have opium, but it is late, and my supplies are low. In my head is the rushing of my blood, all about the moving-through of things. Tonight we took four, slipped from a pauper's hole in Blackfriars, their limbs icy from the enclosing earth. They are cold, the dead, colder than the air, colder and heavier than the earth.

I should go to Arabella but last night we quarrelled: no great thing, but painful nonetheless. She guesses where it is I go now, how my money is made, but she will not speak of it, will not question me. Sometimes she seems to be made of silences, of those things she does not say. Often now I feel unwelcome in that house, as if they hung back from me, almost as if they were afraid of me.

'Why does your woman stare at me so?' I asked her, for as I came in Mary did not rise, just sat before the fire.

'Hush,' Arabella said.

I looked at Mary's face, and then back at Arabella, feeling the way they were joined against me.

'Always she watches me,' I said, 'as if I were a monster.'

'You mistake her,' Arabella said – 'Does he not?'

A moment too long, then Mary slowly nodded.

———

In the kitchen Graves is awake, seated with Rose, the woman who was there the night Lucan brought me here. Though they are not man and wife she shares his bed, but on what terms I do not know. As I enter she juts her chin out in my direction.

'Why, it's pretty boy,' she snorts, her voice too loud, her head spilling back to bounce on Graves's shoulder, loose with drunkenness. I am seized with the desire to strike her, to send her tumbling to the floor. Graves bites his lip, his crossed eyes alight.

'Sit, sit,' he says, standing and pushing back a chair.

I draw it back and sit. Rose snorts again, fighting to keep her head upright. Moving too quickly, too eagerly, Graves takes a glass and fills it for me.

The liquor is hot to the throat, but I drink it anyway, feeling Graves's pressing gaze and Rose's anger. There is something heady in Graves's company, some sense he urges one on with his attentions; and so, despite his manners and appearance, I take the drinks he offers and share in his amusement with Rose's befuddlement. Come five, and we begin to beat a tune upon the tabletop, singing with voices loud and hoarse, calling on Rose to dance, and as I watch her lurch here and there about the room, her arms held high above her head, lost in some imagining of her own desirability, it pleases me, as it pleases Graves.

———

And later, in my darkened room, the sound of the city awake. The seconds slipping, one upon the next and then the one before. On my fingers and my lips the taste of Arabella, the smell of the earth. If I close my eyes I can feel her here, feel her in my arms, shadow with weight, dream made flesh. It is the opium, I know, and yet not. And then somewhere I sleep, and dream.

NEARLY DAWN, THE NIGHT already drawing back. Craven and I have been to Camden Town, where the air was still and clear, caught as if waiting. All night something nagging in my head.

Graves is seated by the fireplace, his face delicious with anticipation. At first I do not understand, and so I stop. Even then it is not him I notice first but Walker, seated in the corner. And then I see him, seated to one side of Graves, his face lit by the light of the lamp which stands on the tabletop. Caley.

'Prentice,' he says.

At first I cannot speak, the presence of him there like something sick inside of me.

'What?' he asks. 'Did you think I would rot forever in that prison cell?'

I shake my head. Then he puts a foot upon a chair and pushes it out so I may sit.

'Drink with us,' he says.

———

Their conversation is of everything, and nothing. A man who broke his neck falling down Foster's Stairs, a woman who bore a child though her husband was these last ten months in Newgate Gaol, a gang who snatched an infant from a mother's house in Bloomsbury. Caley is made different by his months away: thinner of course, and paler too, but that is not the whole of it. There is something newly wild in him, a fragility of mood. Graves sees it too, and hangs upon Caley's words with some unhealthy exhilaration.

Dawn is long past by the time I push back my chair and rise. Outside the grey world all awakening. In my room I fall upon the mattress, my body light with opium and exhaustion. And when I awake they are gone again, and the house is still once more.

Never once does Caley speak of the thing I know is on his mind, the thing that brings him here.

TONIGHT THE THREE OF THEM are already gathered close, laughing, Bridie seated on the carriage-bench, Lucan and Craven lounging by the door. As I approach, they fall quiet, as if they spoke of me. Lucan does not greet me, just lets his eyes meet mine then move away, gesturing to Bridie to move the carriage off. A little thing perhaps, but something hardens inside of me. And in that moment I think I understand, think I perceive Caley's purpose in revealing himself to me. He offers me complicity, a secret knowledge all my own that Lucan cannot touch.

Something has altered, something has changed.

———

We go to Bethnal Green, where the tree leans low over the graves. The coffin lid already broken, my hook clatters loosely into the space below.

At first Lucan just stands staring, Craven too. This cannot be, for we call this yard our own.

Craven pushes me aside. Kneeling, he shines his lantern first into the musty passage we have made, then at the heaped earth atop the grave, seeking some sign of how this might have come to be. His narrow face clenched tight, he looks up and gestures to the nearest grave.

'Check it,' he hisses.

Taking up the spade I back away and do as I am bid.

The soil is loose, and I dig quickly down, the breath coming loud in my chest, the muscles in my back and legs hot with coursing blood. And when at last I strike the coffin top my spade falls through the broken board into the space below, just as with the first.

'This is no accident,' says Craven.

Slowly Lucan turns the lantern back and forth, searching the ground. The beam picks out a pale point amidst the broken earth. A shell, round and smooth, left by some friend or relative, positioned so its disturbance will be a sign if the grave is tampered with. Slowly he kneels down and takes it in his hand.

'No,' he says, 'no accident indeed.'

Suddenly something shifts inside me, and I understand who is responsible and why. My heart skitters, my body growing light.

The shell still lies in Lucan's hand. With a careful motion, he reaches out and places it back upon the piled earth and rises.

'Fill them,' he says.

———

To Kensington, where the leaves lie deep upon the graves and the cows can be heard murmuring and lowing in their sleep beyond the wall. From a tomb beneath a granite slab, the body of a gentleman, one leg missing from the knee.

Then back through the silent streets, his body bound and trussed upon the floor. The whole way Lucan barely speaks. Beside him in the darkness of the carriage I feel something like vertigo, giddy and sick. At Blenheim Steps we wake Brookes and sell to him, then make the split, and with money in my hand I leave them there, eager to be away.

———

Back in the close the drive is dark, the windows shuttered against the fog. From within voices, low and indistinct, Graves's snuffling laugh. Lifting my hand, I find the door locked, silence falling within as I rattle.

'Who's that?' calls Graves.

'Gabriel,' I say.

The bolt slides back to reveal Graves's cross-eyed face, the door opened just enough to admit me.

The lights are low, and Caley sits with Rose and Walker.

'Why, prentice,' he says, 'I had not thought to see you back so early.'

Muddy footprints mark the floor, and through the half-closed door to Graves's room I see the bundles bound and tied.

'You have been at work,' I say.

Caley lifts his eyes to me.

'And if I have?'

By the fireplace Graves draws back his seat, his lips parted in a grin of anticipation.

At last I shake my head. Taking up a bottle from the table Caley passes it towards me.

'Drink with us,' he says.

FOR THREE DAYS the bodies lie in Graves's room, half covered with a canvas sheet. Caley seems not to care what happens to them, happy instead to let them lie and spoil, their flesh eaten by the rats that rustle in the walls and ceilings. I would think them forgotten, save that on the third day I pause to look at them, and see Caley watching me from his chair. He bites his lip.

'Why do you not sell them?' I begin to ask, but his manner stays my tongue.

———

Once, long ago, lost in some childish game high in the loft of the barn, I saw the son of the groom slipping in below. Myself seven perhaps, or eight. Something in his manner, some quality of quietness making me fall still.

Though he was known to me and I to him we were not friends. His father was a serving man, and mine a gentleman, a distinction which made me a lonely figure amongst the children of the house.

Slipping into one of the stalls he unfolded a chaff bag from his chest. In it a half-grown cat I knew as the cook's, a quick ginger thing with a coughing, broken purr. It shook its head as he set it down, the motion kittenish, its body all legs and tail as it started away from him. A hand outstretched and it drew closer, sniffing, then slid its head along his hand. Slowly he let his hand run down its back, once, twice, until it came closer again, and coiled about him, tapping at his arms with its paws.

He was so still that when he closed his hand about its neck the cat seemed to think it mere accident, only growling and moving as if to shake him off. But he did not let go; instead he tightened his grip, forcing it to the floor. Even now the creature seemed not to understand, but I did, my heart tripping as he pressed it down. Lifting a hammer from the bag he raised it, letting it hang for a moment in the air, his arm suspended before he brought it down upon the cat's head, striking hard, first once and then again.

This done he laid the hammer down, leaning back upon his feet as if waiting to see what the cat would do. At first it did not move, its head bloodied and broken, but at last it tried to stand. It moved unsteadily, its movements jerky and uncoordinated, dragging itself away from him. He let it go at first, waiting until it was almost at the entrance to the stall before stepping after it and prodding it so it fell again. Again it tried to stand, and once more he prodded it, and then again, each time blocking its escape. Finally it hissed at him, and tried to bite, its teeth closing on his exposed leg and drawing blood. With a curse he drew back his hand, and swinging back the hammer he struck the cat hard from the side, knocking it across the stall. Around and around they went, he blocking its route, moving faster and faster, until at last he lifted his foot and stamped on it, first once, and then again and again, his face pale with savage glee, over and over. And all the while I did not move nor make a sound. Not because I was afraid, because it was not fear I felt, nor anger, but rather something closer to desire, a feeling secret and horrible and wonderful that filled my hands and chest and groin. Only when he was finished, and the cat was still, its body smashed broken did he stop. And then, and only then, did he turn, look upwards to where I lay, his eyes meeting mine. His freckled cheek was splashed with blood. I could not move, nor look away. He did not speak, nor did he have to, for I realised in that moment he had always known I was there. And then he smiled, and all at once I understood the part I had played in this thing, the heat I felt not that of fear but recognition.

———

Sometimes now I cannot bear her touch. Like a sickness, the knowledge of those others who have touched her, the lies she has told, is always there; it whispers in my ears and follows me through my sleep. And when I hold her in my arms I am filled to overflowing with my loathing, not just for her but for myself, for all of this.

TWICE MORE IT HAPPENS, bodies taken that we thought our own. Each time the work done carefully, so we know it is not simply thieves or amateurs. That Caley is responsible I am certain, and though I do not know where he conceals them he is ever here, and so I suppose they must be too, hidden in some quiet room.

There is some power in his presence, I see that now. Not just in the way he bends Graves to his will or the way Walker submits to him, but in the way his temper fills the room. They are frightening, his moods, and all of us are afraid of them. Always he dares me to strike back at him, to test his mettle, each time I choose silence it seems a victory for him.

Though I am a fool for it, I find a sort of savage glee in seeing Lucan cuckolded thus. That he knows not who is responsible is plain enough, it is in his looks and his words and all that he does, though never does he lose control or give himself away. In another man this might be admirable, but as I watch him taunted by Caley's acts I find nothing to like in it, instead I find only contempt for him and all he has made of me.

———

We have been in Whitechapel, then Clerkenwell. Two smalls, a mouthful of teeth, no great pickings, but Lucan will not make the split. Instead he delays, finding reasons to keep us in his company, though I am irritable and out of sorts, and would have my medicine. Here and there the bakeries are opening, and at Lucan's bidding we buy bread. Still warm with the oven's heat, but my stomach is colicky, and I cannot eat.

Then, out of the mist, a carriage looms. Its driver has laid planks across the mud so a woman might board. She is small, her face obscured by her coat's hood. But as we pass, she turns, and I know her, not by her face but by the way she holds herself. Her pale face meeting mine.

Opposite me Lucan leans his head back against the carriage wall, his hooded eyes dark.

'A man should be careful his tastes do not outstrip his means,' he says. Craven starts to laugh. Staring back I hold Lucan's gaze, wishing only that I might wipe his smile from his face, from all of them.

———

Tenderly she opens my hand.

'How came you by these?' she asks, touching the broken skin on my knuckles.

'An altercation,' I reply. 'Nothing.'

'And this?' she asks, touching my ribs. A bruise, mottled green, and purple.

'It is the work,' I say, 'no more.'

'The work,' she echoes, her judgement hanging in her words. Though she does not move I feel the way she pulls away.

With a sudden surge of anger I push her from me, harder than I had meant to, and she stumbles back. Something flares in me, to see her fall, some pleasure, and for a moment I stare at her, exultant.

ON EVERY SIDE the earth is broken, turned and spilled about, graves open to the air.

'Dogs!' Craven spits, stepping forward, but Lucan stays him with a hand.

'Wait,' he says, 'let us be sure we are alone.'

Craven bends his head, then moves away along the wall.

Lucan is still. Picked out by his lantern a body sprawls, its abdomen swollen huge, face pulled back in a rictus of corruption. Beyond it another one, a woman's corpse, the flesh turned foul, headstone overturned. He lets the light move impassively from one to the other, making no remark on what we see. Stepping back into the shadows I draw my bottle from my coat and take a sip.

'Long gone,' Craven says, reappearing. Lucan nods. He kneels at the body lying bloated on the ground, touching the ruined face with his hand. And then he stands, and walks back towards the gate. As he comes abreast of me he stops, his hand moving so fast I do not have time to react, gripping my wrist painfully.

'Leave that poison,' he hisses, and with a sharp motion he flicks my arm aside so the bottle flies from my grasp. I watch it fall, biting down the urge to grab it back.

OUTSIDE RAIN, AND YELLOW SKIES, the grimy light of dawn on everything. In his room Graves sleeps, his snoring a soft whistle. Beside the fire a bottle lies. Behind me there is a sound, and I turn, half thinking to see Caley. Not Caley though, but Craven, his white eye spectral in the jaundiced light.

'No one here?'

I shake my head. 'Who should be?'

He gives a knowing smile. 'Perhaps you could tell me that very thing?'

'I can tell you nothing,' I say. Slowly he skirts the kitchen walls, pausing by each door to look up or down. By the cellar door he stops, and puts a hand upon the knob and turns it slowly. He does not shake or rattle it, just presses hard enough to know it is locked.

'What do you want?' I ask.

'Nothing much,' he says, drawing a chair out from the table and seating himself. 'A word, is all.'

'Then have it, for I am tired.'

'We have a traitor in our midst,' he says.

'Indeed?' I must fight to keep my voice level.

'Indeed,' he replies, watching.

'Why do you tell me this?'

'You do not know who it might be?'

I shake my head, and for a long time Craven sits.

'You do not look well,' he says at last. 'Are you sick?'

'Just tired,' I say. Slowly he nods.

'Think on my words,' he says, pushing back his chair and standing to go. Once he has gone something begins to rise in me, a wildness. I would run, I think, throw myself against the world, this feeling uncontrollable. My hands are trembling, and try as I might they will not stop.

A T FIRST I THINK I have lived this moment already. Time seeming to repeat itself, to stutter.

Lucan smiles. 'You had not thought to see me here?' Shaking my head I take a step away.

'Why do you back away?' he asks. 'What have you to fear?' He glances round the empty kitchen.   ·

'Where is Graves?'

'Out,' I say, but he does not reply.

'What do you want?' I ask, willing myself to be calm, but some note in my voice catches him.

'What?' he asks, coming closer. 'Such hate?' By the heaviness in his eyes I know he is drunk. 'Have I not been a friend to you?'

'No,' I say, 'not hate,' but he reaches out and touches my face, his rings cold against my skin, the gesture almost tender.

'Hate is good,' he says, 'it makes us strong.' As he speaks something thickens inside of me. Not hate, or not quite, nor fear either, but something more like tenderness, exquisite and painful and violent. He holds my face, swaying slowly, the smell of liquor strong on him.

215

It seems he means to say more, but then on the stairs someone catches their breath, and Caley is there, Walker behind him. At that same instant Graves appears at the door from the yard. None of us moves.

'So,' Lucan says in a quiet voice, 'it is true.'

Caley hangs back, his body tight, like a child in the presence of something long desired but forbidden to touch. In the door to the yard Graves remains utterly still, his mouth half-open.

'What?' Lucan asks – 'you did not think I would find you?'

Still Caley does not answer, stays poised as if ready to flee. Behind him Walker is trembling, his breath coming loud through his ruined mouth. Slowly Lucan lowers his hand, and as he does I back away.

'You thought you might take this from me did you? An Irish guttersnipe like you?'

'No,' Caley says. 'You wronged me, old man.' His voice trembles with fury, but Lucan only laughs.

'I wronged you? By giving you up to the lags?' Lucan snorts and turns away. Caley glares at his retreating form. He seems beaten, but then he draws the knife from his belt and takes a step forward. Lucan turns back and looks for a moment at the knife, contempt written on his face.

'You think me afraid of you?' he asks. Caley shifts from foot to foot, the knife swaying before him.

'Why should it be yours?'

Lucan laughs. 'Because I made it mine,' he says, his voice low. Still Caley is caught between his hatred and his fear. Looking past him, Lucan seeks out Walker's eyes.

'Come, John Walker,' he says. 'Leave here now with me and I will forget your part in this.'

Walker's face is bloodless and drawn, but Lucan has divined something in him. Still, though, he does not move to follow. At last Lucan looks once more at Caley and laughs, and as he does Caley's arm wavers and falls.

'Remember this,' Lucan says, turning once more for the door. Behind him Caley stands staring at the knife in his hand. I am shaking, I realise, my legs weak and loose beneath me. It is over.

And then, quite suddenly, Caley lifts his eyes, his hand tightening about the knife. In a slow shuffling run he begins to move again, Lucan turning too late to see him there, as with one thrust Caley drives the knife up into Lucan's chest, his eyes bright with tears.

THERE IS A MOMENT as the blade enters him when all is still. As if time slowed, and in that moment everything is possible. On Lucan's face a look not of fear, but of disbelief. Pressed close against his chest Caley does not move, as if he himself cannot quite believe this thing he has done. Then from Lucan's mouth a gulp of blood, thick and almost black. Beneath him his knees seem to quake, a convulsive movement. Letting go of the knife Caley takes one step back, and then Lucan's legs begin to buckle, his weight bearing him down onto his knees. Lifting a hand he makes to touch the knife where it protrudes from his chest, his face still set in a look of shock, but the hand cannot seem to close about it, groping instead at the air once, then twice, before at last he slumps face-first onto the ground.

For a long time none of us moves, just stand staring at his body on the ground. He lies twisted on the floor, his chest pressed high on Caley's jutting knife. From beneath him a pool of blood is spreading, spilling slowly out across the stones, thick and dark as oil as it leaks into the cracks.

'What have you done?' I ask at last. The words seem too loud somehow, unnatural.

Caley's face is ashen, uncomprehending. Against the wall Walker too is still. Only Graves is moving, his hands clenching and unclenching as he trembles by the fireplace.

'What have you done?' I ask again, and Caley swings his head. Perhaps he would deny this thing, make some claim of innocence but then something hardens in his face.

'Killed him,' he says, and though his words are certain his tone is not. 'Would that I had done it long ago.'

Something begins to knot inside of me, some anger. Somehow it pleases me, this thing that he has done. He feels it too, it is in his face, the pale look of him, the queasy thrill of possibility. Beside me, Graves has stopped, and stands, staring down, his face flushed with excitement, as if he cannot bear to look away.

WE PLACE HIS BODY, still warm with passing life, in the dark beneath the floor. There is something irresistible in this thing, all of us can feel it. As we bear him down the stairs, Graves flaps around us, reaching in with eager hands as if to help, but each time I push him away.

And later, in the kitchen, he sits upon his chair, rocking back and forth, eyes darting to the stain upon the stones excitedly, his foolish voice running on and on with jokes and plays upon the fact of which we cannot speak. Whatever madness infected Caley earlier is altered now, and he drinks and stares about himself, as if he teeters on the edge of grief, and must drink so to erase this thing. Looking at him I too want to be away from here, away from this, but I cannot go, cannot tear myself away. Only Walker seems not to share in it, his ruined face haggard and drawn. I cannot look at him, for something in his manner, in the pity of his face and nature, seems awful to me tonight.

FOR A DAY OR TWO we linger here, waiting for Craven to come seeking him. He must know something is amiss, and so will come, I am sure. At first I think this frightens me, but as the days leak by I realise I am not frightened so much as numbed, as if Craven has no power to harm me any more.

All the while the presence of his body in the scuttle beneath the house is like a weight that grows with each passing day, heavy as a tide. The knowledge of it seems to swell in Graves, something he cannot forget or put away. He follows me about, and presses himself upon me in his need to speak of it. Caley too is changed, though where Graves has grown needier Caley grows more silent and withdrawn.

Outside the fog is heavy, the days slipping by in a twilight that seems without shape or form. Once or twice I venture out, sometimes to buy opium, sometimes to drink or just to walk, but mostly I simply stay closed in my room. I do not sleep, or not much, the hours flickering by, as if I skate across the surface of my dreams. I know well enough I take too much of it but it seems easier to give into the need for it than to fight.

We work barely at all, though the nights are secret ones, shrouded close by fog and cold. Once we go to Bethnal Green, once to St Giles, but each time we take but a single corpse, a dozen guineas worth, no more.

And one evening his body is gone, spirited away as if never there, the space in the scuttle where he lay made empty.

THEN IT COMES, as it always would. The sound of laughter, a woman's voice. Coming downstairs I find Caley there, and Graves, the two of them standing outside Graves's door in some secret conference. In the corner Walker stands alone, his body knotted in upon itself. Graves looks around, his manner telling me at once something is afoot.

'What's this?' I ask. Graves darts a look at Caley, who smiles as if he has some secret that he means to taunt me with.

'Nothing much,' he says, smiling callowly. His face is pale, with that same look as the other night, that wildness. Inside me something queasy stirs. As if Caley has made a joke, Graves begins to laugh his foolish laugh. My legs tremble as I take a step towards the door; Caley does not move to cut me off, just stands aside so I may pass.

On Graves's bed an old woman sits half-slumped against the wall. She wears a ragged dress, much soiled and wrapped about with a dirty shawl, and in her hand she holds a pint of rum. Hearing me there she lifts her head, seeming to sniff at the air and blinking myopically.

'Tom?' she asks. Confused I look around, and as I do Caley and Graves come closer, past me into the room.

'No,' says Graves, barely able to contain himself, 'just a friend, another friend.' His face shines with some unhealthy glee, his squinting eyes seeming to look everywhere except at me. Advancing on her, he holds one hand out to remind her of the bottle in her hand.

'He'll be here soon though?' the woman asks, and Graves giggles.

'Very soon,' he says, pressing the bottle on her, 'drink up now.' Chuckling, she lifts the bottle greedily, smacking her lips and slurping on its neck. Her toothless mouth is slack with drink, her shrivelled lips wet and horrible. Turning back to us Graves capers a bit, his hands held high to his chest. I can hear Caley's breath moving in and out beside me, hot and quick.

'Who is she?' I ask.

'Did you not hear?' he replies. 'She's mum to Tom.' Then I understand. It is wrong this thing, I know that well enough. But it has a power of its own. And there is a sort of freedom in it too, to give oneself to it. Moving slowly Caley comes close to where the woman sits.

'Tom?' she asks, and Caley gives a laugh. He looks very young, I think, and terrible.

'No,' he says, 'not Tom,' and he puts a hand upon her head to touch her hair. She gurgles drunkenly, in some ghastly parody of girlishness, bending her head to him. Graves is standing, his hands clenching and unclenching, his excitement palpable. Lifting a hand Caley strokes her hair, my skin jumping each time it descends onto her head. Against his body the old woman murmurs something, and Caley chuckles, solicitous. And then just as suddenly he grabs her hair and twists it tight around his hand, forcing her back and down onto the floor in front of me. The movement quick as a

224

snake, shocking in its ferocity. Frightened now the woman gives a cry.

'What are you doing?' she moans. But Caley only laughs, one hand holding her, the other already around her neck.

'Please,' she sobs, 'I have money, a shilling you can have –' but Caley seems not to hear, his grip tightening about her neck. The old woman starts to kick and fight, twisting herself and punching at him.

'Take her,' he cries, 'hold her still,' but I do not move, and nor does Graves. It is awful, the way he holds her there, his pale face and kissing lips. With her fingernails the old woman rakes at his neck, drawing blood, but Caley seems not to feel it, instead crying again to me to take her arms, hold her down. And this time I do, stepping in to help pin her there.

He is whispering I realise now, words that might be endearments, words of love made words of hate.

'No,' the woman moans, 'let me go,' and 'I want my Tom.' Caley takes the corner of her shawl and with two fingers crams it into her mouth. I think she will close her teeth about his hand, but she gags and spits, frantic and terrified, and as she does he stuffs in more and more, cramming it tight until she can take no more. Her eyes are wide, bulging from her face – blue once, I think, now stained yellow as nicotine and veined with red. Caley has stopped speaking, focused in on this task of his with an awful clarity. With his other hand he grabs her nose, clamping it off and twisting it, and though she fights and makes a muffled noise she cannot shake him off. He is very still, it seems, even as she fights and squirms, her struggles dragging on and on, until all at once it is done, and she is still.

For a long time then I do not move. Against my hands she does not strain, or push. At last, unknotting my grip, I release her and rise. All is as it was yet nothing seems the same: nearby Graves still stands trembling with excitement, one hand half extended as if he would touch her but fears to do so. Caley has already straightened, the blood where she scratched his neck beading bright against his skin. From her mouth the shawl protrudes, her face red and eyes bulging. I do not know how I should feel, only that it should not be like this: I am calm, and somehow numb, as if I have done something that was always waiting here, something no more and no less than the act itself. Caley lifts his eyes to mine, and there again is the wildness of the night that Lucan died. But this time I see something else as well, something more like pain, or need, as if he felt something that he sought already slipping away.

WE TAKE HER to Guy's, to sell to Sir Astley's man. Her body loose and lolling in the sack.

'Still warm,' Barker says as he touches her, lifting his eyes to look at us. Caley does not answer, his body tight, the moment stretching on until I am afraid.

'Fresh,' I say, 'is that not what your master asks?'

Barker looks at me, and then he smiles.

'Indeed it is,' he says, 'indeed it is.'

As we make our way back to Clerkenwell through the darkened streets I seem to move outside myself. Strange, but I feel no guilt, nor remorse, just a kind of unreality, as if some part of the world is made different that can never be the same. I might be drunk, or full of opium, for colours and sounds seem brighter, louder, but somehow far away.

———

Such a small thing, to take a life. No harder in the end than to draw a tooth or slip a knife into the flesh. I could say I did it because I feared she would betray us, but I did not. Nor was it for pleasure, or because I lost control, for I was calm, and clear. Rather I did it because I could, because in that moment, in that room, it seemed easier than not. And because in its doing there seemed a sort of escape, as if in the act I was unmade, and for that space of seconds, still, and free.

A WEEK PASSES, slipping by like water. We do not speak of the events of that night, but they are always there, between us, shivering and powerful. Outwardly Graves is the most different, his foolishness somehow reined in, as if he held his breath, his laughter less frequent, his attentions to his visitors less fawning, more demanding.

But Caley too has changed, his temper darker, more certain. Where once the violence in him seemed always ready to reveal itself, now he is quieter, more calm. As the days pass my money bleeds away, as must his own, but he shows no inclination to work, rather sitting in the kitchen with Graves and Walker and myself. There is a watchfulness in him, something that broods and gnaws as might a nest of rats.

When one night Rose appears in Graves's company, Caley does not object, nor threaten her. Graves cannot have kept his secret to himself, and indeed she is wary of Caley now, watching him as one might watch a dog that one has reason not to trust, steeling herself against his smiles and charms with careful looks and cautious hands.

THE NEXT IS A BOY Caley brings to the house. The old woman ten days dead; Rose asleep in Graves's room. Though he laughs, the boy is in an evil mood. Graves and I are in the kitchen, and seeing us there he calls us nancies, and tells us he will put a dagger up our arses if we touch him. He has one too, for he shows it to us: a nasty thing with a chipped and broken edge. Yet he takes the drink that Caley offers and seats himself. Though no word is said I know what is intended here.

We give him rum, and laudanum, and soon enough he grows sly with it. He is a dirty boy, with a face angry with pimples and tufted hair, yet as Caley touches his cheek he does not resist, and only watches me so I will know what kind of boy he is.

'Show us that knife again,' Caley says, and with a knowing smile the boy produces it.

'You'll give it back,' he says and Caley smiles as he takes it from his grasp. Graves has stopped his giggling.

'Oh yes,' Caley says, 'oh yes.'

When the time comes he dies easily, stupid with the laudanum. I do not help this time, just watch as Caley takes a pillow and presses it down upon the face. I might be outside myself, as if it were not me who sat here in this room, as if I were asleep and watched this thing in a dream. Caley's whole being is newly concentrated in the doing of this thing, as if he seeks some answer here, some release. But in the moment the boy dies, as his body kicks and jerks and then grows still, Caley takes a sudden breath, an intake sharp and quick, and I see it is not delight but loss that shudders in him then, a thing gone as soon as it is done.

———

The boy's body we sell to Sir Astley's porter as we did the woman's ten days earlier. Eight guineas we get, a sum that seems too small. Though Graves does not come with the three of us, Caley keeps a guinea for him, slipping it in his hand when we return to Clerkenwell. Taking the guinea from Caley's hand Graves stands with his body poised as if he fears we might snatch it back from him, then with a snuffling laugh he slips it in his coat.

Caley's mood is ugly, seeming to teeter on some precipice. Moving slowly about the room he picks up the things that sit upon the mantelpiece to examine them. He is unsatisfied. Then he pauses by the door to Graves's room. Rose is within, asleep. Stepping through the door Caley goes and seats himself beside her on the bed. She murmurs something, and turns away from him a little bit, still lost in sleep. Graves advances slowly on the door, his cross-eyed face quivering. Beside me Walker is still, his breath whistling in his ruined mouth. His eyes are bright with fear, and tears too, I think. Caley looks up at Graves, then letting his hand fall he runs it across Rose's hair, once, and then again.

———

The next is a cripple called Matthiessen, whom we smother like the boy. Despite his infirmity he fights and kicks, striking me in the face with his fist as we hold him down upon the bed, and loosening one of my teeth. We sell Matthiessen to Brookes, who gives us twelve guineas, remarking on the freshness of the corpse. Brookes does not care for Caley, and though Caley is careful and polite, I see the way he watches us.

———

And afterwards, in the kitchen of Graves's house, the rain outside heavy in the yard, we sit and drink. Caley has a knife, and he presses it into the tabletop, gouges deep across the wood, his arm straining with the force of it. Graves is murmuring something, whether to himself or Rose I do not know. Walker sits apart from us upon the floor, his legs huddled up against his chest, staring up at Caley. His eyes are wide, and wet, and I remember now the way he looked after we killed the boy, as if something he loved had died, and now nothing made sense, not any more.

WHEN IT BECOMES A HABIT I do not know. At first it seems to happen almost at random: a night of drinking, a new friend, the walk to the house. It is like a game, the rules of which we each of us understand without being told. But in truth it is not random, or not quite. All of us know what will come each time it begins, and it quivers in us, the anticipation as irresistible as the act itself.

We sell the bodies where we will: some must suspect but none refuses the goods we bring. Of Brookes alone are we wary, Brookes and Mr Poll. Our takings we split three ways, a third each for Walker, Caley and myself, keeping always a guinea back for Graves's hand. And though we need it, the money sometimes seems more like an afterthought, unconnected to the act from which it came.

After Matthiessen there is a Scotswoman whose name we never learn, brought by Caley on a freezing night with the offer of food and a place to sleep. After her another youth, blind in one eye and half-simple, who begs in the mornings by Clerkenwell Green, and whom we dose with laudanum and choke by pressing closed his nose. An Italian boy named Fido too. There are others, a half-dozen more, too many to remember easily, though with each there seems to be a hastening in us, a sense of slipping down.

It is not that I do not understand the nature of my acts, nor that I feel no guilt. Yet these things are somehow without meaning now, seen as if from another place, another time. Perhaps it is the opium, but it seems not me who commits the acts, or no more me than the sleepwalker who lifts a hand in sleep, without volition, or presence in the limb. As if I myself were hollowed out, and this thing an emptiness inside of me.

A ND SO I RISE, weightless. Sometimes in the shapeless
time of the passing hours I wake to voices from the
other rooms, laughter and sounds of pain, the disjointed
dreams of fever's sleep. Beneath my face the wool of my bedding rank, and thin, my skin icy in the freezing air. Outside,
the world moves by like a void.

They come more often now, twice a week, sometimes
thrice. And still they are so few of all there are. In the cav-
erns of the city perhaps we might do this thing for ever
and for ever and still there would be thousands left. Someone must know, someone must see. But there is no word
of rumour or fear that people vanish from their lives,
snatched away and slipped onto a table for some student's
education. Surely there must be spaces left, I think, relatives and friends who mark their absence? And yet even
when I sit in the shops where gin is bought, or in the
marketplace, I hear no whisper of this terror in their
midst. They might be ghosts, these people that we take, for
others clamour everywhere to fill their places, the waters

of the city closing over them too easily, unremembered and unmentioned, as if they had never been, had never breathed.

I DO NOT NOTICE he is gone at first. He is so quiet, so careful to remain always out of one's way. Caley sits in his chair by the fireplace, a piece of wood in his hand, his knife slipping back and forth as he whittles. Outside the day is bitter, the clouds moving fast against a dead sky. Taking the bottle which sits upon the tabletop, I drink, aware of the way he does not look at me. It is then I realise he is not here, that I have not seen him anywhere. There is something odd in this.

'Where is Walker?' I ask, but Caley's gaze stays on the piece of wood, his busy knife. In my chest a tightness forms.

'What have you done with him?' I ask now, but still he keeps on whittling, his knife moving faster. I cannot take my eyes from the blade.

'Why do you not speak?' I ask. 'What is it you are not telling me?'

In his chair he sets his mouth.

'Tell me.' My voice is harder, and quavering, 'tell me where he is.' I would go to him, put my hand upon his arm

237

and turn his face to look at me, but I am afraid of the fixity of his stare, the motion of his blade.

'*Tell me*,' I say again, and at last he starts to his feet, casting the piece into the corner so it rattles on the stones.

'Gone away,' he says, voice cracking, his expression daring me to contradict the words. He looks very young suddenly, a boy again, scarcely older than myself. Something more like pain than anger in his face – pain, and an intensity so great I think he will do himself harm.

———

Later I wake to find him upon my bed. Though there is no reason for it, he has never entered my room before, always lingering just outside the door, as if he is afraid of what it contains, or of me. Now he sits, his back to the wall, knees drawn up. Perhaps I should fear him, but I do not think he means me harm, so out of place does he seem here. In his hand he holds something. Quietly drawing myself upright, I see it is my locket. With one finger he traces her face through the glass.

'She was your mother?' he asks.

I nod, not speaking. His eyes do not leave her face.

'Did you know her?'

I shake my head. 'No,' I say quietly. 'And yours? . . . Do you remember her?'

His face knots. 'Sometimes,' he says. Listening to his flat, Irish voice I try to imagine the Dublin slum in which he was born.

'If I had a picture of her, perhaps I would remember more.'

'Perhaps,' I agree. For a long time then he looks into my locket. When he speaks again his voice is quieter.

'It was not what you think.'

'What?' I ask.

'I had to do it, he gave me no choice. He did not understand.' He turns to look at me, his eyes seeking my attention, needy of so much I cannot give. At last I nod and look away.

'Yes,' I say, though something in me rises up to contradict my words, 'I understand.'

After he has gone I uncork my bottle and drink, willing myself away, out of here. The opium is bitter, a sour taste in my throat. Yesterday I walked alone through the streets of Bloomsbury, staring in the windows. Men and women moving in their little worlds of light, speaking and laughing, reading and listening. I wished that I might go to them, and sit inside, and become once more one of their kind. But I knew that I could not, that I had moved outside the world, and beyond.

WITH WALKER GONE a difference descends upon the three of us. We are bound together now, all of us know it. Caley seems wilder, his mood more brittle, and yet at once more still. Though we barely speak, an intimacy lies between us two now, some sense that we understand the other's mind better than we might care to.

Graves guesses as well, seeing Walker gone, but keeps his questions back. Where once he fawned on Caley now he seems almost afraid of him, preferring to mutter to himself alone by the fireplace. Once in the hall he comes close to me and, crossed eyes staring into mine, puts a hand upon my chest and asks me what I know of it, what it was that Walker did. But his needy fascination repulses me, and I leave him there without a word, pushing past and on into my room.

That night he is strange with us, distant and peculiar, and when Caley rounds on him he pulls away, lifting his hand and giggling as if unhinged, before beginning then to weep inconsolably. In another I might think these were signs of some repentance, but he revels in the work we do.

I should care, I know, but I do not. With each of them something dulls inside of me. Even as it holds me here I feel a hopelessness, a sense not that this is wrong but that I have failed somehow. Of something once within my grasp and already fled.

THEN BY ST PANCRAS, where the ivy grows upon the wall and the water seeps out through the stone, I hear a noise, the quiet sound of something cocked in stealth. In the shadows up ahead Craven's figure emerges from the gloom. I know him at once by the way he holds himself, the stooping posture of his frame. Behind him Bridie, and another man I do not know. In his hand Craven holds a pistol, and he lifts his arm so it is trained on us.

'So,' he says, 'then it is true.'

In my hands the barrow is heavy; carefully I lower it, unsure of what he means to do. In front of me Caley does not move, just stands staring at the pistol's barrel.

'What business have you here?' he asks.

'I might ask the same of you,' Craven replies. Taking a step closer he reaches down to the barrow, the pistol still held high. With one hand he draws aside the sticks which cover our bundles.

Something troubles him, something he does not understand quite yet. Caley takes a step closer, but Craven aims the pistol towards him.

'Where is your shadow?' he asks then – 'that wretched dog you call a friend?' For a moment I think Caley will lunge at him, but he stays still. And then Craven lowers the gun and turns to me.

'I once said we were fools to let you close,' he says. 'Now I know I was right.'

Once they have gone, Caley and I gather up the cart and move away, neither willing to meet the other's eye. Caley wheels the cart hard, his pace furious. I follow, though not close, something choking up inside me. I can hear Caley's breath, coming rough and hot, and in my head my beating blood, like waves heard from far away.

I AM WITH GRAVES in the kitchen by the fire when Caley enters. Across the table Graves looks up, and in his face I see he is fearful. All night he has been silent, and restless, but until now I have given it no thought.

'Where is she?' Caley asks, advancing on Graves's chair.

'Who?' Graves starts up and backs away.

'Do not lie to me.' Caley grabs Graves's collar and throws him back down. Though Graves is the larger man by half a head, I see the strength in Caley's arm.

'What is this?' I ask, starting to my feet.

'He has betrayed us,' Caley says. 'Telling old Barker he has a body he would sell.'

'No,' Graves whimpers, 'I would have divided it with you.'

Caley shakes his head. 'Where is she? What have you done with her?'

Graves begins to weep, and all at once Caley pulls a knife from his belt and holds it to his throat.

'Do not defy me,' he says, forcing Graves down onto his knees.

'Please,' babbles Graves, 'I did not mean it, it was an accident.'

Caley presses the knife harder to his throat. 'I will not ask again.'

'Mercy,' Graves cries. Caley lets go and Graves stumbles to his feet, one hand fumbling at his neck to check it is intact. Still weeping he looks from Caley to me and back again. Caley takes a step forward, lifting the knife again. Graves backs away.

'No,' he says, 'I will show you.'

He takes us to the cellar, where a girl lies in the coalscuttle, one arm cast back unnaturally, her hand knotted tight in what looks like pain. She is young, and pretty too, though black with coal. Her face is scratched, and her mouth hangs open, but there is no other sign of death. Yet as Caley and I pull her loose we see the back of her head has been bludgeoned in, the skull a filthy mess of broken bone and clotted blood. She is stiff, and we must break the rigor of her limbs, twist them back into some semblance of peace. Behind us Graves has ceased his weeping, and though he will not come close, he addresses us as we work.

'You will pay me for her, won't you?' he snuffles. Caley turns to him then looks away again, his face and arms filthy with the coal.

'I should give you nothing to teach you honesty,' he says.

Graves points at me. 'Yet he shall have half for bearing her to the damned anatomists?'

'Aye,' Caley says, then smiling, he reaches into his coat.

'Here,' he says quietly, drawing out two sovereigns, 'take these now and let this thing rest.'

Sulkily Graves extends a hand, but as he does Caley grabs his wrist and pulls him close.

'Betray us again and it will be your body we sell,' he hisses, his mouth hard against Graves's ear.

IN THE SKY the moon hangs like a pale eye. My skin shivers, alive to the whispering around me. Too much opium again. The night is cold, yet I linger in the streets. I feel a rupture in the surface of the world, and the running forth of what lies beneath.

I come upon him on the street outside a tavern by Clerkenwell Green.

At first he does not see me, but as I approach he turns, and begins to cower, and I know something is wrong.

Two men are with him, weavers perhaps, and they watch me suspiciously.

'No,' he whimpers, 'don't let him near me.'

As he speaks one of the men approaches me, Graves cowering behind him.

'Graves,' I say, 'why are you hiding from me?'

'Because you mean to kill me,' he says. His words make me nervous, but I look at the two men and shrug.

'He is a friend,' I say. 'I mean him no harm.'

'He says he knows the whereabouts of some

resurrectionists,' says the larger of the two men, his tone implying that I must be one of these men.

I shake my head. 'He is a fool with the drink,' I say. Looking past them I smile at Graves.

'Come now,' I say. 'Are we not friends?'

Graves stares at me for a moment, and then lurches to his feet.

'It's not him I was afraid of,' he says in a wheedling voice, sounding more like a child than ever. I look at his protectors one by one.

'I think it would be better if he were inside,' I say. 'It is a cold night and he might come to harm.' For a moment they stand before me, as if undecided, then without a word they step aside, and I take Graves by the arm.

'Come,' I say as brightly as I can. 'I will help you home.'

In the moonlight the snow seems to shine, dark footprints lying in it like pools. As we walk, Graves takes my sleeve. 'I cannot help myself,' he says. 'I am damned, we all are.' I want to slap him, for this idiocy will betray us, if it has not done so already. Instead I march him down the narrow alley to our door. I am not sure what I intend, beyond leaving him here and seeking out Caley. But Caley is already seated within. Seeing him, Graves cowers back, but I will not let him flee, and push him through the door, close it behind us.

'Where did you find him?' Caley asks.

'In a tavern,' I say, 'pleading for his soul.'

'Has a dog a soul? Caley asks, watching him, and all at once I know I have not seen all of this. But then he surprises me by coming up to Graves, and taking his arm solicitously.

'Sit,' he says. Graves allows himself to be led by Caley to his seat by the fire. There, Caley offers him a drink, and briefly all seems repaired between the two of them.

'You must be careful,' Caley says. 'If we are discovered all of us will hang.'

Graves snuffles into his drink, staring at the two of us. 'For what you have done you deserve to hang.'

'You have done it too,' I say.

Graves looks at me. 'Perhaps I have,' he says, 'but at least I'm not a damned resurrectionist.' Then he giggles, the idiot sound incongruous.

Behind him Caley has taken up something in his hand. Perhaps Graves sees my eyes move, for he begins to turn, but even as he does Caley raises his hand and brings a chisel plunging down. It cannot take more than a second, less perhaps, but it seems to occur so slowly that its various parts can be unpicked: the look on Caley's face, the movement of the blade up, then down, Graves's recognition of what is to come; and then, even as they slip apart, they seem to pull back, collapsing inwards, in a sudden rush, only to meet in the sickening crunch as the knife pierces Graves's skull.

Graves does not slump or fall, instead he gives a choking cry and stumbles to his feet. At first I think I must have misunderstood somehow, that the implement has glanced off, or struck somewhere unimportant, but then I see the handle sticking from his head at the back, the blade sunk several inches deep within.

'Oh no,' cries Graves, groping behind him with his hand. 'What have you done?' Seizing the knife he closes his hands upon it, as if not quite able to believe what he has found.

'Give me up,' Caley hisses. 'Give me up would you?'

'I never gave you up,' says Graves, 'and now you've killed me.' He has his hand wrapped about the handle, but he cannot bring himself to try to pull it loose. Blood has begun to bubble from the wound running down to stain his collar.

Swivelling to look at me, Graves holds out a hand.

'Please,' he whimpers, 'help me. Draw it forth.' He lurches suddenly, and his face contorts, tears leaking from his squinting eyes and down across his cheeks. Once again he looks at Caley, then with a sudden motion starts towards the door. For a space of seconds he fumbles with the latch, trying in vain to open it, but then Caley starts after him, catching him around the neck. Though he moves more slowly, stumbling and swaying as if drunk or drugged, Graves still has strength enough to throw him off.

'Help me,' he pleads hopelessly, 'help me,' tears streaming from his face. Looking at him I realise I no longer care what happens here, all that matters is that it be done, and moving calmly and without haste I take up the poker by the fire. As it strikes his lifted arm the force of the blow reverberates through my own, and lifting it I strike again, harder now, hitting him across the face. Still he does not fall and so I strike again, and then again, and at last he stumbles to his knees, and I follow him, beating him with it as one might whip a dog, over and over and over again, until at last he falls forward on his face and is still.

WE TAKE GRAVES to Brookes' house. It is folly, to take a body mutilated thus, but Caley will not be swayed from it. His face set so pale and furious, I am afraid of him as I have not been in many weeks. We hurry down through the shrouded streets, the smell of the river heavy, dank and sulphurous, Caley driving the barrow mercilessly.

Brookes is asleep when we arrive, and so it is his prentice who shows us in. When Brookes appears he is in his nightshirt, as he often is, its filthy folds billowing about his fleshy form. Seeing it is us he nods and rubs his hands together, and I am reminded of the kindnesses he has shown to me. Time seems out of joint tonight, the smell of Graves's blood upon my skin.

'You knew I was short?' he asks, his little eyes studying us.

'Buy this one,' Caley says, 'and cut him close and small.'

Brookes looks at him curiously. 'Let me see him first,' he says. All at once I wish to be away from here, out of this house, and I lift my eyes to the roof of glass above.

'You have some learning,' Brookes says, watching me,

'have you heard tell of the Hindu's belief that life is not a thing lived from end to end but a circle, in which we die only to be born again, over and over?'

I shake my head. 'A strange belief,' I say, and Brookes nods his head.

'Perhaps,' he says, 'perhaps.' He puts out his hand and draws back the cloth to reveal Graves's face. The mouth lolled open, the squinting eyes half closed in death. I am struck by the sadness of Graves being there, of the stilling of his foolish laugh. Poor Graves, I think, tears welling up, uncontrollable. Brookes has paused, Graves's chin held in his fingers. Slowly he lets his hand fall, the back of it brushing the chest beneath the arm. Still warm, I realise, and must hold myself unless I laugh. With his other hand Brookes touches Graves's mangled face, then pulls back a scrap of scalp where the chisel entered. For a long moment he stares at it, then slowly, carefully, he withdraws his hand and wipes it on his nightshirt.

'Go,' he says. 'Take this with you.' Though his voice is level I hear the way he must work to keep it thus.

'Why not?' Caley demands, stepping closer as if to threaten him. Brookes turns to look at him.

'I will pretend you did not ask me that,' he says, drawing the sack back up over the ruined head.

Only at the door does he speak again.

'Do not come here again,' he says. 'I will not have you in my house.'

———

I hear the impact like a dull thud, and turn. At first I cannot tell what has made the sound. Behind me two men stand, a large mirror held between them, halfway between the door and a wagon filled with furniture. They have heard it too, and for a moment we all stand, gazing about.

251

Then I see it. The small corpse dark upon the freshly swept cobbles. The men's eyes follow as I bend to touch it. A swallow, its neck broken, wings lolling loose. At once I know it has flown into the mirror, winging into its own reflection in a hastening arc, only to strike those glassy depths. I lift its broken body, so small it can be held in one hand. Still warm, the tiny heart only just stilled. A small thing a life, so easily broken, and all at once I begin to weep, while above me the men place the mirror on the wagon, and one, with a rag from his pocket, wipes the small mark the bird has left upon the glass.

I DO NOT REMEMBER how I came to be here. It is as if I am slipping out of myself, like a lens falling out of focus. I cannot go back to the house, for Caley is there, and I know he would see it in my eyes. I am by the river, where I used to walk with Robert. I have had no word of him, and miss him. All day I have been walking. I have a decision to make, although in truth I know it is made already. The only question now is how it is to be done.

———

He is not hard to find. The fog is already thick, so he only hears me when I am hard upon him, stepping out from behind to call his name. He wheels around, one hand moving to his belt, his white eye staring blindly.

'It is only me,' I say. He looks as if he thinks to kill me there.

'Run away, boy,' he says. 'You have no business here.'

When I do not move, he takes a step closer.

'Did you not hear what I said?'

'I would speak with you,' I say.

'What could you say that I would want to hear?'

'Intelligence,' I say, 'about the murder of Lucan.'

At the mention of Lucan's name, Craven stiffens.

'You say he is murdered?'

'And anatomised,' I say.

In one sudden movement Craven lunges forward, grabbing my collar and forcing me to my knees. Though he is thin he is quick, and strong, and before I can fight back he has produced a knife and has it against my eye.

'Who did it?' he asks.

'Caley,' I gasp, and at my throat his grip tightens.

'And you?' he demands. 'What part in it did you have?'

'I was a witness,' I say, 'but not a party.' Craven holds me there, the knife quivering an inch from my eye. With the fog behind him he seems shrouded in a jaundiced light.

'Why have you come to tell me this?'

'Because I would see some justice.'

Craven nods, and lowers the knife.

'Why should I trust a traitor?'

'I owe Caley nothing,' I say.

Craven lets me get to my feet.

'Speak then,' he says. 'Tell me what you intend.'

S HE IS SLEEPING when I knock upon the door.

Though Mary's instincts are to turn me away, she admits me. I am not sure what I think to do: wake her perhaps, ask for some absolution. Yet once I am there in her room, I am unable to touch her. It is dim, the soft light of the evening against the drapes. Outside the air is still, and cold, but in here it is warm. She lies upon her side, as she always does, one arm outstretched, her face downturned, one half obscured by the pillow. Where do we go in sleep, I wonder. The self turned inwards, only to find itself absent, lost amongst the inner shapes of its dreaming. I am so full of the wrong of this thing, with the knowledge of my part in it. Yet as I look at her I wish I could say to her that I will make it right somehow, that all that has been done can be undone. I am tired, and would lay myself beside her. After a time, a minute, maybe more, she murmurs, and stirs, pushing herself over onto her back, turning her face away from me, and quietly I step away, out the door and am gone.

WORD IS SENT, telling him it is me who seeks his company. Two days he has been alone, and I am afraid of what he will have done, alone in the house.

As I walk I seem to float. I did not sleep today, and the night is cold, a bitter wind blowing hard against the sky. No opium, I told myself this morning when I woke – I should be clear tonight, and calm – but somewhere I drank, and then again, the depth of it pressing out against my eyes.

I am late, I think as I arrive, or early, or maybe both. We are to meet in the yard of St John's, a narrow place and walled. I have been here, I know, but I cannot find the memory. Time is slipping about me.

And then his voice.

'Prentice,' he says. With a start I turn to see him there.

'What?' he asks. 'Did you not think that I would come?'

I shake my head.

'Where have you been?' he asks.

'Nowhere,' I say, 'nowhere.' He takes a step closer to me, and I step away, and he goes still.

'Why back away?' he asks. 'Are you afraid of me?' I hear the crack in his voice, sharp as a gun. There is something in his hand, some heavy thing.

'No,' I say, 'not afraid.' Then he extends a hand until it almost touches me.

'Then what?' he asks, his voice trembling.

But I hear a sound, and without thinking turn. He too starts, one hand grasping me by the collar and pressing me back against the wall.

'No one,' I say. But as he presses me against the wall I see his eyes are wet with tears.

'Do you mean to give me up?' he demands, pushing me, his body pressed against my own.

'No,' I say, 'I will not give you up.'

His face is full of this thing that is in both of us. I see the way it swells and grows, like tenderness, or love.

'Please,' I say, and then all at once he steps away. At first I think to run, for now I understand. I am betrayed by all.

And then I see his eyes are not on me but on a shovel abandoned by a grave nearby. Taking a step towards it he reaches out, closing his hand about its haft.

'What do you do?' I ask, and he laughs.

'You did not think I would let you kill me, did you?'

'Let me go and you will never see me again,' I plead, and Caley nods. Encouraged I take a step away, but then he yanks the shovel free, pulling it into his hands and around in one long arc, its passage slicing the air only inches from my head as I stumble back. Near the fence a tree grows upwards, and I make for its dark shape, the quickest way across the wall, and am almost there, when suddenly I am grabbed out of the darkness, and go down into the reeking mud. A hand claws at my face, and I struggle upwards, but something strikes me in the head from behind, a massive blow that sends me crashing to my knees. I struggle to rise, but then it strikes me again, sending me down once more, then again, and again. Dimly I know it must be the shovel.

Then a hand grabbing me, my body rolled onto its back, the weight of a knee upon my chest.

'Betray me, would you?' he demands, and I hear the way his voice is breaking. All I see is red and sparking light. Then taking me by the throat he dashes my head down upon the stones, and consciousness ebbs and all is dark.

I WAKE WITHOUT WAKING, merely rising from a kind of stupor into a different darkness. Where I am I do not know. Above me is the sky, although I do not recognise it at first. A girdle of light, dark cloud scurrying fast. For a time I lie, staring upwards. I can feel the earth beneath me I think, moving in the void. I am cold, and everything is slipping upwards, like heat lost into the night. The slivered moon. I try to move, but cannot, or not my arms, and so I twist my head back, and then I see the lantern, the opened grave. I am floating, smooth as a stone borne in the mouth.

Then I am above, the grave open beneath me. A pauper's hole, the bodies wrapped and stacked one on the other, nameless in the earth. With a strange clarity I understand what is happening, what Caley means to do. One by one he pulls the bodies forth, lining them around the pit. Then I see him take the one I recognise as my very own, and pressing his face close to it to whisper something I cannot hear, he pushes it into the waiting pit.

I am above and I am beneath.

Then one by one the bodies falling in upon me there, their swaddled shapes rolling in on top of me. And all at once I am afraid, and I start to strain and fight, but my body is not mine, it will not move, and so I try to shout, but my voice is mute, as if this was a dream, and one from which I could not wake. From overhead the earth still falling, the close stink of it, as my body seems to fall into the smothering dark, its pressing weight, as if I am not to die but to be unborn, and unmade, returned to the womb from which I came. And all at once I think I understand. Time is not a river, but a prism, in which we are broken and divided like light. Then the last earth tumbles from above, and all is still.

THE KINGDOM OF THE BIRDS

New South Wales, 1836

AT FIRST IT IS NOTHING, or less than nothing. A sort of hesitation in the air. Bourke has fallen still; all about is silence, the only sound the breathing of the bush. In the depthless mirror of the water's surface the clouds stream by, a silent motion, the dipping flight of a currawong moving crosswise to their current like a stone forever falling but never striking. On every side the world unspools.

Turning my hand I look at it. It is part of me, and yet it seems another lives within its skin. The water spilling down from it, beaded glass, as slowly as a feather might. My blood moving past inside of me.

Lifting my eyes I see them. Silent on a rock upon the creek's other side; so close we might speak. How long they have been standing there I am not sure: though it is only now that I have seen them, it seems that they have stood there all along, or even are already gone, as if the fault lies with my senses or with time itself.

In his hand, each holds a brace of spears, light and slender things which give the impression of flight. And yet they seem dressed not for the hunt but for some ritual, their faces and bodies painted with circles and lines of white, lending them the appearance not of men but of ghosts, which perhaps they are.

Unfolding myself I rise. They do not speak, or move, though for a moment I think perhaps they will utter some words which will give this sense, in some tongue known to all of us. But they do not, instead they stand, and watch, their eyes deep and liquid beneath their painted brows.

How long we stand like this I am not sure. A few seconds only, no more, though time seems to stretch impossibly. And then, quite suddenly, a flicker in the light, as if a shadow moved over us. In the water's rusty depths a shaft of light slips upwards and away. Too quick, I think, as if it were just a bird that moved against the sun. But it is enough to break whatever spell it is that binds us here. Across the creek the smaller of the two steps backwards, his eyes passing over me and away. Then the taller too, and without a sound they are gone, slipped away into the bush.

———

When at last I turn from the space that they have left, I see Bourke still standing there, his horse's bridle hanging in his hand. His eyes meet mine, and briefly we are equal in each other's gaze. And then he looks away again as if some intimacy has passed between us and we were made closer by it than we might care to be.

Only later, as we come acrest the road towards the settlement does he speak of it. It is growing late, and overhead the birds shoot and wheel against the fading sky.

'They thought us spirits once,' he says, not turning in his saddle. 'They took the colour of our skin for the pallor of the dead and imagined us their ancestors, lost and wandering in the living world once more.'

Though it is a story I have heard before, the memory of the silent way they stared at us across the creek, the spectral masks of their painted skin rises unbidden in my mind. Then all at once he turns to me.

'You have never felt it?' he asks. 'That sense we are not quite real here? That this land is not our own?'

In the failing light his face is unreadable, and so I let the question hang unanswered.

I AM WITH JOSHUA, upon the hill, when I see the horses on the path, moving slowly up the slope. Lost in the act of drawing, Joshua does not notice them at once, his eyes moving from the view to the page and back again. Only when the quality of his attention changes, do I know he has seen his father there. Then, looking down again, he returns to his work, determinedly, though the fluidity of before is gone, his hand moving awkwardly upon the page.

As they approach I lift my arm to shade my eyes: the day is clear, and bright, Bourke reining in his horse and greeting me with a hand upon his hat.

'I had thought to find you here,' he says, though I am sure it is not me but Joshua, still bent over his book, that he had thought to find.

'You ride out?' I ask, and Bourke nods.

'Not far.' Then with a hand he indicates his companion. 'You have met our new neighbour?'

'I have not had the pleasure,' I say, still shading my eyes.

'Edmund Winter,' says the figure on the horse. He is a thin

266

man in his early thirties, dark-haired and precise in his saddle, and though he is careful enough in his words he does not
offer me his hand. Joshua sets down his pen.

'Thomas May,' I reply. I turn to look down the hill.

'You have bought the Wemys property?'

Perhaps he finds my questioning distasteful for he lets the
question hang unanswered a moment longer than is polite.

'And the land upon its northern boundary.'

'But you are new to the colony?'

Winter stares down at me. 'I am,' he says. His mouth is a
little wide and full in his high-boned face; in another it
might lend an air of sensuality to his looks, but in him it
seems somehow cruel.

'Sydney's gain is Hobart's loss,' Bourke says, good-
humouredly, but Winter glances at him as if this revelation
displeases him.

'How do you find it here?' I ask.

Winter smiles thinly. 'Handsome enough,' he replies.

———

Once they are gone I direct Joshua to return to his sketch.
Westward I can make out the border of the land that was
once Major Wemys's. For three years it has lain deserted, its
fields left to go to seed, its stock sold by the executor while
the cousin he had willed them to was found and informed
of his good fortune. A solicitor in Somerset, I have heard, or
Surrey, but with no desire to see this land he has come into
unexpectedly. For a time Bourke himself thought of buying
it, as did others hereabouts, but one by one they each
declined, and so the agent was bound to seek buyers
elsewhere.

Beside me Joshua sets down his pen again, interrupting
my thoughts. The image on the page before him having

faltered I refrain from directing him to continue, telling him we will finish for the day.

Walking back to the house Joshua talks, and laughs, the encounter with his father seemingly forgotten. By the gates he asks me to accompany him inside, assuring me his step-mother would be happy to see me, but I shake my head and tell him I have business of my own, and so we part.

It is a delicate thing, my relationship with the Bourkes. In the three years that I have known them I have gone from a thing bought and sold, to being their employee and, finally, a friend. And yet between us there is much unsaid, omissions and questions unpursued. When first I sought work it was Bourke who engaged me to educate his son, and, later, Mrs Bourke who found me work with the ladies of the settlement. This would be enough to place me in their debt, but still they treat me as one might a friend, a kindness I am uneasy with.

———

I make my way back down towards the road, my portfolio upon my back. At the sound of approaching hooves, I step aside and turn, expecting to see Bourke come after me to pass on some word or make some request, but it is Winter. Pulling his horse about he stops in front of me.

'Mr May,' he says, 'I had thought to find you at the house.'

I shake my head. 'I have other business that needs attending to.'

He nods almost imperceptibly.

'Your lesson with the boy is done?' he asks, and I nod.

'Bourke says he has talent of a sort.'

'He draws well,' I say, 'and finds pleasure in the act.'

Winter looks me over. 'You take other pupils, I understand?'

'I do,' I say.

'I have a sister,' he says slowly then, 'unmarried, and with too little to fill her days. It would do her good to have some accomplishment to find pleasure in.'

Something in his manner makes me hesitate. 'You have discussed the question with her?'

He smiles coolly. 'She is my sister, Mr May, I think I know her mind.'

Drawing a card from his jacket he places it in my hand. 'Call on us,' he says. 'Next week, if you will.'

I place the card inside my jacket. 'Very well,' I say. Then pulling on the reins Winter turns the mare about and sets off across the hill.

M Y HOUSE IS QUIET when I return, the shadows long about it on the ground. In the air the smell of the eucalypts, the dusty fragrance of the bush. Setting down my portfolio I loosen my waistcoat and collar, drawing water from the bag that hangs behind the door, its wetness coming cool and close with the memory of the stone from which it sprang. Before me the evening stretches out in solitude, an unbroken space.

There are those to whom it would seem strange that privacy should be a luxury in such a place. The colony is small, and the roads between the settlements and the houses long and little travelled. But solitude and privacy are different things: though a man may easily go a week here without crossing another's path, in truth it would be easier to pass unseen amongst the press of a London street, to lose oneself in the throng of the passing multitudes than to go unnoticed here in solitude, for in this place all know the business of their neighbours, and gossip travels far, and fast.

It is a strange kind of solitude then that I have found for

myself here. I am one amongst the people of the colony, and yet not. My profession grants me entry to their circles and some measure of trust, but for all of that I still keep myself apart, for I find no ease with them.

This is not a privilege I have always enjoyed. For the space of my sentence I lived and worked with other men, sleeping rough upon the ground, and later in beds six to a room. I was not happy thus, nor unhappy, instead I learned to mind myself, to make a place inside of me where my thoughts might be my own. And when my time was done, Bourke gave me first a room, and, later, the lease upon this house and land adjoining his estate.

Though it is small, with little in the way of amenity, the rent was cheap and the neighbours few, and so I took it gratefully. It had been an officer's, a man returned to England five years past, and had been abandoned long enough to be reclaimed by the bush. Cockatoos nested in the chimney and possums scuttled in the roof, and leaves and dung were scattered on the floors. No doubt it was convenient for Bourke to have me here, for I cleaned it out and fixed the roof and walls, and kept the blacks from burning it or escapees making it their own, but his was an act of kindness nonetheless.

Another might be lonely here, but I find pleasure in the solitude. I have little taste for company, travelling only when I must to take specimens for those who commission me, or to teach amongst the ladies of the settlement. No doubt I could make a better living other ways; there are many who would have me make their likeness, or those of their loved ones and family. Many too who desire portraits made of animals they possess: most often horses, but sometimes cattle and dogs, and even once or twice a pig of great consequence. But I have no taste for this work; though I am a fair hand at the rendering of the human form there seems something false and overweening in this desire to have one's likeness set down for posterity. And so instead I teach, helping guide the hands of ladies who would attain some degree of accomplishment in the art of drawing and water colours. For though it requires me to gild my words and to flatter them, there is an honesty to it nonetheless, a truth in the moment when a student finds something perfect and true in a line, which brings me happiness. But more importantly, through my teaching I am left alone, the world I hold inside and my other work kept private and inviolate.

A WEEK PASSES before I find time to call on Winter. The day is fine, the unearthly song of the cicadas shimmering in the air. Though I have passed it many times I am not familiar with the property, only with the house as is visible from the road. Approaching up the winding drive I look about myself at the gardens, half-wild with neglect. Once this was a place such as an English gentleman might feel at home in – save for the immensity of sky and the annihilating light, the shrieking parrots in the trees – but left on its own it has grown wild and strange, snakes slipping in along the branches, wattle trees and native bushes seeding themselves amidst the dainty English roses.

Upon the step I knock, and in the quiet that follows I hear from somewhere within the sound of a pianoforte, the tune gentle and sad. Then footsteps, the door opening to reveal a woman in a housekeeper's uniform, her face hardened first by the memory of some London slum, then by the unforgiving sun of the antipodes. She regards me dubiously as I tell her my name, looking hard at the card I give to her, then taking it she directs me to a little parlour by the door and leaves me there.

Left alone I listen to the music from above. The tune is not known to me but it suggests itself in such a way that I almost feel it might be. Still listening I set down my portfolio and look about. The room is small and plain, two walls decorated each with a painting in the style of Gainsborough, a shelf of books against another wall. Above the fireplace hangs another painting, a portrait executed in a cruder hand. Stepping closer to examine it I see a man of middle years dressed in the fashions of twenty years ago. The painting is of no great artistry, its flat and awkward composition betraying some untrained hand; nonetheless it captures some quality of kindness in its subject and though its subject is an older man, and heavier, I fancy I see Winter's face in his.

Lost thus in the picture I am startled to hear the voice of the housekeeper behind me in the hall, remonstrating, then another voice, quiet and firm. Overhead the music has stopped, I realise, and turning towards the door I see a woman standing there. I am not sure what I had expected her to be, but I know at once it was not this. She is young, not more than twenty-two, and dressed in a pale dress of great simplicity, her ash-blonde hair tied back in a manner quite unlike the showy styles so popular with the other ladies of the colony. Like her brother she is slim, but where his face is imperious hers is gentler.

'Mr May?' she asks. I would take her hand, but something in her expression repels that familiarity.

'Your brother told you I would call?' I ask, and she gives a little nod.

'It was his wish I give you instruction in draughtsmanship, so you might have something with which to fill your days,' I say.

'Yes,' she says, 'he spoke of it.' Behind her in the hall the housekeeper is observing; following my eyes Miss Winter turns to her.

'Thank you, Mrs Blackstable,' she says. The housekeeper lingers, then nods sourly, and turns back down the corridor.

'I am sorry you should be greeted in such a manner,' says Miss Winter, turning back to me. She gestures at a pair of crates which stand opened in the corner of the room. 'As you can see we are not yet fully settled in the house.'

I shake my head, telling her there is no need to apologise. 'I am told you are late of Van Diemen's Land? You are a native of that place?'

'I was born there,' she says, her voice dropping away at the sentence's end, leaving little doubt as to how her parents made their way across the sea. But lifting her eyes she looks at me with a sudden, steady gaze, as if defying me to find some shame in her. At last she looks away.

'You are a painter then?'

Stepping forward I take up my portfolio from the table-top. 'I may show you some examples if you need references.'

She looks at the portfolio for a second or two. 'No,' she says, 'I do not think that will be necessary. Has my brother discussed terms with you?'

'Not as yet,' I reply.

'I am sure they will be acceptable. No doubt he will confirm them with you when he returns.'

Resignation and defiance are so strangely mixed in her manner I am unsure how to respond. Groping for some common ground I set down my portfolio.

'I heard music before, the pianoforte. It was you that played?'

She looks up, her expression suddenly wary, and at once I fear I have misspoken, breached some barrier. But then she nods.

'Yes,' she says quietly.

'I thought it very fine,' I say, but she looks away.

'Thank you,' she says. I think she will say something more, but instead she lifts her eyes to mine, the challenge they contained before returned and altered in some subtle way.

'I will look forward to your brother's letter,' I say. But at the door she steps after me.

'Mr May?' she asks. 'What is it you paint?'

I look out through the doorway.

'Birds,' I say at last, 'only birds.'

Enclosed in the cage of my hand she trembles, a hot weight, scarcely heavier than breath. Only moments ago she fought and shrieked in the net's entangling strands, now she does not move, her body poised motionless within my grasp. Not stunned, or injured, merely stilled, her tiny form seeming to quiver with the arrested urgency of flight.

Though my hand is closed about her it is but loosely so. Were I to open it she would spring away, her body cast into the air on beating wings and gone, quick as memory. But while held she does not strain; instead she waits, as if for some sign from me.

It is a dreadful sort of power this. To hold a life so small in your control. And yet it is not the power to give or take that life which makes it terrible. After all, to live, to die, each is a simple thing. Rather it is the intimacy of it, the way that in the possession of such power you are made naked in the gaze of another, as they are in yours. And for that brief second it is possible to glimpse what it might mean to leave the cage of the self and touch another, to know them as you know yourself.

Behind me in the air the net shifts upon the breeze, its silken strands barely visible against the fading light. On every side the birds are in motion, magpies and lorikeets, screeching cockatoos. And closer in, her own fellows, their tiny bodies shooting round about me in desperate circles. With each dive they cry out, urgently and ferociously, in a panic for her life, the grace of their bodies marvellous as they arc and wheel on the air. What must it be to live like that, I think, a life as hot and quick as blood, all its meaning concentrated in the moment of being?

In my hand I feel her tense, and looking down again I see she is watching me. Beneath my thumb her body seems to flicker, the mothbeat of her heart quicker than a child's pulse. Moving faster now her flockmates spin and turn about the two of us, their cries coming sharper from their chests, more urgently. With each cry she seems to start, as if with a half-remembered pain. I feel it too, I think, an ache inside of me.

Willing the other's cries away I lift my hand, slowly tightening my grip about her tiny form. She is so light she might be naught but heat. Beneath my thumb now the dome of her skull, fragile as an egg. She must realise what I intend and yet she does not fight, not even now, her eyes just watching mine, liquid dark. I could close my eyes, or look away, or cast her up into the air so she might fly again, but I do not. Instead I let my thumb press down against the tension of her neck, gently at first, and then harder, until at last it gives a little pop, and in that moment she is dead.

———

Though the days are not yet hot I pack her quickly, for the heat that lingers in her body will not last. Already her eyes are dull; in an hour she will be cold, her legs gone stiff, feet curled back, in a day spoiled. Though it brings me no pleasure to take her life, later I will imagine her back into being, learning from her body's details, erasing the deceptions of the eye. Though one must know the habits of their kind, the way they move and hold themselves, the trees in which they rest, life will tell only so much about the semblance of a bird. To make an image which is true one must also know the way a throat is banded, where the colours of the belly give way to the tail. Just as the brilliant white of the cockatoos is in truth shot through with yellow, this same hue lending the feathers their unnatural clarity, so too those birds which might seem dull black or drab brown will reveal colours within themselves when held in the hand, midnight blues and viridian, shades which shimmer and shift.

———

It is a fragile thing, the line within an image which contains the whole. Yet in its finding it transcends all other considerations. Like a note played clear and true it reveals itself as if already there, plangent and unadorned. And in its finding we may move without awkwardness or artifice, somewhere outside of language, outside of care.

THOUGH WINTER'S TERMS when they come are generous, my first impulse is to send the letter back, reject his offer outright. I have no reason for this, only the feeling that his generosity is too easy to accept, its taking buying my complicity in some purpose I do not fully understand. But something in the memory of her manner decides me otherwise, and so by letter I accept, and set a time to call three days hence.

On the day appointed I have a lesson at the Robertsons' first, and so it is mid-afternoon before I may call. These past days Winter is much discussed by the ladies of the colony, who would know more of him, more of his intentions here. At the boundary of his property I see a group of men moving raggedly across the hill, bearing tools upon their backs, as if to start the work of repairing nature's damage these last years. They are Company men, I know at once, not by their clothing but by the way their gaze follows me without ever meeting mine, the uneasy questioning of their eyes.

Nearer the house, work has begun as well, the lawn now

cut, limbs lying here and there, lopped from the overhanging trees. The door is open, a girl standing within; greeting her I give my name and business and a moment later Miss Winter appears. She has that same look of broken defiance I remember from our first meeting. Then she nods, though whether in greeting or disappointment I am unsure.

'My brother's terms were acceptable then?' she asks, and something in her voice reminds me of my barely articulated revulsion against Winter's note, its too-generous terms.

She holds my eyes for a moment longer than is necessary, and then sets her mouth.

Ushering me in before herself she leads me to the parlour where we met a week before. On the table lies a portfolio; setting my own down beside it I touch it with my hand.

'This is yours?' I ask, and she nods.

'You will not mind if I look?'

She shakes her head and so I open it, leafing through the pictures it contains. A picture of an abbey, all romantic ruin, a pair of hands, the face of a man. The pictures a girl would make, I think, and old, besides.

'You have had instruction before?'

'When I was a girl there was a man in my father's employ called Davidson.' For a brief second she hesitates, before adding, 'A convict.'

Looking around I indicate the portrait above the fireplace.

'That is his work?'

'It is.'

From the door comes the sound of a throat being cleared. The girl who admitted me is standing there. She is a thin thing, her dress hanging loosely on her narrow frame, and she averts her eyes, fixing her gaze upon the floor. Miss Winter does not make any movement to prompt the girl, and so at last when she speaks it is an ecstasy of embarrassment.

'Please, Miss. Mrs Blackstable said I should sit with you and the gentleman.'

Still Miss Winter says nothing, and so, embarrassed for the girl, I direct her to a chair and tell her to sit. Glancing back at Miss Winter I see she has looked away, out the window into the garden, her body tight.

'Miss Winter,' I say, and she turns.

'Shall we begin?'

As we work the girl sits staring at her hands. At first I think it is something we have done that has unsettled her, but as the hour passes I realise I have misunderstood: her discomfort lies not with Miss Winter's silence, but in whatever purpose lies behind her presence here. For a time I speak to Miss Winter about the principles of composition, trying to gauge how much she already knows, asking questions, watching the way she answers, and then I set her the task of sketching a bowl of flowers which sits upon the table.

While she works I take up the drawings in her portfolio once more. They are awkward, and pedestrian, all too evidently full of a girl's restless longing and the desire for life to be more than it is. Lifting my eyes I look once more at Miss Winter. The task I have given her is of no great worth, a drawing to be made and then forgotten, but still she works at it with an intensity that is almost painful to observe. I want to lift a hand, to still her, yet it is difficult to set aside the sense that even her seriousness is somehow an act of defiance, though one enacted without care for consequence. It frightens me somehow, as if she might do herself harm in her desire to lose herself in this. Her hands are lined and reddened, the hands of a woman twice her age, and this small detail makes her appear more vulnerable than all the rest of it. I find myself gripped by the desire to ease whatever it is that she fights so hard against. It is a strange thing, tenderness, how near to pain it is, as if it were itself a sort of loss, a longing for a closeness we can never know.

'Mr May,' calls Mrs Bourke as I take my leave of Joshua a week later. Surprised, I turn and see her on the stairs, Miss Lizabet skipping down below her.

'You are leaving?' she asks, beginning to descend, but I shake my head.

'It was your husband's wish that I attend on him before I go,' I say, 'but he is still occupied with Tavistock.'

Mrs Bourke purses her lips in a gentle frown. I have heard her complain good-naturedly her husband might have married Tavistock, the farm manager, had he thought the other man capable of giving him an heir.

'He will not be back for some hours yet, I think,' she says. 'Do not wait for him.'

I am uncomfortable with breaking my word to Bourke, but I have come to trust Mrs Bourke's judgement in many things, her husband most of all.

'Miss Lizabet would play, I think. Perhaps you might walk with me while she does,' she says as her daughter shakes the little doll she holds, her face fixed in a frown.

'I have work –' I begin, but Mrs Bourke places a hand upon my arm, and gives me a little push.

'And you shall get to it,' she says, 'but not quite yet.'

Though we are separated by the barrier of our places in the house I am fond of my employer's wife. She and Bourke were but newly married when I was first bonded here, she herself little more than a girl, still fresh from England's shores and heavy with the child who would become Miss Lizabet. Just sixteen when Bourke met her on a visit to England, barely a year older when she arrived here as the wife of a widower fifteen years her senior with a son only ten years younger than herself. I remember glimpsing her as I went about my work, walking slowly through the gardens of the house, careful in her own company. Even then I admired her, I suppose, so young and so far away from all she knew, not just for her kindness but for her tact and lack of ceremony.

'We have not seen much of each other of late,' she says as we make our way across the lawn.

'I have been occupied,' I reply, and she smiles.

'You have not been too much alone?'

I shake my head. Of those few I might call my friends only Mrs Bourke would ask this of me.

'I have my work.' In front of us Miss Lizabet is spinning in slow circles, her doll held out in one hand, lost in some childish game.

'Bourke says you give lessons to Miss Winter,' Mrs Bourke says then. Startled I look at her, but there is nothing prying in her face. Perhaps my expression tells more than I mean, for there is an instant when she looks at me, and then away.

'You think her fair?' she asks.

'You have not met her yourself?'

She shakes her head. 'Bourke has. Her brother keeps her close, I think, though I know not why.'

284

'You do not care for him?'

She ponders. 'I think he is a man who cares very much for how the world sees him,' she says.

As she speaks Joshua appears. Miss Lizabet runs towards him, her doll held high, eager to tell him some secret she has discovered or perhaps to have him partner her in a dance. Mrs Bourke gazes at the two of them.

'I am told Joshua grows more like his mother every month,' she says.

I look at her in surprise. 'Bourke says that?' But she shakes her head.

'He would not say such things.' Joshua lifts Miss Lizabet onto his shoulders provoking a delighted squeal. 'But I know he sees it too.'

NO DOUBT THERE ARE SOME who would laugh at the airs of those who are exalted in these colonies. Bigamists and kidnappers, cattle thieves and gamblers. There are men amongst us here worth more than baronets who speak with the commonest cockney tongue, women in the finest gowns who have sold their bodies on London's streets. To laugh at them, or mock, however, is no easy thing, for what lies in their pasts is there for all of us. And so we conspire not to enquire, nor to tell, as if by this silence we might forget what was and make a life without a past, as if this were a land without history, a country founded on the air.

And yet the past is ever there. In the land and in ourselves. There are things that come to us without words, movements in our selves. As real as thought, or memory. But without words they cannot be, without names they are not given life.

These past weeks she is ever in my mind. Not the look of her but her presence in that room, the sense of some secret. It hums in me, something I cannot put aside. I am distracted in my work, distracted with my pupils, and yet I will not put a name to it, will not give this feeling shape. Still, with each passing week I find myself thinking on my next visit, wishing I might find a way to pierce whatever barrier it is she sets about herself. In the images that I make, in their colours and their lines, I can feel her pressing, feel the way she is wound into their making. But I will not speak the word that might unhinge it all.

It is Bourke who tells me of his wife's invitation, speaking the words almost as a joke.

Turning I ask that he repeat himself.

'An evening of musical performances,' he says again. 'She bids me tell you she would find your presence gratifying.'

'I have work,' I demur, but Bourke is not to be so easily refused.

'She asks it as a kindness to herself,' he says.

And so it is that two nights later I find myself at the Bourkes', moving uncomfortably amongst the guests. Their faces are known to me, their business too. They laugh too loud, coarse and crowing, the women overdressed and bejewelled, their faces hardened by the sun. We speak in words polite and undemanding. And then I lift my eyes and see Winter at the door, his sister by his side. He enters the room with his head held high, and though he shakes the hands of his hosts there is little warmth in the greeting that I can see. His sister looks ill at ease. She holds her head high as well, but looks like a woman who is here against her will.

If Mrs Bourke sees this in her manner she ignores it; instead she extends her arm and draws Miss Winter closer, speaking to her as if they were already intimates. Winter's eyes do not leave his sister's back, but with a smile Mrs Bourke bids him leave them. There is a moment when Winter might resist, but then he gives a nod, his face a mask, and turns away from the two of them.

Placing Miss Winter's arm inside her own Mrs Bourke leads her off across the room. Though she wears a gown of pale green which suits her well beside Mrs Bourke she looks awkward and sad. That this should be is the stranger because she is fine-featured, and possessed of a dignity which draws the glances of the men and the scrutiny of the women as she is introduced. Even once the music starts, and the singer, a pretty girl recently arrived from India, begins, I see the way they look at her from behind their fans, and too the way she ignores their stares, gazing ahead, this careful attention of theirs only acting to place her further apart, as if she were a stranger in this place.

Then comes Bourke's voice at my shoulder.

'Your pupil makes a pretty picture with my wife.' His eyes are upon the two ladies. Though he is a good husband and a faithful one, he is a man who appreciates the charms of the fairer sex and is comfortable in their company. I begin to compose a reply, but then her brother is standing there at Bourke's side.

'Mr May,' he says, his voice inviting no familiarity.

'Mr Winter.'

'How does your sister find her lessons?' Bourke asks. Winter regards me carefully.

'She has not said she finds them unsatisfactory,' he says. Bourke chuckles.

'A rousing endorsement, to be sure. And you, May, how do you find her as a student?'

'She shows some promise,' I say, 'though I am not the first

to offer instruction to her.' Then, turning to Winter, 'There was another tutor, a convict, she said.'

'An employee of my father's,' he says abruptly.

'Your sister says he was the author of the portrait which hangs in your drawing room.'

'He was a man careless in everything,' says Winter. I hold his eye with my own.

'Yet he taught your sister well, I think.'

'My sister takes instruction well enough when it pleases her,' Winter says. Suddenly I am angry for her.

'That is true of all of us, is it not? It is not a habit of our species that we thrive under the yoke.'

Winter regards me coldly, but before he can reply the singer finishes her aria, provoking a scattering of applause. The girl bows prettily, and Mrs Bourke steps forward, hands raised to quiet the audience.

'Perhaps we might find another amongst our ranks who would perform for us?' she asks, looking around. There is laughter from a pair of men in one corner; fixing them with a stare Mrs Bourke shakes her head. 'We'll have none of your sailors' songs, Mr Wilkinson, I'm sure. I've heard more than enough of them down by the docks.'

Grinning delightedly at the general amusement which greets this remark, Mrs Bourke lifts her hands again. 'Well?'

People shift and murmur, but when no one steps forward Mrs Bourke extends a hand to Miss Winter.

'You play, do you not?' she asks. 'Perhaps you might do us the honour?'

Miss Winter seems to grow very still, though she does not shrink from the request.

'No,' she says, 'I think not.'

Mrs Bourke shakes her head. 'Please,' she replies, 'we crave accomplishments in this place. And I am sure you will have talent possessed by none of us.'

Standing there, I feel a sort of tenderness, Miss Winter seeming still to hesitate. But then she bows her head and consents.

With Mrs Bourke beside her she takes a seat upon the piano stool, her hands resting on the keys.

'What should I play?' she asks. Mrs Bourke looks down at her solicitously.

'That is a matter for you to decide,' she says. And so Miss Winter gives a nod, and then slowly, carefully, begins to play.

———

Her playing is not elegant nor even terribly fine, but she plays with such intensity, such longing, that it hardly seems to matter. What it is I do not know, only that it is as sad and wonderful as anything I have ever heard. She does not look around, nor seek the eyes of these watching her, just plays, and plays, sometimes dropping notes or faltering here and there as she goes, but it is almost as if this awkwardness is of a piece with her manner, the intensity of her longing made the more painful to hear by this clumsiness. And when she is done I lift my hands and clap, watching as she bows her head not to the audience but to the piano in front of her, then rises, and after clasping the hand of Mrs Bourke for a moment slips away.

———

For a long time after she has gone I stand watching the space where she last stood. All evening I have sought to avoid her gaze, whether out of sensitivity to her or myself I am not sure. But now I find I would speak to her, though I do not know what words I might say. And so, with a word or two to those I pass I follow her out through the doors into the garden. Outside the air is cool, and smells of dust and smoke, the sandstone of the courtyard worn and golden in the light from the lamps. Two men are standing, smoking quietly. She is by the steps down to the lawn with her brother, the two of them in conversation with the Bourkes. Though he speaks amiably enough I see the way he holds her arm, the anger in him. Her face is turned half-away, and she cannot see me; motionless I will her to turn my way, to look at me. But she does not, instead taking the hand of each of the Bourkes in turn as her brother bids the two of them farewell. Only as they reach the drive does she turn, and her eyes meet mine, before she looks away again and they are gone.

———

Perhaps it is the memory of her music, but tonight I cannot sleep. All night her presence here, the sense that in her quietness there lies some sympathy. Overhead, possums scrabble on the roof, nightjars hoot and cry. It frightens me, to be so possessed. Come three I rise, thinking to work, and light the lamp upon my desk. In its glow insects move, points of light which dart and weave. One by one I open the boards between which I keep my drawings, following the lines of the birds I have sketched upon these pages. In their making they brought me happiness, but now they seem clumsy things, poor transpositions of the life. They do not move, nor call. Looking up I see my reflection distorted in the window's glass, a chiaroscuro in the lamp's golden light. Its features familiar, yet strange, as if the face were not my own but a mask, and beneath it only emptiness.

I AM IN THE ROBERTSONS' DRAWING ROOM with Amelia when her mother enters. Glancing round I wish her good morning, then return my attention to Amelia's page. Behind me Mrs Robertson seats herself, and I can feel her observing us.

'I am told she is a pupil of yours,' she says at last.

'She?' I turn to her. Mrs Robertson smiles, as if my question amuses her.

'Miss Winter, whose playing so enraptured everyone the other evening.'

I keep my gaze steady, but Mrs Robertson has seen what she sought, and taking up her fan flutters it at herself.

'What do you make of her?' she asks.

'She shows promise,' I reply, but Mrs Robertson only laughs.

'You are most politic. What of her character?'

'You are not acquainted with her?'

Amelia has turned to listen. Mrs Robertson raises a hand to shoo her off.

'Leave us,' she says, and with a bob to me Amelia stands. Only when she is well outside does Mrs Robertson give me a look which might charm another man.

'I know her brother is said to be worth forty thousand.'

I just sit. Then, with sudden carelessness, she gives a laugh.

'Really, Mr May, I sometimes think you are even more of a hermit than you say. Do you not know of the scandal surrounding her?'

'Scandal finds many, given time,' I say, but Mrs Robertson is not to be denied.

'It is said her brother left Van Diemen's Land on her account. She bore a child to an officer, a man married with a wife back in England.'

Perhaps the effect of this news upon me is visible, for Mrs Robertson smiles unpleasantly.

'There is no child that I have seen,' I say quietly.

Mrs Robertson laughs. 'No. I am told it died, no doubt fortunately.'

I think for a moment to walk away, leave Mrs Robertson there, but that would reveal more than I suspect she already guesses.

'Yet you have introduced Amelia to her brother,' I say instead. A cold silence falls, and I know without another word I will not be welcome here again.

'There is much forty thousand will forgive,' she replies, then, rising, brushes her dress.

'Finish your lesson,' she says. 'I wish Amelia to accompany me in the carriage.'

OUTSIDE I WALK QUICKLY. It is three hours till the time appointed for our lesson but remembering our last meeting I want to go to her immediately, as if I might offer her some absolution, some forgiveness, though for what I do not know. Only as I reach the road towards her gate do I pause, knowing that to arrive in such a state would merely compromise the both of us.

Mrs Blackstable greets me and, leaving me to wait in the parlour, goes to tell Miss Winter I am here. Left alone I pace about, looking now and again towards the portrait above the fireplace.

She appears at the garden doors, a beaded shawl wrapped loosely about herself.

'I had not expected you so soon,' she says. 'I was in the garden, and must apologise.'

I shake my head. 'There is no need,' I say, 'the fault is mine. I am early.' Although I have spent the past few hours imagining this meeting, now I am here I am uncomfortable, and she oblivious to the changes in the way I feel.

'Shall we begin?' she asks, stepping closer. I nod, a little brusquely I suspect. She looks at me as if I have betrayed her in some way.

'Perhaps outside,' I suggest, and with a wary glance she bids me wait while she fetches her portfolio.

Walking across the lawn we seek out a place in which to sit. At last we choose a little arbour framed by a pale-skinned eucalypt, and, setting down the chair I have carried from the house for her, I wait as she seats herself. Taking up her board then, she begins to sketch, but it is clear at once that something troubles her, for she is distracted, unable to lose herself into her work.

'Your playing at the Bourkes' –' I begin, but she turns, too quickly, then looks away again.

'I am sorry for that,' she says. 'I am a poor musician at best.'

'No,' I say. 'I was greatly moved by it.'

She nods, the gesture dismissive. 'My brother thinks my playing indulgent.'

When I give no answer she lifts her eyes to mine. For a few moments we sit thus, unspeaking.

'I think you mistake me.'

'No,' I say, 'I do not think I mistake you.'

'You know something of me then, of my past?'

'Of the child, and the officer, yes.'

For a long time then she is silent. 'Yet still you come to visit me?'

At that moment I hear a sound. Mrs Blackstable is standing there.

'Your brother wants you in the house,' she says. Miss Winter gives her a look of hatred but Mrs Blackstable does not flinch.

Closing her portfolio Miss Winter rises to her feet.

'You must excuse me,' she says. 'Perhaps we may resume this next time we meet.'

I nod, standing as she turns and walks away. She holds her head high, and will not bend.

'Miss Winter,' I say then, and she turns.

'Yes?'

'We are none of us without a past.'

She pauses for a moment, watching me, then she lowers her eyes and, turning, continues on. For a moment Mrs Blackstable lingers. I do not speak to her, nor do I need to inquire how much she heard for as she turns to go she looks back at me, and smiles.

ON THAT FIRST DAY, as they led me from the ship onto the dock, I do not know what I had thought might lie ahead. Four months by wind and sea, halfway across a world, and yet I had no care for where I had arrived, all things seeming equally flat and unprofitable.

After the dimness of the hold, the creaking coffins of the beds in which we lay, the light of the day seemed impossible, the flashing water and the shrieking birds cacophonous. We were ragged and pale, our bodies wasted by the months beneath the decks, and as we stumbled and shuffled up through the streets in our chains, the people turned and stared. I had thought they might jeer, but they did not; indeed, beyond a boy who ran beside us, pulling at our sleeves and murmuring offers of meat or bread or liquor for a shilling, scarce a word was uttered in the time it took us to pass.

Though I had been almost five months in their company I had no friends amongst those men I marched beside, each dragging his feet beneath the weight of our bonds. Another man perhaps might have found friendship there, yet I had no taste for it. And so as we lay upon our beds in the Barracks I could only listen as the others schemed and speculated upon what fate awaited them.

That I could read and write I had made no mention of, and so I thought I would be bound to the service of the colony, a government man, condemned to burning lime or digging coal. Though this was the fate most abhorred by the other men it held a sort of power over me: to be made the lowest amongst the lowest had a sort of morbid symmetry.

Yet I was not bound to the colony, but rather to a grazier called Tavish. This news came only with the order that I rise from my bunk and shuffle to the yard, where, with five men I did not know, I was set to walk behind a wagon bearing provisions north. Though we had a hundred miles or more to walk, across hills and valleys, streams and rivers, the chains were not taken from our legs, lest we should try to escape, and so we stumbled, hungry and thirsty, our ankles chafed raw by the shackles, our backs burned red by the sun overhead.

Though there are masters who treat the men assigned to them decently, Tavish was not one of them. He had been a soldier once, and I am sure in that life too he was hated by the men who served under him. Handy with a whip, he took delight in tormenting those bound to him, as if by making beasts of us he answered some absence in himself.

His land lay south of Newcastle, amongst the lakes and marshes, and he worked the property with his son, the man responsible for our enforced march. Though the earth thereabouts was sandy, and poor, it was their intention to open the country, so it might carry sheep, and cattle, and to this end we were set to clearing it. The work was brutal but neither Tavish nor his son seemed to care, feeding us barely enough to keep life and soul together, and driving us until we fell.

They had no right to do this we knew, yet we had no place to go, no authority who might help us.

But those cruel months somehow wrought another change in me. Out there, where the hills sloped down into the water, and the sunlight fell like glass, I found a measure of quiet I had never known. Often I would pass whole days alone, or simply in the company of those others bound with me, and though the work was hard, we each of us were glad of the space and air. Sometimes as we worked I would grow conscious of other life nearby, egrets and water birds, until there came one day in particular when I turned to see a grey heron, moving with liquid steps across the pools not far away, its long neck poised and ready to strike. I know it saw me, for it fell quite still, watching me warily, the two of us held there in that moment for what seemed a heartbeat or an eternity before at last it turned away, stepping off across the water with an unhurried pace. Only then did I feel the breath leave me in a rush, and realise I had been holding it.

In time I learned to move quietly enough to avoid the interruption of the lapwings, whose shrieking cry can send every bird for three hundred yards clamouring into the air; and I began to learn the habits and manners of the birds that lived here on every side, the kingfishers and lorikeets, the whipbirds and wattlebirds and honeyeaters. To watch them rise upon the wing, to watch that lightness of form, was itself a kind of freedom to me, yet this was not all I saw in them: I saw something sharp, and dangerous, creatures who lived outside the realm of man, torn by hunger, and desire, a different Creation.

Perhaps that would have gone no further, had Tavish not come upon a bundle of paper. Like many masters who take pleasure in the ruining of those men bound to them in the colonies, Tavish sought often to make what pay he must to us in kind, and then in goods of no use or value to those who lived as we did. This paper no doubt seemed to him to be such a thing: what good could we make of it, we who could not read or write even the names we called our own. The others cursed his name, and were for burning it, but I argued that we keep it, and, giving up a ration or two, took also what the others had been given.

From the housekeeper I bought a pen, and ink, and some pencils, thinking perhaps to keep a record of my days. And so at first it was a journal, a chronicle to remind myself that I was really here. Yet the notes I made were of so little consequence, tired lists of trees felled and stumps dug up, of fences built and trenches dug, that instead, piece by piece, I began to write about the birds. Describing them, counting their numbers, enumerating their habits as I came to know them from proximity. It was not science, or not quite, for in these words I found a sort of poetry, as if in them I might capture something that eluded me, an inner thing whose presence was wrought in the birds' living heat. I do not know what I thought these words might be, simply that there seemed in their making some secret I needed to unravel. Soon words turned to images, and clumsily at first I tried rendering their likenesses. Not with wholes at first, but with smaller things: the speckled eggs of the moorhens on their platforms of reeds; the feathers of the pelican; the open wing of a swallow, fallen dead from flight into the grass.

But in those I worked beside my journal drew a different reaction. One might suppose amongst men such as ourselves all would be made equal, yet we were not, nor had we ever been. Sometimes as we lay not far from sleep, our bodies aching from the day, they would speak of the homes they had left, of streets, and women and sons and daughters left far behind. Of the six of us I was the only one with a mere seven years: these others had sentences of fourteen, and twenty-one, and there were two who might never return, and as they spoke of home I heard the true meaning of this exile we shared, their voices rising in that anonymous dark soft and dreamlike with no trace of anger, as if they were wary lest they sully these things with that. Of we six, only I never spoke of my life before, and though none would ever demand of me that I reveal myself, my silence set me apart. Yet the revelation that I could write, and draw, seemed to come almost as a betrayal of some unspoken trust. I felt them withdraw, shrinking back from me and away.

After two years on Tavish's farm my labour was sold to another, a man called Donaldson, who had a farm near Liverpool. I passed three years there, then I was sent to work for Bourke. And in Bourke I found a man who sought to understand this country too, who had made a study of its animals and plants. Somehow he heard of my note-taking, and one day he called on me in the quarters where we convicts slept, asking if he might look at what I had done. Until then I had shown no one the work, but I opened it, and handed my notebooks and sketches to him. He turned through them carefully, as I stood stiffly by, my cheeks hot and my stomach light. And then at last he turned to me, and told me I had a gift for drawing.

Though it pleased me to have such compliments, I felt exposed somehow.

It was at Bourke's suggestion that I first took commissions for specimens. In my last year in his service he had come to me one afternoon, bringing with him a letter, and asked me if I would earn an easy pound or two. He was my master then, and so I accepted his offer. I winced at it, the sound of the gun, the concussion as the bullets struck the birds, their spinning tumble earthwards. In those first months each death seemed a part of me, and yet I learned to steel myself to it. They are all architecture, these birds, light as paper on the wing, warm as air. With their bodies in the hand, I learned, one might draw them more carefully, and so this act of violence might itself be something closer to love.

IT IS MRS BOURKE who tells me of Mrs Robertson's anger at me.

'We did not speak the other night,' she says, seating herself opposite Joshua and me.

'I am sorry for that,' I reply. 'You seemed more than occupied.'

'What did you think of the entertainment?'

'Miss Honoré was most pleasing,' I say.

'And Miss Winter?' she inquires.

'She played well, I thought.'

Mrs Bourke smiles and turns to Joshua. 'Might you fetch Miss Lizabet for me?' she asks. Joshua stands, leaving the two of us alone.

As he heads out the door Mrs Bourke watches him affectionately. In the last six months he has grown as many inches, and he is uncomfortable with the fact of it, awkward and difficult.

'I am told you have made an enemy,' she says once he has gone.

'Of whom?' I ask.

With the candid look that I admire in her she says, 'Mrs Robertson.'

'Indeed.'

'You knew then?'

'Not that she had spoken against me.'

Mrs Bourke nods. 'I have heard it from two friends. She will not say what it is you have done, only that she will not have you in her house again.'

'I am sorry for that,' I say.

When she speaks again her voice is quieter.

'Joshua is nearly fourteen,' she says. 'His father will soon want to take him more under his wing.'

'I have expected as much,' I reply.

'You do not approve?'

'I think he is a boy not suited to the life he must make his own.'

'His father cares for him.'

'I do not doubt it,' I say. 'You mean then to terminate my position here?'

She shakes her head. 'No. Only to tell you it will not be forever.'

WITH OUR NEXT LESSON whatever bond it was we found when last we met seems to have abandoned us. Miss Winter is ill at ease and seems troubled by my presence. Not once but twice I suggest we take ourselves away from the house, so we might sit once more in the open air, but both times she pleads the weather's inclemency, the threat of approaching rain. At first I think I have offended her, and carefully I seek to find some suggestion of what I have done. Then Mrs Blackstable appears, busy with some silverware in a cabinet. Irritated I turn, meaning to remind her of my injunction that we not be disturbed. But Miss Winter lifts a hand.

'Please, Mr May,' she says. For a moment she meets my eye, then shaking her head she goes back to her drawing, and I understand. By the cabinet Mrs Blackstable has paused in her work, and is watching us: seeing the way Miss Winter's attention fixes on her drawing she goes back to the business of the silverware.

I do not speak again until she is gone, just sit willing her to leave. Only when I hear the sound of her feet receding down the hall do I rise, and crossing to where Miss Winter sits kneel down beside her.

'I am sorry if I have caused you pain,' I begin, but she lifts a hand, dismissing my words.

'You are not the cause of it.' She looks at me. Gazing into her grey eyes I feel a need to hold her so powerful I do not think I shall be able to resist it. But after a moment she looks away.

'Do you never wish to be free of this place?' she asks, with sudden vehemence.

I shake my head. 'I have nowhere else I might go,' I say, 'not any more.'

She looks as if I have disappointed her somehow. 'Yet I have done nothing,' she says, 'and I am imprisoned here as surely as the rest of you.'

'I am not a prisoner.'

'It is all a prison, can you not see that?' she demands, turning to me. Without thinking I reach out, and touch her cheek, but she does not melt or bend. At last she covers my hand with her own.

'This cannot be,' she says, and taking my hand she places it back in my possession.

As I OPEN THE DOOR I feel it, the creeping sense that another has been here. A heavy silence in the air, the space inside the room still as the surface of a pond after drowning. The room looks as I left it, its contents undisturbed, the remains of my breakfast upon the tabletop, my gun above the fireplace. Yet I cannot shake the certainty that someone has been in here, looking for something. In the next room, which serves as my study, my papers lie much as I left them, books and painting albums still where they were. On the bench the mounted skin of a lorikeet stands arranged for painting: placing one hand on it I run my eyes across the shelf, where the materials for preservation sit. Arsenic, and scalpel blades. Beneath my fingers the lorikeet's feathers are soft, and lifting my eyes again I gaze out, through the window at the trees.

Then quite suddenly I hear a sound, a foot placed carelessly upon a board, and turn quickly, one fist already clenched, only to find Winter standing there.

'You choose to live in some seclusion, Mr May.'

'I do not care for visitors, as a rule,' I reply.

'No,' he says, 'I see that. The house is Bourke's, is it not?'

I nod, and Winter steps forward, into the doorway. 'I thought to see these images of yours,' he says.

'Indeed?'

'What did you think I sought?' Winter asks, glancing round.

I shake my head. 'I do not know.' Uneasily aware of the meagreness of the things I call my own I watch him take in the bare walls, the simple table and chairs.

'These are yours?' he asks, stepping past me into the room and pausing before a small pile of papers. On top there lies the image of a honeyeater upon a grevillea. As he speaks he looks up: seeing me nod he turns back to them, slipping the image aside to expose the one underneath, and then the next, pausing each time to inspect with the same quick, closed attention, examining and dismissing each in turn. There is a tightness in my belly and throat, a sense I am intruded on.

'Would you have a drink?' I ask, uncomfortably.

'No.' He sets down the last of the drawings. Then he moves slowly about the room, examining each part of it in turn.

'Is there something you would discuss with me?' I ask, and at this last he turns to me.

'No doubt you know something of my sister's past,' he says. I say nothing. Perhaps taking my silence as agreement he continues.

'The reputation of a woman who has such a past is a fragile thing, Mr May, ever subject to gossip.'

'What is it you imply?' I ask, perhaps too hotly. Winter does not flinch.

'You would do well to be careful not to give cause for others to take interest in her.'

I wish at that moment that I might throw an accusation back at him, but to do so would only be to give up all hope of seeing her again.

'I am a man of some substance,' he says. 'The errors of my sister's past might yet be corrected by an appropriate union.'

'I would think that should be a matter for her.'

'Much is forgotten here.'

'I do not think I understand.'

At first he does not answer.

'Why is it you live alone here, Mr May?' he asks at last. 'What is it you are hiding from?'

'I do not grasp your meaning.'

'It is only that we all have secrets, things we would rather were left in the past.'

When I do not answer he takes up his hat and smiles.

'We understand each other then.'

———

He leaves me there, disappearing on his horse along the path into the dusk. Alone again I should feel released, but instead I am unsettled, my privacy and the refuge of my home somehow violated. Angry too, at him, at myself, though whether for her sake or for my own I am not entirely sure. Bound in cotton on the sill is a pair of honeyeaters, caught this morning just after dawn. Then they were warm; in the hours since they have turned cold, their bodies gone stiff, and wretched, their tiny legs bent back in the death grip of their kind. They must be cleaned, and quickly too or they will spoil, and so, hoping to put these feelings from my mind, I light a lamp.

I work quickly, my hands moving with the knowledge of a task done so often it comes almost without thinking, calming me: the knife along the belly and around, the skin peeled away from the flesh, careful not to damage it, arsenic rubbed inside the skin to cure it. They are so small, these birds, so light, their twig-like legs so thin it can touch me like grief to see them caught thus in death.

Outside darkness comes, and yet I do not stop, my hands moving on. Packing them away and then taking down pen and sheet I begin to draw, my eyes straining in the yellow light of the lamp. Ordinarily it brings me some measure of quiet, this work of mine, but tonight I work almost angrily, the pictures that I make jagged and filled with pain. Though the clock ticks and chimes on the mantel I do not notice the passing hours, and it is almost midnight when I stop, my hands and back knotted, the room shadowed. Outside the wind has risen, and on every side the bush moves with a sound like water, or waves. Though the knowledge that my home has been intruded on presses in, my mind is not drawn to that, but back to Miss Winter, her distress. What should I have said to her? That this life is so thin, so small, it might be lost in a moment without thought? That the worst prisons that we build are not of stone, or even space, but of our own making? That nothing done may ever be truly undone?

I WOKE TO DARKNESS first. Later I would remember other things: the trickle of the earth against my face, the taste of my blood in my mouth. The clammy press of the bodies all about me. Now all I knew was fear, a sense of dread and panic which clamped upon my chest. Frantically I scratched and tore at the bodies above me, heads and bodies and tumbled limbs, tears choking me as I scrabbled upwards, seeking the surface as a drowning man might from deep beneath the water. Their weight and skin upon me. And then, quite suddenly, I was free – gasping up into the freezing air.

My hands were bloodied, my nails ripped. About me fog, and falling rain.

Dragging myself over the lip of the pit, I stumbled off seeking only to be away. Nothing about me seemed solid, my mind was blank, and all I desired was escape from that pressing dark.

Of those first hours I remember little: flight, cold, a gnawing hunger in my chest and hands and throat. When I realised I did not know my own name, that where my self had been there was naught but emptiness, I am not sure; all I recall is the confusion of it, the way the unremembered seemed to tremble on my tongue.

In the fog all seemed alike, as if the city were a waking dream without substance or depth. Carriages loomed like ships upon the shrouded sea, coming huge and all at once, the sound of the hooves and wheels made strange by its muffling veils. And then again the rain began to fall, soaking through my ruined shirt, and like some creeping filthy thing I sought the shelter of a doorway.

An hour passed, maybe two, then from the dark there came a light, a hooded lamp, two muffled shapes. They took their time, coming close, pausing, then all at once they were in the door, their bodies close to mine. Though they made no threat I was afraid, as if some instinctive revulsion of them rose in me, some sense their interest was not kind.

'Who's this then?' I heard the larger of them say, touching my face and turning it so they might see me by their light. I murmured something, and tried to writhe away, but too slow – the hands of the smaller one already slipping here and there beneath my shirt. If I had coins they took them then, though their hands were so light and quick I would not know.

'Mad,' said the smaller one, 'or simple.'

'No,' the larger one replied, 'not mad.' Then, as if reaching some decision, he took my arm, and lifted me. 'Here, take him,' he said.

Though I knew they meant me ill I did not fight. Instead I let them bear me off, to the lair they kept. Of it I saw little, save the room in which they kept me, which was a low place, too hot from the fire they kept stoked. My two companions set me down in a corner, a filthy nest of ancient straw and reeking blankets. Then from the fireplace there came a woman, fat, and cruel-looking. In one arm she held a baby, barely a month in age, and already drunk with the brandy on her finger. Reaching down she took hold of my hair and hoisted me up. Then she gave a little laugh.

'He'll do,' she said, and left me there alone.

How long I lay there I am not sure: an hour, a day, all was the same. Sometimes I slept, trying to find order in the chaos of my mind. It seemed without memory or substance, no more real than a shadow on a wall. What I had been was not forgotten, but unremembered, and I myself a thing of disorder and absence. And yet I could feel my past, my self within me still, though I could not reach it or hold it, for the act of holding seemed to burn it almost to nothing, like an insect caught in a child's glass. Or a dream brought back into waking.

In time I realised I must escape. And so I lay, feigning madness and insensibility, until I saw my moment: an open door, a back turned, and leaping up made a dash out into the dark. I knew not where I was, nor where to go, and so I ran, and ran, stumbling through the fog-choked streets, until at last I felt the darkness change about me, and heard water, and smelt the warmer scents of cows. Though I did not know it I had come as far as Hampstead Heath, where now I wandered. Half mad with hunger and with fear, at last I saw a house, and not knowing what else to do crawled in and found a place to sleep.

I must have eaten first though, for the next thing I knew I was woken by a man who held a musket, and a pair of lads who swore they would have the law on me. It was their kitchen I had entered, their food I had eaten, their fire by which I had slept, and now, taking me for some vagabond, they dragged me to the magistrate, and sought that I be bound in irons and sent down.

I HEAR THEIR VOICES from the library, first Winter's, then Bourke's, then another I do not recognise. Beside me Joshua looks up.

'I did not know your father had company,' I say.

Joshua shrugs, but before he can answer Bourke appears in the door. Seeing him I rise.

'Winter is here?' I ask, and he nods, smiling then.

'He is,' he replies. 'And he would speak with you.'

I glance around at Joshua.

'Leave the boy,' Bourke says, 'he does not need you watching him as he draws.' Across the shining floor, Bourke stands aside so I may pass.

Winter waits in the drawing room, his back to the french doors which are open to the garden. As I enter, his eyes meet mine for a moment before sliding off towards the right. Following them I turn, thinking to see Mrs Bourke, but instead a man stands there.

'Robert Newsome,' says Winter, 'this is Thomas May, our artist.'

For several seconds there is silence. Opening his mouth to speak Newsome seems to catch himself, then shakes his head as if confused.

'I do not understand . . .' Winter begins. Newsome glances at him, then back at me.

'Thomas May,' he asks. 'Your name is Thomas May?'

I nod my head. 'Yes,' I say, regarding him steadily.

'You are acquainted?' Winter asks. Once more Newsome hesitates.

'No,' he says. 'My apologies. There has been a mistake.'

Bourke and Winter glance at one another.

'What sort of mistake?' Bourke asks, but Newsome shakes his head.

'This man is not the man I thought I knew,' he says, looking first at Bourke and then at me. 'I am sorry, sir, for any confusion I have caused.'

I nod, uneasily aware of the way Winter observes us.

'Please,' says Newsome then, 'it is nothing.'

That Newsome is discomfited by me is clear enough: though he seeks to hide it, he is confused, and injured too, I think. Winter is eager for him to sample some of the pleasures of the colony, and to that end has suggested he inspect my collections. Yet our conversation about the birds is strained and uncomfortable, a fact that does not go unnoticed by Winter and Bourke. In the end I make my excuses and leave.

———

But in the hall outside he comes after me, catching me by the arm.

'Gabriel,' he hisses, 'do you not know me?' His voice is not pleading, but almost angry.

Lifting a hand I step away from him.

'Do not do this,' he says. 'It is I, Robert, your friend.'

'My name is Thomas May,' I say, as slowly and emphatically as I can.

Then, with a look of betrayal in his face, he lets go my arm, and backs away.

'Very well,' he says, 'let that be how it is.'

———

Back in my house I take down my gun, and pack my bag. I must have specimens I think, making my way eastwards, seeking out the shelter of the blackbutt trees, the foliage beneath them where the smaller birds dwell. I move quickly and quietly, watching the birds as they shoot and spring and fly. I have no orders I must fill, no specimens that I need, yet still I go, letting my gun follow them upon the air. My shots are not careless, but there is a wildness to them, as if I do not care what I hit, the sound of my shots echoing through silences which last a moment and then are replaced by the frantic calling and crashing of the birds. The first I take is a figbird, then a pair of pardalotes, then at last a little wren, her tiny body falling to the leaves on the forest floor with a sound so soft it is almost inaudible. When I reach her I realise that she lives yet, her breast stained with blood and her wing hanging helplessly. Yet as I reach for her she flutters and cheeps, seeking to avoid my grasp. Twice I must grab, and then a third time, until at last I have her in my hand, and even then she still beats her wing. I know what I must do, but as I stand holding her I find that I cannot. Despite her suffering I am unable to make it happen, unable to do the thing which will take this to its end. Standing there I feel a sort of hopelessness, a loathing for this thing I am, this half-thing of lies and circumstance.

THOUGH I AM SICK with it come the next morning I rise and dress, so I may go to her. I know not how to do anything else – almost as if in her I see some way of holding on to what I am.

The hour is early, yet it is she who answers the door.

'Mr May,' she says hesitantly.

'Miss Winter . . .' I begin, but then Mrs Blackstable appears behind her.

'Come,' Miss Winter says, 'let us walk.'

Together we cross the lawn. When at last I find words to speak my voice is ragged.

'There is something you should know of me,' I say, but she has anticipated my words, her face seeming to beg that I unmake what she has already guessed.

'This Mr Newsome,' she says, 'he is known to you?'

I hesitate. 'He has said this himself?'

She shakes her head. 'No, he has said nothing of the sort. But my brother says his manner made liars out of both of you.'

I do not reply. She looks at me. 'You are acquainted, are you not?'

'Once,' I say, 'long ago.'

'Yet you denied it before my brother and Bourke.'

I nod.

'And Newsome too.' She pauses, watching me. 'What lies between the two of you?'

'He has done nothing wrong,' I say.

'He was surprised that you were not the man he thought you were,' she replies, looking away.

'He was,' I agree.

'And yet he knew you. How? By some other name? Someone else's name?' For a second or two she hesitates. 'Why? Why take another's name? Why should you choose to disappear like that?'

I open my mouth to speak but can find no words, and then I see some knowledge dawn in her.

'No,' she says, quietly. 'Not that.'

I can see the way she strains against this sour knowledge.

Eventually, 'What was it that you thought to say to me today?'

'Only this,' I say, 'so it should not be from another's lips that it comes to you.'

For a long time we stand, and then at last I bow my head, and turn away.

'I would see these paintings of yours,' she says.

I turn back, shake my head. 'Why?'

'For then I feel I might know you as I cannot now.'

I laugh, more bitterly than I mean to. 'There is naught of me to know.'

'No, I do not believe that. There is kindness in you.'

This time she looks away. 'We should say goodbye now,' she says, 'for I think we shall not see each other like this again.'

ROBERT COMES IN SEARCH of me that afternoon. I have been by the creek, filling my water bag, and return to the cottage to find him seated on the step. Only when I stand before him does he rise, dusting his trousers.

'I suppose I should not be surprised,' I say, and he shakes his head. His anger of the night before seems gone, replaced by something else, something kinder.

'We parted ill,' he says. 'For that I am sorry.'

For a second or two I do not reply, then with one hand indicate the clearing.

'What would you see?'

'Only you,' he says.

'Then come,' I reply, 'walk with me.'

We go down, past the creek and towards the beach. He walks quietly.

'How come you here?' I ask at last.

An expedition, he says, into the Pacific. 'I am to be their surgeon and naturalist.' I nod. 'That is how I heard of your work, of your drawings,' he continues, watching me. 'It was always a talent with you, your skill with a pen.' He shrugs. 'I had nothing of the artist in me.'

We come to a halt. For a moment I see the kindness in him. But then a wallaby springs from the bushes, the sudden sound making me jump.

'What do you guard against?' he asks.

'Nothing,' I say. He knows I am lying.

'Miss Winter . . .' he begins, but I shake my head. 'She is dear to you, is she not?'

I nod.

'Yet you know something of her past?'

'She has suffered for her mistakes,' I say, too hotly.

'That was not my meaning,' Robert replies. 'Merely that she should not suffer twice.'

'What have you said to Bourke and Winter?' I ask.

'Nothing,' he replies. 'Though they guess enough of it to come to the truth soon enough, I think.'

I cannot look at him.

'You will be gone soon, then?'

He pauses. 'I am not your enemy, Gabriel,' he says. At the sound of the name I stiffen, despite myself. 'Or would you rather I called you Thomas?'

'Call me what you will,' I say. 'It is all the same.'

Almost immediately I regret my tone. But when he speaks again his voice is not angry.

'To become another man, it is a dreadful thing.' When I do not reply he continues. 'What is it that frightens you, Gabriel? What are you hiding from?'

'Nothing,' I say, too hotly, 'nothing at all.'

FROM WHERE THE NAME CAME I could not say. The fabric of my mind was still unstitched, a jumble of half-comprehended memories which unravelled even as I reached for them. But as I spoke I felt something begin to form inside of me.

At first I thought the bailiff would object, or some other raise their voice, but the magistrate merely raised a hand, glancing to the clerk to indicate the name should be entered in the book.

I am not sure it was a lie, not then, for my own name still seemed as if it were another's, but as I stood and listened to the bailiff read the charges out, I began to understand what I had done, the realisation not horrible, but almost liberating, as if some part of me were left behind by my words.

Only later, as I was led back to my cell, did I feel the lie of it clotting on my tongue. Not my name, but another's. But there was something else as well, less easy to describe, some sense in which it had altered me. What I had been, what I had done, made different, part of some other self. Not gone, never that, but somehow easier to accept.

———

I had lain a week in that cell, my body consumed with fevers and visions. Perhaps I might have died, what little remained of my mind and body burnt away in that animal pain, indeed sometimes I fancied I had. I dreamt of boring things that dug their way beneath my flesh, of shit and bile and fire in my belly, of nameless horrors which crawled upon the roof and upon the floor, weeping and gibbering and clawing at the walls and door. Now though, on that icy stone, I was removed from myself, the horrors of those last days witnessed in a dream.

There were others in that cell with me. It was one who had been with me before the magistrate who first used the name. 'Who's this?' asked a newcomer. 'May,' he said.

There was time to reflect upon my lie in the days and weeks that came after. At first the name fitted me uneasily, a thing ill-made, and my mind seemed weak still, the fabric of my self grown thin and flat. I spoke little to the others in that place, and they in turn kept their faces from my own. But as the weeks passed I found the name grew more easy on my tongue, and then the past began to slip away.

Perhaps another man might have taken more than the name, might even have borrowed or invented a past. But I wished only to be free, to live without past. I might have been born not a mewling babe but full-grown, rising from that fresh and clotting earth to begin again. And if at first it was a lie, then in time it became something less than that, and more. Another life, newfound, another name which I came to know as my own.

What became of my erstwhile friend I could not say.

322

Perhaps he prospers yet in some London street, ignorant of this shadow life of his I live. Would he know me if he saw me now? Would he understand what I did, what I took? After all, they are such little things, these names of ours, scratches of sound and ink, impermanent. It is so easy, to forget one's self, to mistake the masks we wear for the truth of us, to become a name which is not our own, to leave a life behind and be reborn.

THERE IS NO WRIT or proclamation of banishment, but it is done, nonetheless. One by one my pupils are withdrawn from me, my lessons cancelled. Some do it with the glint of pleasure in their faces, others less gladly, as if they performed a duty regrettable but necessary. In the street faces are averted when I pass, gentlemen falling into too loud conversation with their fellows, ladies pursing their lips and turning away, only to whisper once I am past.

This is not the doing of Winter alone. Others have taken their part willingly, I am sure. There is a peculiar brutality to the way the unspoken law is kept here, a vengefulness, as if to fall among the fallen is a sort of weakness which must be expunged. Sometimes I have thought the coarseness of the manners in these colonies, the hardness of the spirits that they breed, springs not from the lives we lived so long ago but from the denial of those lives, almost as if the silence we conspire to share is itself a sort of violence we do to ourselves.

Of course my crime is none that all here are not guilty of.

I have taken another name, another life, made myself anew. But there is some quality to the way that I have done it, some unspoken transgression that may not be borne. I see it too, I feel the way it denies us all.

Without pupils I may not earn, which is ill for me. I have money, for now, enough for food, but it will not last. There is other work I might do, commissions for specimens I could fill, but these last weeks I find I cannot bring myself to do what they demand. To take a bird from the wing with gun or snare seems horrible to me, something which I may no longer do, nor wish to see done. Of course a man may earn a life in other ways: there is work for all here, and in time I may come to push a plough or walk the boundaries.

The last of my students to be taken from me is Joshua. Bourke does it with a gruff declaration that it is time for the boy to learn more of the running of the estate. He does it quickly, seeking no argument, and I give him none, though I see he has made the decision against his own nature. Perhaps it is as Mrs Bourke said, and in the boy he sees his former wife, some possibility he cannot acknowledge, but it is plain the decision is one that has cost him part of the easiness with himself and his family he once enjoyed.

Nonetheless it is to the Bourkes' credit that they do not abandon me entirely. Despite the scene with Newsome, despite the story of my dismissal as Miss Winter's teacher, the truth of which they must half-guess, neither has pressed me for an explanation. And though for others my name is now a source of endless speculation and scandal, the Bourkes have not made me unwelcome in their home.

Yet it is plain to all three of us that some fundamental trust is broken. Bourke's friendship was always of the distant kind enjoyed between those of unequal station, and so it seems less altered, but with Mrs Bourke the change is more easily seen. Though she is as kind to me as she ever was, now her kindness has a different quality. She speaks as to someone who was once a friend, but with whom one has suffered a schism, now resolved but never to be repaired; as if she is determined not to pry within me, not to dig too deep.

And of her who lies at this thing's heart there is no word, only the news of her brother's instruction that I not be received in their home. What she knows I cannot guess, what she guesses I cannot bear to think upon.

THERE ARE THOSE who would tell you that to make the likeness of a bird you must begin with the head, then proceed to the throat, and hence along the breast-line to the legs. The wing must be started at the pinion line, then the outline of the tail last of all, the details filled in only once the lines are made. But in truth there is no rule for it, no system. The line speaks to the page, and back again: drawing forth the image that is borne within the mind. And this image, for all the precision that it has, is as much one of impression and of feeling as of craft, a thing that takes its life from its line, until it brings itself into being, a thing new born, and new made.

———

Late afternoon, a knock upon my door. The intrusion of this human sound into the air of the house seeming to jar. I sit, arrested in myself, and then it comes again, less certainly.

Rising, I cross to the door and open it, clearing my throat so I might speak. Days have passed since last I had human company. Outside the blueing light of the afternoon, the rising branches of the trees. And then I see her standing there.

At first she does not speak, and nor do I. Her face looks somehow different, as if I have misremembered her. Older perhaps, and thinner too, more ordinary. Perhaps I look the same to her, for she stares as if I am some sort of ghost, a husband or a brother long thought dead and now alive again, but altered from the image carried in the mind for so many years.

A life might be lost within the time we stand there. When at last we speak the first words are hers, coming nervously, as I have not heard her be before.

'Mr May,' she says, clasping her hands.

'How came you here?' I ask, looking past her towards the path.

'It is no great distance to walk,' she says. 'May I come in?' and, confused, I step back to let her pass.

Her eyes move here and there about the room. She stands like this for a space of seconds, her back to me, then turns to me.

'Why . . .?' I begin, my question fading out, incomplete.

'I would see the paintings that you promised me,' she says.

Not knowing now what I might say, with a lifted hand I gesture to the little room where I keep my desk.

I am nervous, with her here. We cross towards the papers on the desk, but I push them aside.

'Which ones would you have me see?' she asks, and so, selecting one, I place it on the table in front of her. For a long time she contemplates it. Then she moves it aside, and I pass the next, and then the next. My throat is tight.

Finally she sets aside the last of them. She straightens, touches the things I keep upon my shelf. Watching her I sense she approaches something in her mind, something she is unsure of how to broach. Then at last she turns to face me. Her face is tired, but I see in it some decision reached, something she will not now put aside.

328

'Would you know how he died, my boy?' she asks.

'There is no need,' I say, shaking my head.

'Yes,' she says, 'I would have you know,' and so I nod, and she pauses, and then starts.

'I did not love his father,' she says. 'Not even then. He was not a wicked man, but a foolish one, the sort who does what pleases him and then feels a fine regret for his actions afterwards, all sorrow and self-abasing shame. He began it, I suppose, though I understood well enough what it was he sought of me, and I did not discourage him. I knew he had a wife, but he flattered me, and the rest of it was more like carelessness. I am not sure what I thought I might find in it. Some sort of pleasure, I suppose, some sort of feeling.'

She looks at me, and I understand that what she tells me she has told no one else.

'There was not much joy in it, not for me, nor even I suspect for him, but that was not the worst of it. The worst of it was that when it was done and all was changed I was still on my own. Sometimes I have wondered, were I to have that time again would I do the same? – if I am honest with myself I know I would, save for the hurt that it brought to those who were close to me.

'When it was clear what the result of my indiscretion was, I was sent away to where I would not be visible. A farm near Launceston, kept by friends of my father's from another time. Good people, and Christian too. I spent a winter there in their company, unvisited, forgotten, or so it seemed. My father wrote to me when he could, but his letters grew more infrequent as the months of my confinement passed. From Edmund there was no word, but that seemed normal to me then, for even when we were young there was little warmth between the two of us.

'The child came at the winter's end. I pressed him from my body in the dark of the night, watched over by a doctor brought from the town. When they put the little one in my arms I did not know what it was I felt; something fierce, and so like pain I thought I might weep.' Lifting a hand she wipes it against her face, though there are no tears that I can see. 'I called him Thomas,' she says, 'the name you bear.

'I think my brother thought we might give my boy away, perhaps my father too, bring me back into society, pretend I had merely been away somewhere, until the story was forgotten and I might be married off quietly. But as I held him in my arms those thoughts did not occur to me.

'It was almost a month before my father came to visit me, and when he did I understood the reason his letters had not come more frequently, for he was ill, and had been for many months. But I saw the way he took my child in his arms and cradled him, the way he spoke to him. He was a gentle man, and kind, and I saw the joy he took in the boy. He promised he would come again – but he never did, for that very week he suffered a seizure of the brain, and for the month that he lived on after had neither speech nor movement in his limbs.

'After he was dead my brother brought me back to Hobart so I might live once more with him. I thought at first it might have been an act of kindness, to have the child there, but I soon understood he merely wanted me where he might watch me closest, so I could not cause him any more disgrace than I already had.

'Though Edmund never spoke to Thomas, save when he could do nothing to avoid it, he was not cruel to him. That is not his way. And yet Thomas worshipped him. He was a quiet child, not much given to playing with the other children, which perhaps I liked more than I should. It is a strange thing, to be cast out: with so few who were prepared to see me, I was largely on my own, and he came to mean so much to me. Too much, I suppose some would say.

'Nonetheless it worried me, that he would be too often

on his own. But our housekeeper had a brother, a man not long out of Port Arthur, and he brought a pup. It was not handsome to look upon, just a ragged thing, but my boy loved it. He would play with it for hours, chasing it, making it bark. It was so unlike him, this happiness, that I did nothing to keep them apart. Then one morning, I came down to find the two of them in the yard, Thomas running back and forth, so the pup would chase him. Because the men were in the yard that day and I saw he would be troublesome I sent him down past the house to play with the dog there, meaning to follow him immediately. But then I thought to fetch a book, so I might have something to read, and going in I went upstairs for the volume from my bedroom where I had left it the night before. Wordsworth, it was, poetry.

'When I came down the path I could not see him anywhere, but I could hear the dog. There was a little creek in the gully behind the house, its water black with the tannin from the fallen leaves, and so I followed on, seeking for the dog and for him. And then I saw the dog, standing by the creek's edge, barking and barking. I knew then, without needing to see, the knowledge of it so powerful I thought that I would choke, and yet I cast aside the book, and ran, tripping over the grass towards the edge of the creek. And then I saw him, face down, his body drifting below the surface of the water. He did not float, and for a moment I though he might still be saved, and so I went in after him. The water was not deep but it was cold, and I pulled him out onto the bank, and striking his chest and fumbling by his lips I tried to put the breath back into him. But it was no use, because he was dead, and drowned, and I knew, I knew what had happened, that it could not be undone.'

———

When she is done there is silence, a space larger than words. Though she does not look at me I know what my part is, what part I should now play. Yet even as I see what it is she needs of me I know that I cannot, that there are no words to mend this thing. And so at last she looks away, her hand straying onto a painting which lies beside the window sill.

'I would keep this, if I might,' she says, turning to me. Her eyes are wet.

I nod, and she steps away. I follow her towards the door. At the last moment she turns back to me.

'Your name,' she asks, 'what is your name?'

I feel myself naked in her gaze.

'Gabriel,' I say, 'it is Gabriel.'

'It is a fine name,' she says. I think that she will weep, but she just stands, holding herself so she does not shake.

'We are none of us without a past,' she says at last, leaning forward to let her lips brush against my cheek. And then with an abrupt movement she turns away from me.

———

I stand there for a long while once she has gone, staring out along the path by which she went. Outside the day is drawing to a close, and overhead the birds are gathering for the night, calling and chattering as they move between the trees, their cries rising on the air. How many times have I heard them thus, the chirruping of the lorikeets, the whirring sound of the honeyeaters, the long echoes of the currawongs. It might be yesterday, or tomorrow, each day the same. How long has it been, I think, how long have I been thus alone? It weighs on me and chokes, something I cannot undo, cannot forget, nor live without.

Sometimes when I am alone out there, in the bush, or even here in my house, it seems almost possible that I might lose myself; there in that silence where there is no need of words or discourse. I have heard it said that there are men who have lost their minds to it, reason drained away into the dissolving space of sea and sky. And indeed while there are times when this place is full of life, a raucous cavalcade, even then there is a sense of emptiness, as if some ancient silence lingers in the fabric of this place, something alien, and unknowable.

Do I dream of them at night I wonder, standing here? The answer is no, or not often. Rather I sleep as might the dead, almost without dreams, or none borne back with me from that place. Instead it is in the days that I remember them, when I am alone, amongst the trees and hills. Then they come back to me, summoned as if from some other life. But even then I feel no guilt, only emptiness, as if all feeling were drained from me, and I was made unreal, transparent as the sound of the wind upon the trees.

Overhead the birds are calling, their cries seeming to fill the air. As I watch they rise, flinging their bodies against the sky, intent upon the moment, spinning and turning like embers or smoke upon the air. I envy them, this life of theirs, the way they live so free of themselves. They are without past, without future, an exaltation of life beating in so many parts, rising up into the infinity of space. Watching them I find I want to weep, and yet I have no tears. And anyway, what would these tears be for? That I cannot fly like them? That I am not free? We are all of us made like this, I see it now, to live and die and live again, our hands and bodies cages which can bind as well as keep. I would rise like them, forget myself, and be released. And then all at once I do begin to weep, and I think I understand what it is to be reborn, what it is to be remade. So many lives, so light.

Acknowledgements

I would like to thank all those who assisted in the writing of this novel. For taking the time to read various drafts and offer advice I am grateful to David Malouf, Hilary McPhee and Delia Falconer; similarly I am indebted to the doctors and students who allowed me to observe as they worked and who allowed me to learn first-hand what it is like to spend time with the recently-dead. Though their subjects could not consent I owe them and their families a special debt of gratitude. For support of a different kind I am grateful to the Literature Board of the Australia Council for the provision of the Fellowship on which much of this novel was written, a gesture which bought me time and space I could not otherwise have hoped for, and to Fiona Inglis for her support through much of the time it took to write. But most of all I would like to thank my agent at Rogers, Coleridge and White, David Miller; my publisher at Picador Australia, Nikki Christer; and my editor, Judith Lukin-Amundsen. And last, but certainly not least, Mardi McConnochie, without whom it would never have been written.